ZENN DIAGRAM

ZENN
DIAGRAM

WENDY BRANT

KCP Loft

KCP Loft is an imprint of Kids Can Press

First paperback edition 2018

Text © 2017 Wendy Brant

Tea analogy used with permission from Emmeline May, from her original blog: http://rockstardinosaurpirateprincess.com/2015/03/02/consent-not-actually-that-complicated/

Kids Can Press gratefully acknowledges the financial support of the Government of Ontario, through the Ontario Media Development Corporation, the Ontario Arts Council; the Canada Council For the Arts; and the Government of Canada, through the CBF, for our publishing activity.

Published in Canada and the U.S. by Kids Can Press Ltd.
25 Dockside Drive, Toronto, ON M5A 0B5

Kids Can Press is a Corus Entertainment Inc. company

www.kidscanpress.com
www.kcploft.com

The text is set in Cambria

Edited by Kate Egan
Designed by Kate Hargreaves (CorusKate Design)
Cover background courtesy of iStock

Printed and bound in Altona, Manitoba, Canada, in 1/2018 by Friesens Corp.

CM 17 0 9 8 7 6 5 4 3 2 1
CM PA 18 0 9 8 7 6 5 4 3 2 1

Library and Archives Canada Cataloguing in Publication

Brant, Wendy, author
Zenn diagram / written by Wendy Brant.

ISBN 978-1-77138-792-7 (hardback)
ISBN 978-1-5253-0026-4 (softcover)

I. Title.

PZ7.1.B73Ze 2017   j813'.6   C2016-902744-9

For Jimmy, Emma and Nathan.
Love you forever and eva.

CHAPTER 1

I HOLD JOSH'S TI-84 IN MY LEFT HAND, press a few buttons just for show and wait for the vision to come.

The TI-84 is my favorite lower-end calculator. Not many teenagers have a favorite calculator, much less favorite calculators in different price ranges, but I'm super cool like that. My dream calculator is the TI-Nspire CX CAS Handheld graphing calculator with full-color display. I yearn for it the way some girls my age might obsess over a cute pair of boots.

Yeah. I'm into calculators like most teenage girls are into footwear.

Have I *mentioned* that I'm super cool?

But the appeal of the TI-84 is completely lost on Josh. From the looks of my newest tutee, I'd guess he uses it mostly to spell out upside-down words like *hell* (7734) or *boobies* (5318008). I doubt he appreciates the fact that it can do complex calculations faster than he can send a text.

I glance over at his square jaw, his thick forearms, and then down at the calculator again. What a waste of a finely engineered piece of equipment — both Josh *and* the TI-84.

I type in numbers — 53177187714 — just to entertain myself while I wait. Some visions take longer than others and I often need to buy time while they gel, but Josh is too busy checking his phone to notice I'm stalling. Everyone is always too busy with their phones to notice anything.

We could have used the calculator app on his beloved phone instead, but if he'd asked (he didn't), I would have insisted that we use the TI-84. The visions I get — I call them algos (short for algorithms: nerd alert!) — from his calculator tell me all about Josh's math issues: where he's struggling, what he gets and doesn't get. They lay out a nice little road map for me to follow on our path to eventual trigonometry success. I wish I could take credit for being a tutoring genius, but the algos are the only reason I'm such a rock star (mathematically speaking). I don't control the visions any more than I control the weather: it rains, I get wet. I touch the calculators, I get the algos.

Josh looks up from his phone long enough to notice the number word I've typed and he grins, probably surprised that nerdy math girl has a sense of humor. Sometimes it sort of surprises me, too.

"Hillbillies." He laughs. "Classic."

I nod and think about making a joke, but the familiar light-headed tickle has started, the vague dizziness and dull headache that signal the algo is close. I tense up a little, hoping it is just an algo vision and not the other kind. Usually the other kind won't ease in so politely, but you never know.

Once in a while a vision will start like an algo and then go all Jekyll and Hyde on me.

But this one stays mellow. I let myself relax into the familiar and almost soothing patterns, the unexplainable language of symbols and colors, and when I look up a moment later, Josh hasn't even noticed the pause in conversation because he's back to gazing at his phone. I set the calculator on the table, clear my throat quietly and reach for my pencil. The calculator algo gave me more information in just a few seconds than sitting with him for hours would have. I mean, I'm good at math and everything — awesome at math, actually — but without my little visions the process would be tedious. While I'm good at figuring out numbers, I'm not so good at figuring out people.

Coaches love me because I can get a flunking athlete eligible faster than you can say *football scholarship*. I can't really take credit for it — I don't cause the visions any more than I cause my own fingernails to grow. But I get the credit.

And of course the shit that sometimes goes with them.

"So, you drew the short straw, huh?" Josh says, putting down his phone and spinning his pencil across his knuckles with a flick of his thumb. I wonder how he learned to spin it like that, like a little yellow baton floating around his fingers. It's quite impressive actually. I suppose it's what he does in trig instead of paying attention.

"Hmmm?" I flip through his book, looking for the right section. His algo told me he's just not grasping the idea of basic trigonometric functions: sine, cosine, tangent. Easy peasy. I feel a happy anticipation that I'll get to unravel it for him. In the beginning I'm always optimistic that I can make everyone love math, like when you try to convince someone to watch your favorite TV show. Eventually I realize that my tutees are not usually the right audience for math appreciation, but in the beginning I am the master of hope.

"I suck at math," he says apologetically. "Like, big ol' legit bucket of suck."

I shrug and try to offer some consolation: "I suck at football."

He silently flips his pencil again as I find the right page. When I glance up, he's looking down at the tabletop, the tips of his ears a little red, a small patch of pink on each cheek. If I didn't know better, I'd say he looks embarrassed. Maybe even ... ashamed. Is it possible for boys like him — football-playing boys with pecs and blue eyes and basketball shoes that cost more than my dream calculator — to feel embarrassed about not being good at math? I thought boys like him *reveled* in not being good at math.

Whatever the reason, he looks kind of embarrassed and any other girl might reach out, touch his arm to reassure him. But for me, touching his arm would unleash God-knows-what kind of shit storm, so I fold my hands carefully in my lap and try to reassure him in a different way.

"Lucky for you," I say, my voice purposefully cocky and light, "I'm *awesome* at math. Wait till you see. You're going to. Freak. The freak. Out."

This makes him smile a little. His pencil stills in his hand.

I clear my throat. "Cosine," I say, and start to copy a problem onto the paper. "It's not just something your dad does on loans." He laughs a little, the pink in his cheeks fades and we get to work.

During our session the surprisingly polite Josh offers me a piece of gum, his pencil when I break mine in my overzealous scribbling and his notebook when I need another piece of paper, but I decline every time. My aversion to touching other people's things, and other people for that matter, has earned me the unfair reputation of being a germaphobe, but I'm not trying to protect myself from germs. Hell, I'd lick a toilet seat if you promised me a TI-Nspire CX CAS Handheld graphing calculator with full-color display. And it's not the algos I'm trying to avoid; those are actually almost pleasant to a math dweeb like me. No, it's the other visions — the fractals — I try to stay away from.

The algos I get from his calculator tell me about math and math only. I mean, who (besides me) has any kind of emotional attachment to calculators? Calculators are used for one purpose and they pretty much soak up only a person's math-related struggles. But the visions I would get from touching his phone, or pretty much anything else of his, or especially *him*, would tell me about *all* the rest of his issues. Seriously. *All* of them. Instead of any kind of helpful road map it'd be more of a chaotic flood of personal information, a monsoon of crap that has nothing to do with math. Stuff about his childhood, about his insecurities and fears, about his past traumas. And instead of enabling me to help *him*, those visions would just leave *me* feeling helpless.

Calculator visions are harmless drizzle compared to the tsunami I get from cell phones, with all their teenage emotional baggage. All the drama of Instagram, Twitter, Snapchat; all the texts, all the photos. When I hold someone else's cell phone, I'm immediately dripping in cold sweat, swept away in a hurricane of things I really don't need to know.

I need to know about the math and the math only. I've learned a few things in the years I've been doing this, often the hard way. Don't touch. Don't take on everyone else's burdens. Don't try to fix things. Just keep your damn hands to yourself.

Before we're through with our session, I hold Josh's calculator again to check in. The algo comes more quickly this time, as if the calculator now recognizes me as some kind of BFF. It whispers, in the weird language only I understand, that we're heading in the right direction. We'll have to keep meeting for a while, but I estimate that Josh will eventually lift his grade up to a solid C, which will be good enough for both him and his coach. How a C is good enough for *anyone*, I'm not sure I'll ever understand. But somehow he will be satisfied by his own mediocrity, I'll be thanked for getting him football eligible and we'll both go on our merry way.

By the time Josh gets up to leave, his phone-checking detachment is nearly gone. I'm not exactly a warm-and-fuzzy girl, but Josh has grown comfortable enough to let down his cool-guy vibe a smidge.

"So. You and trig got a thing, huh," he says, more a statement than a question. I don't speak Teen as well as most of my peers, but I'm smart enough to figure out that he's complimenting me, and a compliment about math is always enough to make me blush a little.

"Trig. Calculus." I shrug. "I'm kind of an all-around math slut."

He laughs and nods. "That's cool."

I'm sure I don't need to explain how very *un*cool having a

thing with trig is, but I am flattered anyway. I snap his book closed and slide it toward him across the table.

He hesitates to take it and when I glance up to see why, I find him studying me more closely than he has in the entire half hour we've been together. I shift uncomfortably under his gaze, unfamiliar with this level of male scrutiny.

"You know, you're actually pretty cute in, like" — he pauses and tilts his head, trying to find the right description — "a hot-librarian sort of way."

This one catches me off guard.

"Oh." I look down and brush eraser crumbs off the table. "Okay. Thanks?" A much more traditional compliment about my looks is buried in this observation somewhere, but it's diluted by the surprise in his voice, the word *actually*, and the librarian comparison. But I sense he thinks I should be flattered to get this little nugget from a guy like him.

I mean, I have to admit he is one of the more attractive kids I've tutored, although his purposeful effort at it is a bit of a turnoff. He does these little head flips to keep his boy-band hair out of his eyes, which ends up coming across like some kind of tic. His Nike T-shirt, with the word *Determined* emblazoned across the chest, makes me think it should have an invisible subtitle: *to get in your pants*. The Axe sex potion he has liberally doused himself in floats around him like a haze, smelling pretty good at first, but then eating away at your mucous membranes until all you can think about is fresh, unscented air. He has put a lot of effort into looking and smelling the way he does, but all I can think is that if he put that much effort into math, he'd probably get a higher grade than a C.

I hear the opposite kind of feedback about my looks: that *I'd* be pretty if I tried a little *harder*. Wore my contacts more often, put on a little more makeup, showed some skin. But to me, being pretty isn't something worth *trying* at. It would be like trying at being tall. So I focus on accomplishments I can master: running a six-minute mile, solving the Riemann hypothesis, picking up dropped items with my feet. But putting an excessive amount of effort into being pretty? Not worth my time or my money. My beauty routine is limited to good hygiene, clothes that won't get me picked on and the occasional coat of mascara when I'm feeling nutty. I mean, I'm not *Amish*, after all.

I guess my indifference to my own appearance is unusual. Most women could make a full-time job of trying to be prettier, and sadly beauty is the one thing that we, as a gender, work at the hardest.

Josh has thanked me and left by the time my friend Charlotte peeks her head into the room, glancing around quickly before her eyes settle on me. God love her, she smiles and tries to act happy, but I know it's killing her that she's missed Mr. Determined.

"All done?" she asks with a forced lightness. "I'll give you a ride home." She has private cello lessons with her orchestra teacher after school on Fridays and always checks in with me before she heads home, today more eagerly than usual.

"I have one more. But thanks."

Charlotte nods and lingers for a moment. It takes everything in her not to ask.

"He was ... nice," I tell her, somewhat reluctant to admit it. "Nicer than I expected. You could fumigate an entire apartment building with his cologne vapors and I think maybe he thought he was doing *me* the favor, but he was polite at least."

She raises her eyebrows innocently. "Who?"

God, she is *such* a bad actress.

I roll my eyes and give her a look. Charlotte has recently rekindled a middle-school crush on Josh and she flipped out when she heard I was going to be tutoring him. But honestly, there is no Venn diagram between his social circle and ours. Josh's friends are football players and cheerleaders, kids who go to parties that involve cases of beer, kids to whom homework is an afterthought, an optional side effect of education. Charlotte and I hang with the straight-A orchestra geeks and mathletes, whose parties involve intense games of Catan and cans of Monster instead of beer. Really, our circles only intersect in Josh's far-reaching olfactory cloud, which isn't saying much because kids in Minneapolis might actually be able to smell him. His scent is a phenomenon that crosses state boundaries.

Charlotte hesitates a moment longer, hoping for more, but I have another kid due any minute. When she realizes I won't be indulging her any further, she shrugs nonchalantly.

"Cool," she says. "Text me."

She turns to go, bumping her shoulder roughly against the door frame and then tripping into the hall. Clumsy as hell, that one, but unlike most girls, Charlotte is pretty without even trying. She's all long, lean legs and flat stomach, symmetrical features, toothpaste-commercial smile. Her thick blond hair is cut in a cute short pixie, the anti-haircut of every other teenage girl in a hundred-mile radius. You'd think her supermodel good looks would be enough to make her popular, but when they vote for things like homecoming court, quiet, smart, statuesque Charlotte is overlooked in favor of loud cheerleaders with big boobs. So boys like Josh don't really pay much attention to her. One of my frequent and fervent wishes is that boys get smarter with age.

I have the sinking feeling I'm going to be terribly disappointed.

I'm overlooked by boys, too, but not because I'm taller than they are or unnervingly beautiful (which I'm not), or because I'm unusually unattractive (also not). Mostly it's because I'm a little weird and love math the way most girls love Starbucks. Plus, as I mentioned, I don't create a welcoming atmosphere with my seemingly germaphobic tendencies. I don't place my hand flirtatiously on muscular arms and giggle. I don't hug everyone for no reason or push at firm chests in mock aggression. I keep my hands to myself, and I know for a fact that that's *not* where teenage boys generally want a girl's hands.

CHAPTER 2

I START ON MY HOMEWORK while I wait for my next customer. The kid is already a few minutes late, but I've learned not to expect ... well ... *anyone* to be as prompt as I am. After giving him another ten minutes, I figure he's probably forgotten. Math isn't exactly something normal people look forward to on a Friday afternoon. Me, I save my math homework for last, like it's dessert.

I take off my glasses and rub my eyes and try to remember if this kid was going to pay me, like Josh, or if he was part of my looks-good-on-college-applications-pro-bono-client list. If he was supposed to be a paying customer, I'm out twenty dollars on top of my wasted time.

Great.

I squint down at my phone again, decide he's not coming and start packing up my books. I jump when the door bursts open.

The guy stops short when he sees me, maybe surprised that I'm still waiting.

"Sorry," he blurts, slightly out of breath. "I'm late."

I look up at him but without my glasses I can't make out anything other than a human-shaped blob — maybe a grayish T-shirt and dark hair. I'm tempted to say something sarcastic to let him know my time is just as valuable as his, but I've been trying to work on my warm fuzziness. Instead I mumble, "That's okay."

Sadly, that's about as fuzzy as I get.

I slip my glasses back on and, since I don't want to let him off the hook *too* easily, I avoid any polite eye contact.

He drops his trig book on the table with a heavy thump. Out of the corner of my eye I see him take off his jacket and hang it on the back of his chair. He wipes his forehead with one hand and I guess I have to appreciate that he rushed enough to break a sweat. He plops down and rubs his hands on his thighs and, since I'm still avoiding eye contact, that's what I notice first.

His hands.

Tan, sturdy wrists, scratched-up knuckles, long and calloused fingers. His fingernails are fairly clean, but I suspect it took some effort to get them that way. His hands look a little like they've been tumbled around in the washing machine with gravel and then put out in the sun to bake to a golden brown.

They make me look up and notice the rest of him.

Well, hey.

He's not bad. Better than not bad, actually. But not at all in the same way as Josh.

His very short, nearly black hair reminds me of an animal pelt: so shiny and thick that I wonder if maybe water would bead up on it, like it does on an otter or a seal. His eyes are dark, but more of a deep gray than a brown, with impossibly long, thick lashes. He blinks once, twice, and I realize that if I had been wearing my glasses, I definitely would have noticed his eyelashes first. Holy crap.

The overall darkness of him is striking. My eyes have to adjust after the Scandinavian golden glow of Josh and Charlotte. Like Josh, this kid is objectively attractive: symmetrical features, straight nose, full lips. But like Charlotte, he's not trying too hard. No hair flipping. No overwhelming body spray. Just the lucky recipient of a desirable gene pool.

Unembellished. Nothing fancy.

He inhales and lets it out in a heavy sort of sigh — the kind my mom makes after a day when my siblings have sucked every last ounce of maternal instinct from her exhausted body — and then he inhales again. He probably smells the remnants of Josh's cologne.

"The kid before you," I say. "He's pretty fond of his Axe."

His mouth twitches in a near smile and he rolls his eyes. "Let me guess: Josh Mooney?"

I can't help but laugh. "How'd you know?"

He shrugs. "He's in my gym class. Has a gallon-size tank of that shit in his locker. I'd know his stank anywhere."

I feel my guard lowering. "Someone needs to tell him that more is not necessarily better."

"To a kid like that? More is always better." He shrugs again. "Unless it's IQ points."

I like that this kid isn't impressed by Josh's brand of

High-School-Musical popularity. The fact that Mr. Sexy Hands is not the president of the Josh Mooney fan club makes me think that he and I might just see eye to eye. Late or not, he's forgiven.

I don't even smell the cologne anymore. All I smell is a soapy mix of Safeguard and Tide, and maybe a hint of mint emanating from my new pupil. His clothes are clean but not new or trendy: just a gray T-shirt from Judson College (which became Judson University several years ago) and jeans that look worn out from actual overuse rather than some Hollister marketing strategy. The green canvas army jacket he hung on his chair looks about twenty years old, probably a Goodwill purchase. You can still see where a name patch was once attached to the chest.

He scrubs one beat-up hand over his close-cropped hair, which looks like maybe he cut it himself with clippers. He also has a small scar, a tiny crescent moon like a baby's fingernail, just under his left eyebrow.

"Did you bring your calculator?" I ask.

"Huh?" He looks up at me. Again with those eyelashes! "Shit," he murmurs. "I forgot. Sorry."

I push down the panic. The calculator itself is not the issue; I have one in my backpack. It's the algos I really need. Without his calculator, I'll actually have to spend time trying to figure out where he struggles with math.

I look at his hands again. His eyelashes. And I think maybe that wouldn't be so bad, spending some extra time with this one.

"It's okay. I think I have mine." I reach for his trig book instead, hoping it will give me some insight into where we need to start. Books don't usually work as well as calculators; something about paper is less ... absorbent? And while kids struggle with their math homework, the book usually sits on the desk, oblivious to their frustration. A disinterested observer presenting a problem, not an active participant trying to find a solution. Calculators have witnessed the battle firsthand, clutched tightly in nervous fingers, wrong formulas entered, wrong answers given. They know. But sometimes, when I'm desperate, books will give me something to go on. I press my palms firmly against the cover and wait ... but there is nothing. Not even a flicker. Given the fact that he needs a tutor, I'm guessing he either never opens his math book or it sits on his locker shelf 99.9 percent of the time and hasn't had a chance to absorb the feelings that go along with his math frustrations.

"I'm sorry ... I forget your name." To be honest, I didn't pay much attention when Mr. Haase told me about this kid. Blah, blah, blah, new to the school, blah, blah, blah, needs help with trig. Same story, different student. I think his last name is Bennett, but his first name was something weird ...

"Zenn," he says. His voice is like gravy. Like ... melted peanut butter.

"Right. Zen. Like ..." — I pinch my middle fingers and thumbs together and place them, palms up, on the table — "Buddha?"

"Kinda. But two n's. Like ..." — he makes a circle with each of his hands and overlaps them slightly — "Venn diagram."

Oh, lordy. He's using math analogies. I think I'm in love.

"That's an interesting name."

"Yeah." He nearly snorts. "I have interesting parents."

"Ha. Who doesn't, right? I'm Eva. Like ..." — I put on my gangsta voice and hold my hands in what I can only assume is a gangish symbol — "you neva met a girl named Eva?" It's the kind of thing a girl trying to be pretty probably wouldn't do. But we've already established that I'm *way* too cool to worry about such things.

He full-on smiles now, with both sides of his mouth. I can't tell if he finds me amusing or if he's a little embarrassed for me.

"Neva Eva," he says. His gangsta voice is much more street than mine.

I blush, even though it's not like he said I was cute in a hot-librarian sort of way. I'm not sure why I blush, actually. I look down at the trigonometry book and stammer, "I, um, I'm named after Évariste Galois? He was a French mathematician."

"Ah. So I must be in good hands, then. Mathematically speaking."

I blush a little more at the mere mention of hands.

Good lord, what the hell is wrong with me? I'm turning into Charlotte!

I stall, trying to think of how else I can figure out where he's struggling with math. I think Mr. Haase said he does okay on tests but rarely turns in his homework, which makes me think he's either cheating on the tests, or he's lazy. But his hands are not the hands of a lazy guy.

Crap. Without the algos to help me, I have to rely on my people skills, which I've already mentioned is *not* my strongest skill set.

"Is there something in particular you're having trouble with?" Asking someone what they don't understand is kind of pointless, but I'm not sure what other tack to take.

Zenn doodles shapes on his notebook paper. I can't seem to tear my eyes away from the tip of his pencil or the hand that holds it.

"Time management," Zenn offers, and I look up. His mouth is quirked in that half smile and I can't tell if he's joking. "Well, that, and graphing amplitude and period cosine transformations."

Aha! Now we're talking. I grab my pencil and draw two axes on my paper. "*That* I can help you with."

I work through a problem, catching his eye occasionally to make sure he is not distracted, but his eyelashes end up distracting me. I lose my train of thought twice.

Jeez. Pull it together, Eva.

We get through a couple of problems but I feel inefficient without my calculator visions, like I am wasting his time. I plod on, reminding him more than once to bring his calculator next time.

When our half hour is up, he stands and stretches, thanks me and grabs his book in one of his rugged hands.

"See you next week, cleva Eva."

I'm starting to wonder if my flushed cheeks will ever cool off. "You bet."

You bet? When did I start saying *you bet*? Weird.

He's already out the door and down the hall by the time I notice that he's left his jacket behind. I grab it and I'm halfway across the room when the fractal hits me hard.

CHAPTER 3

HOLY SHIT.

They usually don't come that fast or that hard. Even fractals usually creep up slowly, like a migraine, and then spread like when your hand has fallen asleep and starts to regain feeling one tingly bit at a time. But this one, it does not creep. It does not tingle. It hits me like a cement truck of inky-black lightning bolts, a crimson hurricane, and I am on my knees on the linoleum floor before I even realize what caused it.

I toss the jacket away from me like it's covered in tarantulas. I was so hypnotized by Zenn's cute-without-trying looks and charm-without-effort manner that I picked up his coat without thinking. Like a normal person would.

I rub my forehead and find it slick with a fine layer of sweat. For a second I think I might throw up, but the wave passes. Eventually I stand again.

That one was nothing like an algo. It was a full-out massive whack of a fractal, a chaotic, messy jumble of dark feelings as heavy and real as my dad's fifteen-passenger church van. Nothing specific, nothing clear. Just the weight of a concrete block on my chest.

This is why I don't touch people's stuff. Even really cute people's seemingly harmless stuff.

I hook his jacket on the toe of my boot and kick it back toward the table. I'm in the process of trying to lift it, with my foot, back to its spot on the chair when I hear the door open behind me.

It's him, isn't it? I know it's him.

I try to think of how to make this — me balancing on one foot with his coat dangling from the other — look less weird, but my mind is completely blank. I kick the jacket back to the floor, lower my foot and turn around.

"I just ..." I gesture lamely to the floor. "You forgot your jacket."

"Yeah." Zenn steps closer. I hadn't realized how tall he is, a good six inches taller than my five feet seven. Also hadn't noticed how nicely the gentle swell of his chest highlights the *Judson College* on his T-shirt. If I were a normal girl, I'd push against it flirtily to camouflage my embarrassment and distract him. But I'm me, so I don't.

He leans over and picks up the jacket. I reach out apologetically to brush my footprint off it, but then realize that would likely trigger another vision. I tuck my defective hands safely into my pockets.

"Sorry. I just ... clearly have some issues ..." I try to make my voice light, jokey, but he looks away.

"Don't we all." He gives me that half smile again, slips the jacket on and lifts his hand in a small wave as he leaves.

"Bye," I mumble, and push up my glasses. Another sweating episode has caused them to slide down my nose.

Yeah, not sure if I could *be* any more cool.

I finally stumble out of the room, woozy and exhausted, and head home. I try not to spend too much time thinking about his fractal. I've learned that it's best to put them out of my mind, because dwelling on them only makes things worse.

I used to call them *feeling scribbles* when I was little, because that's exactly what they felt like: scribbles of feelings. Mostly hurt, shameful feelings. Mostly dark, heavy scribbles. When I got a little older, one of my many doctors referred to them as visions, and that term stuck for a while, even though it wasn't quite accurate. I mean, I don't see the future or anything. I'm not 100 percent sure I "see" anything at all. Even the shapes and patterns and colors are more feelings than visions. But when I eventually learned about mathematical fractals, that name stuck.

Fractals are exactly what they are. Never-ending patterns, like ice crystals or the spiral of a seashell. Mathematical fractals are formed by calculating a simple equation thousands of times, feeding the answer back in to the start. They are infinitely complex, which means you can zoom in forever and the pattern never disappears, and never gets any simpler. When I touch people or their stuff, that's what my visions are like: patterns that go on forever, engraved, etched, carved so deep they can't be erased. I get these glimpses into people — the insecurities and struggles that make them who they are — but only a bit at a time. One tiny part of the pattern that hints at the bigger whole.

The more I touch someone, the more I can see and understand, and the more I think I can help. But that's my mistake. I *can't* help. You can't "fix" people like you can solve a math problem.

I couldn't fix Jasmine Ortega, whose fractal told me that she'd been date-raped when she was fifteen. I discovered that back when she was my partner in Biology and we had to study our saliva, our hair and a drop of our blood under a microscope. After weeks of holding those glass slides of her DNA, her fractal became pretty clear. Nothing I could do would make that pattern go away. Nothing I could say would fix it. I had to keep looking at her every day, knowing that shame would haunt her for the rest of her life. We were just Biology partners, we certainly weren't close enough friends to talk about it. I couldn't even tell her I knew. Hell, I had no idea who the guy was that raped her, so I couldn't even turn him in or make his life miserable. I was helpless. All I could do was know that bit of truth about her, and hurt for her.

I couldn't help Trevor Walsh freshman year, when I learned he was gay from holding his sweatshirt during gym class. I see him now, nearly three years later, still dating Julia Ford, and there isn't much I can do to save either of them the heartache that I know is coming. I'm not going to "out" him to his super-religious family. He would probably deny it anyway. All I can do is watch and wait. And hurt for him.

Not all fractals are so dark, so secret. Some people live happy lives without much trauma or struggle. Some people get over things quickly, or never let them sink in to begin with. The problem is, you can't always tell which camp they are in just by looking at them. You can't tell if their fractal will be a pink ray of sunshine or an inky mass of mountain ridges. People tend to hide all their darkest secrets, and somehow still look fine on the outside. This is why I keep my hands to myself: because you never can tell what's beneath the surface.

I used to be more curious. I would touch people just to snoop. I'm not proud of it, but once in a while I'd want to know what made someone tick and I couldn't help myself. I don't do that much anymore, though. I learned I can't control what information I get. Sometimes it's like I'm stuck in a current and can't swim free. I can't give the information back once I have it, can't erase it from my mind, so these days I keep my distance as my classmates goof around and hug and touch and just ... live.

I try to block out the memory of the overwhelming darkness that came from touching Zenn's jacket. Instead, I count sidewalk squares and hop over each one that is a prime number.

I could have called my mom for a ride, but it's easier and quicker for me to walk. She'd come, of course, but she'd have to drag my quadruplet brothers and sisters along with her. By the time she got all their shoes on, grabbed snacks, buckled them into the car ... It's just simpler for me to walk. Any time I can make things simpler for my parents, I do. They've already done enough for me.

When I finally walk into the house, Essie and Libby greet me with lots of jumping and a flood of chatter. Well, Libby jumps and chatters. Essie just holds her pudgy, sticky, three-year-old hands out to me and I pick her up. Libby bounces in protest.

"EvaEvaEvaEva," she chants. "Metoometoometoometoo."

Libby never says anything just once. One day I counted and realized she repeats most things four times. Once for each sibling? Or just a way to endear her to a math-loving and slightly OCD older sister?

"Hold on, Libby Lou." I drop my backpack by the front door and scoop her up with my other arm. Back at the same level, the girls start patty-caking with each other. I wonder if I'd be more of a people person, more warm and fuzzy, if I had grown up with siblings when I was younger. These four, they just get one another without any effort at all. Could be the nearly eight months they spent squished together in the tight quarters of my mom's uterus, I guess.

"Where're the boys?" I ask them.

"They in the bathroom on the *potty*," Essie reports confidently, her *th*'s coming out like *d*'s and *f*'s. She always has her finger on the heartbeat — and the bowel movements — of the family. She prefers to report the details in a loud and emphatic voice to anyone who will listen.

"Both of them?" I ask.

"Yep!"

"This I gotta see."

I put the girls down and they follow me to the bathroom where, sure enough, Eli and Ethan sit back-to-back on the toilet, legs hanging over either side, pants hanging around their ankles. My mom is lying in the empty tub reading her Bible.

"Tough day?" I ask.

Her smile is tinged with exhaustion. "The usual."

I nod at the boys, each with a board book on his bare lap. "Any luck?"

She's been trying to potty train them for weeks now, but they refuse to be tamed. Essie and Libby were bribed with sticker charts and new toys, which was good for my parents' diaper budget. I just hope it doesn't mean they'll grow up to be slutty girls who give it away to any cute boys who buy them dinner.

"Ethan went a little peepee," Eli reports.

I look to my mom for confirmation, but she shakes her head. "That's what he *says*. I didn't hear a drop, and the water is as clear as a country creek."

"I did!" Ethan insists. He squeezes his eyes shut in concentration and sure enough, I hear the very faint trickle of something from beneath him.

My mom hops out of the tub pretty nimbly for an almost forty-year-old. "Ethan! I heard it that time! Nice work!" She lifts Ethan off the seat, taking away Eli's support and nearly making him fall back into the bowl. I grab his arm just in time.

Eli glances up at the excitement but then returns to his book. This one might still be wearing diapers when he's my age.

One boy's urination is enough to satisfy my mom at this point. I get the feeling that she's been in the bathroom for a good part of the day. She lifts Eli off the toilet, too, tugs up his Pull-Up and tells them both to wash their hands.

"Why so late today?" she asks me. "Don't you have student council on Friday *mornings*?" Keeping track of my schedule *and* four preschoolers is just too much for her most days. I'm impressed she has any clue when I have student council.

"Tutoring," I answer, rolling up Eli's sleeves so they don't get soaked under the faucet.

"Oh, right!" She gives a towel to Ethan, who has started drying his hands on his shirt. "It's barely October. Is a month enough time for kids to get that far behind?"

"Some kids," I answer, with a bit of unintended conde-scension in my voice, and I immediately feel guilty. They may suck at math, but they have other strengths. Like, most of them have more than one close friend. Most of them can touch a jacket without nearly passing out.

I herd the kids out of the bathroom and head to the kitchen to help my mom make dinner. She's not much of a cook, but she manages to throw together a decent meat loaf. My dad comes home while I'm mashing potatoes. He kisses my mom and gives my shoulder a squeeze. I lean in to his touch, greedily accepting his affection. I'll take whatever touch I can get; I just can't give much of my own. Well, except to the kids, who are still sweet and innocent enough that their fractals are bright squiggles of pastel. I can touch the kids, but I hug my parents tentatively, my hands balled into fists away from their bodies. I know if I touch my mom it will only take a moment to feel all those years of loneliness, all that sadness, all the frustration that she so carefully camou-flages with good Christian optimism. I don't doubt that she is a pretty happy person now, but my visions dip deep into the well of past feelings. The kinds of feelings that neva eva really go away.

CHAPTER 4

THE BLUE CUP WOBBLES PRECARIOUSLY. Ethan reaches to steady it but in his panic he tips the whole thing over, sending milk across the table for the second time in five minutes. I grab the damp rag that is always my dining companion. We only fill up each cup about an inch, which means more frequent filling but lower-volume spillage. But even an inch of milk in the cup becomes a puddle on the table. My mom is determined to get the kids drinking out of regular cups. The sheer number of sippy cups we use multiplied by their difficulty to clean has led her to this frustrating mission, which results in at least two spills per meal, three meals a day. That's 186 spills a month, or 2,190 spills per year, at a minimum. I joke that we should make a tablecloth out of ShamWows that would just absorb spills, or maybe a table with a drain in the middle, so we could go on eating without interruption. Maybe we could even recycle the spilled drinks, saving money along with our patience. But until we invent one of these alternatives, I mop up the milk and suppress my sighs.

"Sorry," Ethan apologizes, his apology even cuter and more pitiful because his *r*'s come out like *w*'s.

"S'okay," I say. "Just ... pay attention to your octopus arms, okay, bud?"

He giggles and tucks his elbows in obediently. For now.

My dad refills Ethan's cup while my mom corrals the peas that have rolled off Libby's plate. Dinner at the Walker house. Good times.

My dad is telling us about a Bible study he led this morning focused on the story of Martha and Mary. I know the story. I know *all* the stories. I mean, I am the daughter of a pastor after all. But this is one (of many) that vexes me a little. Jesus goes to visit sisters Mary and Martha, and while Martha is running around cooking and cleaning and trying to impress Jesus with her *Martha* (coincidence?) Stewart entertaining prowess, Mary sits at Jesus's feet, fawning all over him. Finally, Martha loses it and is like, "Jesus! Will you tell Mary to get her ass in the kitchen and *help* me for a minute?!" But Jesus goes, "Chill out, Martha. You are stressing about everything, but only one thing is needed and Mary's got that figured out."

So of course it's a sort of carpe diem/be-in-the-moment/don't-miss-the-forest-for-the-trees message. And I get it. Sorta. But I think about poor Martha running around and trying to be responsible while her lazy sister sits on her butt, flirting with a boy. It's one of those stories that doesn't sit right with me. Like the story of the prodigal son: The responsible son stays home and works for his dad, while the other goes off and wastes his inheritance on hookers and booze. But when the slacker son slinks home, ashamed, does the dad give him a talking-to? Tell him he messed up? Um, no. The dad throws him a party. Kills the fatted calf for him. The responsible son is pissed off and is like, "Um, hello? Do you even give me a sickly little goat when I want to party with my friends? But you kill the fatted calf for my loser brother?" And the dad says, "You're a good kid. You've always been a good kid. Everything I have is yours. But your brother, who I thought I lost, is back. We've got to party!" I mean, I *get* it. It's a message of forgiveness, of joy in finding someone who was gone to you, of grace. But I don't necessarily like what it says to lazy, greedy, irresponsible people. Do what you want and somehow it's all good in the end? Yeah, that's not how the world works. Or that's not how it *should* work.

I guess I have issues with a lot of biblical messages. I keep these issues mostly to myself. I keep a lot of things mostly to myself.

Anyway, my dad is telling my mom about the Bible study and how so-and-so said this and so-and-so said that and, in the brief respite between milk spills, my mind wanders back to Zenn and the vision. That's the thing about fractals; they are pretty hard to forget.

That jacket was a doozy. Some things, like grocery carts or doorknobs or even car keys, just aren't held long enough by one person to develop any kind of attachment. They're sort of neutral. Things that are held only while performing certain tasks, like calculators, seem to soak up only algos associated with that task. Tools or kitchen utensils or sports equipment, stuff like that. I hold my dad's softball bat and all

I get is his frustration that his home-run days are over. But the other stuff? Cell phones and jewelry and jackets, things that never leave a person's side: those are the things I avoid. Those things are witnesses to an excruciating array of human trauma. I avoid them like I avoid mushrooms and olives.

The algos I get from people's calculators are generally calm, neat, orderly. Tidy formulas in organized rows, like a set of instructions to follow. But fractals are chaotic, overwhelming, heavy. Sometimes scary and intricate, like competing whirlpools trying to swallow chunks of jagged metal.

I remember the first time I tried to do something about a fractal. In fifth grade my friend Lauren and I were on the school playground. We'd been best friends since the beginning of the year, and that day we were dangling upside down from the monkey bars, swinging by our knees until we could build up enough momentum to fly off the bar and land on our feet.

We counted together as we prepared for launch:

"One ..."

"Two ..." Lots of giggling and holding our shirts down so they wouldn't show our sad little training bras.

"THREE!"

Off we flew, but instead of landing gracefully like the gymnasts we thought we were, we landed in a pile on top of each other, giggling at our own clumsiness. I stood up and brushed the dirt off my skinny jeans, and then reached out to help her up.

When she put her hand in mine, fear and uncertainty flowed from her body in waves of orange and neon blue like an electric current. I didn't understand what it was trying to tell me, but it was as real and as solid as the metal bar I reached for to steady myself.

I was used to getting visions from adults. I hadn't named them at that point, but I knew what they were, and I had learned to avoid touching grown-ups because of them. But I had never gotten one from a kid, and certainly never from one of my friends. At first I thought it was from our fall — that maybe she was embarrassed or hurt and that was what I was sensing.

"Are you okay?" I asked her.

She laughed and stood up. "Yeah, I'm fine."

"Are you sure?"

There must have been something in my voice, something different and more serious than usual, because she looked at me and her face grew stony, hard to read.

"Yeah." But her eyes didn't quite meet mine.

I reached out and touched her arm and the fractal struck again, just as strong as the first time. It made me sad in a way I couldn't explain, gave me a sense of unease in the pit of my stomach. She looked at me funny.

"What're you doing?" She pulled her arm away, wary.

"It's just ..." I searched for a way to describe it, but couldn't. I had never told her about my visions. I had never told anyone other than my parents and various doctors. How could I tell her that I *knew* something was wrong even though she hadn't told me a thing?

"Stop being a weirdo. What, are you *gay* or something?"

We had just learned what the word *gay* meant, and by the tone of her voice I didn't think she meant it as a compliment.

I wanted to touch her arm again because the puzzle was starting to come together. Something about her parents.

About their house and maybe about money. But I knew not to touch her again. I knew I was being weird. She was already backing away from me, but not because she really thought I was gay. I could see in her eyes that it was because she sensed that I already *knew* whatever it was she wasn't telling me.

I just didn't know what to do about it. A couple of days later our teacher asked me to help the kid who sat next to Lauren with his math. Even back then, I was always helping people with math. Lauren and I switched desks for the hour, which wasn't unusual, but this time I found when I placed my hands on the desktop, when I lifted the hinged lid, the fractal was there, too.

I told my mom about it and she gave me a sad look. She was familiar enough with my visions to know they were real, no matter how much she wished they weren't.

She'd been dealing with them since I was a toddler, when I cried whenever someone held my hand or when I touched pretty much anything besides other children or my toys. My mom thought I had some kind of arthritis or skin sensitivity or rare pediatric joint issues. She had me wear gloves, spent hours massaging my fingers (which only made it worse), took me to specialists who, after skin tests and X-rays and MRIs, never could find anything wrong.

When I was older I tried to explain it to her, but I must have sounded like a possessed devil child because she immediately started having the whole church pray for me. When that didn't seem to work, she took me to a psychiatrist. No luck there either. So by the time I was six or seven, I learned to just limit my contact with grown-ups and keep my mouth shut. But my mom knew it was still there: her daughter's psychic weirdness. She saw how I avoided handshakes, how I'd pretend not to notice when someone dropped something so I didn't have to pick it up. She knew.

She knew that whatever I had sensed from Lauren was real. And she already knew what the problem was.

"Lauren's parents are getting divorced, honey," she told me gently. "I'm sure Lauren is upset about that."

After that I tried to be an even better friend to Lauren, but a couple of weeks later she wasn't in school for a few days in a row, and then one day her desk was cleaned out and rumor had it that she had moved away.

I wonder what happened to her sometimes. I'm not sure what I could have done to help, but that's the problem with fractals: you have these secrets, this information that you are not intended to have, and no matter what you do with it, it's not enough.

So instead I've learned to just avoid them because it's like opening a can of worms. Once you know something about someone, you can't unknow it again.

If you Google *mathematical fractal* you'll get images that look like lightning, or haunted snowflakes, or solar flares. Scary and beautiful, creepy and intriguing. That's how they feel, too. The line between fascinating and frightening is a thin one. Lightning is cool to look at, but no one wants to get struck.

We've exhausted specialists and therapists and at this point I think the only hope I have of getting cured is to find the cure myself. My plan is to study neuroscience and see if I can't figure it out. Take matters into my own vision-inducing hands. I'm good at solving puzzles — maybe it's not such a

far-fetched idea. Maybe the person with the problem is the
only one motivated enough to solve the problem. It's really
my only option because frankly I'm not sure I can live with
this for the rest of my life.

"Eva."

I hear my name and glance up from the dinner table. My
dad is looking at me expectantly.

"Huh?" I spaced out in the midst of the Mary and Martha
story. Whoops.

"Could you pass the potatoes? Please?"

"Oh! Sure. Sorry." I reach for the bowl, carefully avoiding
the minefield of small cups.

"Everything okay, Ev?"

I wave away his concern and take a bite of meat loaf.
"Fine," I tell him. I smile and chew, and my nonchalance seems
to appease him. I don't tell him about Zenn or the haunting
weight of his fractal.

What's to tell, really? High school is rough on people and
it's not like Zenn is unusual. Sure, that fractal I got from his
jacket was a little darker than most, but what if it hit me hard
because I'm out of practice with anything but algos? I've been
particularly careful lately.

I decide to test it out.

My dad's cell phone sits on the table next to him, always
on hand for pastoral emergencies. I debate picking it up, but
I've learned my lesson with phones. His would be especially
awful, with all the prayer requests he gets daily. Dying parents, sick kids, cheating husbands, drug-addicted friends —
you name it.

So instead I take his glasses, which he only wears for reading. Without him noticing, I slip them off the table and hold them in my hands on my lap. The vision comes gradually, not in an instant like the one from Zenn's coat. And it's definitely a fractal, but a simple one, mostly a deep teal swirled with gray blues, a pattern like a chain. There is some darkness, a sense of heavy responsibility, but overall it feels manageable, sadly hopeful, cautiously positive, like all the books he reads while wearing them. I sneak the glasses back onto the table. Compared to that, Zenn's jacket fractal seemed like something out of a Stephen King novel.

I decide to try my dad's phone anyway. I press my fingers on it, as if I'm just sliding it across the table, and a darker fractal comes more quickly. It's blackish green and clumpy, like seaweed. I see flashes of navy and crimson swirled together like blood and oil. It feels like divorce, death, heavy sadness, cries for help.

But still it is nothing like Zenn's.

I remove my hand again and realize my mom is watching. She is nodding at something my dad just said, but she is studying me intently. She looks like she is about to say something when Essie bumps over her pink cup and I grab my handy milk-soaked rag.

After dinner I help with baths before doing the rest of my homework. Bath time is at least a two-person job at our house, and my dad is off the hook tonight because he has to be back at church for a meeting. So my mom and I rock-paper-scissors for who does washing and who does diapering and PJs. I usually don't mind either job, but tonight, after all the spilled milk, I just want the driest job.

My mom fills the tub and strips the girls down while I put

on a *VeggieTales* video for Ethan and Eli. I watch with them for a bit and Larry is singing one of his silly songs about a hairbrush when Essie waddles back into the room wrapped in a towel, her pink cheeks shining.

"C'mere, Esther Faith." I wrap my arms around her and jokingly wrestle her to the ground. She giggles, but quietly. She's the hardest one to rile up. I wouldn't dare do any roughhousing with Ethan this close to bedtime or I'd never get him to sleep. I pat Essie's silky skin dry and put on her nighttime diaper while she lies perfectly still, batting my dangling hair like a cat might play with a piece of yarn. We count together backward from twenty while I rub pink baby lotion on her skin, enjoying its warmth and softness. I don't mind the mini-fractals she gives me, like little rays of orange sunlight. Her fractals are simple. Pleasant. Still untainted by the brutal world. I tuck her pudgy arms into her fleece pajamas and then sit her up so I can comb out her wispy hair.

Libby is next, and she barrels into the room, loud and naked. "Boysboysboysboys!" she yells. "Your turn!"

Ethan groans. "But I watching *VeggieTales*!"

"Mommy!" Libby yells. "Mommy! Efan is not listening to me!"

Essie sits patiently on the floor while I drag Ethan to the bathroom. Libby stops fussing as soon as he is gone. It takes about an hour, but eventually all the kids are bathed and dressed, tiny pearl teeth brushed, and in bed. My mom seems on the verge of saying something once the boys' bedroom door clicks shut behind us, but I quickly excuse myself to finish my homework. If she thinks I'm having a rough time with the fractals, she'll offer to take me somewhere else, to some psychiatrist or specialist she read about in a magazine at the doctor's office. But I'm tired of dead ends and false hope. I'll figure this out myself. So I give her a light smile and whatever she had been about to say is overruled by my false display and her overwhelming exhaustion. She collapses on the couch and I finish my math quickly so I can cross it off my list. I wouldn't be able to savor it tonight, anyway.

It's nearly eleven when I think about college applications for the thousandth time. One of these nights I'm going to have to tackle them. But not tonight.

CHAPTER 5

ON SATURDAY CHARLOTTE DRAGS ME TO a horrible-sounding Nicholas Sparks kind of movie that I'm afraid might make me vomit if I go with a full stomach.

"Come on ... it has Bradley Simon in it!" she whines. "With his shirt off! You'll get your money's worth for that alone!"

"These movies are all the same, Char. Hot guy, beautiful girl. Impossible love. Bad dialogue."

"Yeah, but there's kissing. And partial nudity."

I laugh at the way she raises her eyebrows playfully. "What has happened to you, friend? You used to be so sexless and levelheaded."

"I know." She sighs, almost sadly. "Things were *way* simpler back then."

So we buy our tickets and camp out with our popcorn. As I suspected, the movie is horrible. I'll admit Bradley Simon looks good without his shirt on, but that is truly the movie's only redeeming quality. I could write a better script, and I'm a math nerd.

Although, if I'm totally honest with myself, it's not just the poor quality of the dialogue that makes me hate the movie so much. What really gets me is all the touching. Hand-holding, strokes on the cheek, arms wrapped around each other. There's one moment when the actress — some waify blonde with doe eyes and perfect perky boobs — grabs Bradley Simon's face while they kiss and I want to gouge both of their eyes out with my ticket stub. All it does is remind me of all that I will never have: simple touching. Warm skin on warm skin. No fucking fractals.

I'm understandably a little cranky when we get frozen yogurt after the movie. I pile Reese's Peanut Butter Cups and chocolate-chip-cookie-dough bits in my dish with a heavy, bitter hand.

"Why do you even bother getting yogurt, Ev?" Charlotte studies my paper bowl. "If all you wanted was candy, we could have gotten that a lot cheaper at Walgreens."

I stick out my candy-coated tongue at her.

We go to the beach to eat — our favorite spot. Lake Michigan is more like an ocean than a lake. You can't see across it and on nights like this the waves crash against the sand so fiercely that we can barely hear each other. I have to give Charlotte credit: she doesn't gush on and on about Josh. She knows my situation leaves me with a limited amount of patience for unrequited love. Given my circumstances, her heartache tends to fall on deaf ears. I only have so much sympathy for girls who could find a boyfriend if they wanted to, but instead keep liking unattainable guys above their social station. It's why Charlotte loves Jane Austen and I stick with nonfiction books about science and anthropology.

"Homecoming is soon," she says.

"Yep."

"Do you think we should go this year? I mean, we *are* seniors."

I shrug. "*You* should go, if you want to."

"You don't want to?"

I shrug again. "What's the point?"

"I don't know. To make memories? To have fun?"

I sigh. She's probably right. I only make my situation worse by wallowing in it. Maybe if I tried a little bit I could enjoy my senior year instead of just enduring it. But the thought of watching all the other couples slow dance while I stand alone along the wall, my hands carefully protected behind my back, is too depressing.

"Maybe ..."

Apparently my nonanswer appeases her because her mood lightens and she's back to talking about the ripples of Bradley Simon's stomach muscles and how he looks like he'd be a really good kisser. I concentrate on the peanut-buttery goodness of my Reese's and try not to think about the kisses I've never had or what stomach muscles might feel like under curious fingertips.

CHAPTER 6

SUNDAY MORNINGS ARE THE WORST FOR ME. Not because I have to go to church, although sometimes that's a real buzz kill, or because I wake up knowing my precious weekend is nearly over. No, Sundays are hard for me because of the never-ending affection of church people. The hugging, the handshakes, the *love*. Most of our congregation is aware of my aversion to touch and give me sad half smiles of pity instead of handshakes. But some don't know me yet, or they do and they think all I need is a good squeeze to cure me. A little "laying on of hands," if you will. So I endure intense fractals from people who look like they haven't a care in the world, but are really just as full of heartache and pain as non-churchgoers. Often much, much more.

It's a brutal way to spend your priceless morning off.

This morning I'm hiding out in the nursery with the quads and a handful of their little friends. It's the safest place for me after the service, when all the good Christians are pumped up by a motivating sermon and a moving hymn. I'm on the floor pretzel-style playing duck, duck, goose when my mom peeks her head in.

"Eva, can you take the church van and run to Piggly Wiggly for me? I just found out Mrs. Effertz broke her hip and I don't have any cream of mushroom soup at home. Or chicken. Or those crispy onions."

This is how the mother of quadruplets talks: in riddles that leave out a lot of important information. Luckily I speak this language as well. I get that she wants to make a casserole for poor Mrs. Effertz, but is missing, well, *all* the essential ingredients. I bite my tongue to keep from saying that Mrs. Effertz's hip will be the least of her worries if she eats my mom's casserole.

Instead, I groan. "The Loser Cruiser? Why can't I take your minivan? Or Dad's car?"

"Mine's got the car seats. Unless you want to take four kids with you," she threatens. I shake my head vigorously. There isn't much worse than taking four preschoolers grocery shopping. "And Dad needs his car to go to the hospital for chaplain duty."

Jeez. Sometimes it's tough living in a family of do-gooders. "*He* can't take the van?"

"There's no room for groceries in his car, Eva!" She's losing patience with me. I see it between her eyebrows. "It's so loaded up with sh —" she catches herself just before a *shit* escapes in front of seven bat-eared preschoolers, "shoes for the shoe drive."

Nice save. Sometimes I wonder if my mom would swear like a truck driver if she weren't married to a pastor.

"Fine." I reluctantly stand up and ruffle the hair of my two closest circle friends. "Gotta fly, ducks. Goose you later!"

They all laugh hysterically. This is the problem — I can fool myself into thinking I'm hilarious because I hang out mostly with three-year-olds who laugh at *everything*.

I sneak out the back to avoid the hug-happy coffee klatch in the narthex, and there it is, waiting. If a Care Bear and the Magic School Bus procreated, their offspring would be the Loser Cruiser. Poorly painted clouds dot a bright blue background so it looks like headless sheep are floating in the sky along the side of the van: a bloodless horror movie meets mattress commercial. There's a Bible verse on there, too, in uneven, messy, microscopic script. Luke 9:24: *For whoever wants to save their life will lose it, but whoever loses their life for me will save it.* I keep telling my dad we should repaint the bus and use a verse that is less confusing in a font size people could actually see. But who has the time, or the money, or the talent? And they'd have to call a heated church council meeting just to decide which Bible translation to use.

The door is never locked, because who would want to steal this monstrosity? And how far would they get, anyway? It's not exactly like it blends in with all the other cars. I pull the door open and climb up. I may not be particularly cool, but even I'm aware of how horrible this van is. I duck low behind the wheel and drive.

At the grocery store I load up my cart with the makings for my mom's infamous chicken-and-rice casserole (the only ingredient we actually have at home is the rice). As each item goes into the cart, I subtotal the bill in my head. It's easy for me, and oddly fun. Charlotte sometimes calls me Casio because she says I'm a human calculator. I pick up two gallons of milk (one of which will no doubt end up splattered across our table), bananas, Rice Krispies, Huggies and anything else I think we might be running low on. As I said, shopping with four three-year-olds would be appropriate torture for terrorists, so I'm trying to postpone my mom's pain a little longer.

I add the 5.6 percent sales tax in my head and smile in the checkout line when my half-full cart of groceries comes to $104.23: exactly what I figured. I use the $50 my mom gave me and dip into my tutoring money to cover the rest. That money usually goes straight into my college savings account, but occasionally I use it to help out my parents. I'll conveniently lose the receipts, put the groceries away before my parents get home and let them somehow believe we are living within our budget. Frankly, the money is probably better spent on bananas and milk than my impossible college dreams.

I load the groceries into the back of the Loser Cruiser, wedging the bags under the last row of seats.

"Can I take your cart, miss?"

"Oh, sure, thanks." I remove the last bag and push the cart toward the guy who has offered. I look up to smile my thanks at him and find myself face-to-face with Mr. Eyelashes himself.

His gray eyes focus on me, there's a slow-motion blink of the never-ending lashes and then recognition registers.

"Hey." His reaction is friendly. Not necessarily enthusiastic, but at least he acknowledges that he knows me. He remembers my face. That's something, right? Is it sad that I think that's something?

"Hey," I say, with an identical level of enthusiasm — no more, no less. This is how teenagers work, I've learned. Only give back what you're given.

I assess my situation: in my church clothes, unloading diapers and applesauce into a bright blue van with a Bible quote on the side. Yep. If only I had a big box of tampons still in the cart. And maybe a mammoth zit right on my chin. Now *that* would be awesome.

Zenn doesn't notice the van. Or at least he doesn't comment, because how could he *not* notice? He takes my cart, and I note that he is wearing a bright orange safety vest over his green army jacket, which makes us slightly more even on the embarrassment scale. The vest doesn't erase the memory of the fractal I got from his jacket, though. Just seeing the sleeves poking out reminds me of the heaviness, the darkness.

"You work here?" The most obvious question of all time.

He nods and adds my cart to the train he already has. "Unfortunately, it looks that way."

"That's cool."

He glances down at his orange vest and gives me that little smirk. He doesn't beam, doesn't often full-out smile. Just quirks his mouth a little on one side in a sarcastic compromise. "Yeah."

"Hello? Have you *seen* what I'm driving?"

Now he does smile with his whole mouth — both sides. I relax a bit.

"That is *quite* a ride. What are those?" He squints. "Sheep?"

"Clouds. I think. Very poorly drawn clouds." I study the side of the van. "Or maybe they are sheep. I really have no idea."

I turn back to him, but he is still studying the van. Light weekend stubble covers his jaw. His insane eyelashes blink once, twice. "I think your church should get a refund for that paint job."

"I know, right? It's ugly as sin, ironically."

He nods and gives me a sideways smile. "It's pretty baaaaad."

Oh, my God. Did he just make a sheep joke? I laugh, trying not to be too obvious about how much I love that. We stand for a moment in post-awkward-joke silence, glancing alternately at our feet and the hideous van. I'm just grateful that he doesn't ask why I'm driving a church van in the first place.

"Well," I say, slamming the door shut. "I should let *ewe* get back to work."

Zenn looks at me, a sparkle in his eye telling me he's quick enough to get my joke, and goofy enough to appreciate it. "Right."

"I'll see you ... when are we meeting again?" I know perfectly well we are meeting on Tuesday afternoon. I think his eyelashes have made me turn fake dumb.

"Tuesday?"

He remembered! My face *and* our meeting time!

"Right! Tuesday. I'll see you then."

"I'll try not to be late this time." He gives me one last half smile before pushing the line of carts toward the store.

"And remember your calculator!" I call after him. I secretly hope he will forget it again. Any excuse to spend more time with him.

He calls back, "I will," but it sounds suspiciously like "I wool." Which makes me think I might consider bearing his children immediately.

I climb back into the van and take a deep breath and let it out slowly. Calm down, Eva. Just calm. The hell. Down.

CHAPTER 7

CLASSES START LATE ON MONDAY MORNING, so Charlotte and I meet at Java Dock before school. There is a Starbucks by the highway, but Java Dock is downtown by the water and the owners make their own muffins that are as big as your head. I always vote for Java Dock.

We split a Granny Smith muffin with streusel topping — Charlotte is a sucker for streusel — and sit on one of the sagging sofas with Charlotte's cello case taking up the spot next to her. Sometimes she does this to keep older men from hitting on her. She may not attract the attention of high-school boys, but middle-aged men *love* Charlotte.

It's kind of gross.

"Hey, new earrings?" I ask.

She touches them briefly. "Oh! Yeah. I got them at the farmers' market. They're made from sea glass they find on the beach."

"Our beach?" The glass is a pale, translucent blue that matches Charlotte's eyes. I reach out to touch them and then think better of it. Even the most beautiful things can hide secrets.

She nods.

"They're pretty," I tell her. Most girls in our school would not be caught dead wearing earrings bought at a farmers' market made out of recycled garbage. This is why I love Charlotte: she is not most girls.

As usual, Charlotte grills me about my college and scholarship applications. She knows I've been procrastinating. Even though it's barely October, she's already completed her early-admission applications for three different schools, including Northwestern and Georgetown. But she's an only child, and her family has some money. If she gets in, and I'm sure she will, she can go. I can't say the same thing for myself.

I try to change the subject with a slow sip of my café mocha — the mocha is the only thing that makes coffee drinkable for me — and debate telling Charlotte about Zenn. I rarely talk about boys, so any mention of a male would distract her from hounding me about my applications. I wouldn't tell her about his fractal — I don't usually talk about those — just about his mere existence. Most girls spend most of their time talking about boys so it wouldn't be weird for me to do it once in a while.

I don't know. Maybe it would be weird.

Charlotte beats me to it. "I can't believe you got to sit with him for a half hour. *Alone.*"

I shrug but can't help smiling. A half hour alone with a

cute boy talking about math. Doesn't get much better than that for me.

Then she says, "I'm so crazy jealous."

Oh, right. Of course. She means *Josh*, not Zenn.

I shrug again. I can almost smell his cologne just from the mention of his name.

"When's the next time you meet?"

I swallow a bite of muffin. "Today."

"Again? Already?"

"He's ineligible, so I have him every day until he gets his grade up. Coach's orders." I say this to hint that the guy is no rocket scientist, but that doesn't seem to deter Charlotte. When it comes to Josh, attractiveness has always outweighed intelligence. I decide to throw her a bone. "Do you want to meet him?"

Her eyes grow big.

"Come by before, like, three forty-five. I'll introduce you guys."

"That would be weird. Wouldn't that be weird?"

"Why? You're just giving me a ride home."

She thinks about this for a minute and then makes a decision. "Okay." Her cheeks are pink with nervous excitement. I'm worried for her. She's usually a wreck around popular boys. But we'll see.

Josh and I are just finishing up when I hear a light tap on the door. Charlotte peeks her head into the room.

"Oh!" she says, fake surprised. "Sorry!"

Huh. Maybe she's a better actress than I thought.

"That's okay. Come on in." I turn to Josh. "She's my ride."

Charlotte steps into the room and the first thing I notice is her mouth. It's pale pink and shiny. Is she wearing … lip gloss?

I'm so distracted by her shiny lips that I momentarily forget my promise. She opens her eyes wide and wags her head toward Josh while he's facing the other way. My God, she's wearing eyeliner, too!

She clears her throat. Oh, right. Introductions.

"Josh, this is my friend Charlotte. Charlotte, this is Josh."

Charlotte manages to make it across the room without tripping. She holds out her hand and I nearly roll my eyes. A handshake? Most kids just lift their chin and say hey. What is this, a business meeting?

But to my surprise Josh stands up and takes her hand without missing a beat. Maybe he has one of those dads who has forced him to shake hands since he was a toddler. I shudder at the thought. Thank God my parents were lax in the social-niceties department.

"Nice to meet you, Josh," she says. I can definitely see the eyeliner. I blame Jessica, one of her fellow cello players. They probably did a makeover during orchestra.

"Yeah. You, too."

Josh and Charlotte make a striking couple: tall, blond, all-American. If you dressed them in denim and put them on a beach with a golden retriever, they'd be a freaking Ralph Lauren ad.

Josh squints at Charlotte in a charming, almost flirty way. "You … play the cello, don't you?"

Charlotte looks stunned. "Yes. Yes. I do."

"My little sister plays the violin. Her name is Lilly?"

Of course Charlotte knows this. She's only spent the first month of school plotting 1,001 ways to use Lilly Mooney to get to Josh, but she's too nice a person to employ any of them. The fact that Josh knows something about her has caught Charlotte off guard.

Maybe boys aren't as stupid as I think.

Josh further chips away at my stupid-boy theory by saying, "I like your earrings."

Charlotte touches them self-consciously. "Really?"

He nods. Suddenly I feel like I'm the third wheel. I hadn't expected Josh to do more than give Charlotte a dismissive *S'up* and be on his way, so I'm not sure how I feel about this development. I want Charlotte to be happy ... but with Josh? Poster boy for popularity and the in crowd?

I close Josh's math book with more force than I have to. I don't think we're going to make any more progress today. Not with math, anyway.

Josh glances at the clock, then almost reluctantly picks up his book and calculator. "Damn. I gotta go. I'll see you tomorrow." This is directed at me.

Then he looks at Charlotte and says her name like it's a secret. And a statement. And a promise.

I see her whole body soften, like her bones have liquefied.

"See you around?" he adds.

"For sure," she says, a little too enthusiastically.

I cringe. She is such a goofball.

But Josh doesn't seem to notice. Or he doesn't seem to care. He touches her arm lightly as he walks past.

The door closes and Charlotte collapses into a chair. "Oh,

my *God*! That went *so* much better than I thought it would."

I want to agree with her, but it would be rude to admit I was expecting a disaster. "See?" I say. "He's pretty nice."

"Pretty nice? He's, like, utter and complete *perfection*." I don't know if Charlotte's rosy cheeks are from excitement or from Jessica's well-stocked makeup kit. "He knows I play the cello! And he likes my earrings!"

"He's observant," I give her, reluctant to join the lovefest because, yes, I admit it: I feel a little jealous. Not about Josh in particular, but about feeling desired. Having someone look you in the eyes, say your name, know something about you. It's been a long time since I've allowed myself to think about that possibility.

Well, it's been about two years.

During sophomore year, I went on the only two dates of my life. The first was with seemingly sweet Chad Morgan, who had dimples and blue eyes and looked like he could have been on some Disney Channel show playing the slightly nerdy but stealthily cute neighbor. We went to a movie and everything was going great — he laughed at my lame jokes, he bought me popcorn. Then halfway through the movie he slid his small, damp hand onto mine and it was ruined. I tried to ignore it at first, concentrating on the story on-screen. But the longer his hand sat on mine, the clearer the fractal became. Orange-and-red hot bolts of anger issues. Bright green streaks of competitiveness to the point of dysfunction. I pulled my hand away in the guise of eating popcorn, but blue-eyed Chad was done for.

Not too long after that, class clown Logan Boggs asked me out and, even though he wasn't really my type, I figured at least he'd make me laugh. Then he held my hand as he walked me home from the frozen yogurt shop and I was overwhelmed by what I suspected was a dark cloud of racism. Or homophobia. Something heavy that scared me away from him immediately.

I know not every boy has those kinds of issues. Logically, I know that. But everyone has *some* kind of issue. Some insecurity or bias or stubborn shortcoming. Later in a relationship maybe that kind of stuff isn't so deal-breakery. Usually by the time you learn about people's "damage," you've become attached, maybe even see it as endearing. But to learn about someone's dark secrets right away, when any red flag can send you running for the hills? That's a whole lot harder. And it's a big part of the reason I've decided I just have to be alone ... for now.

Most of the boys in my school aren't interesting to me, anyway. They try too hard, they care too much about things that don't matter to me, they just seem immature and ridiculous. Until now, no one has lured me out of my cocoon of denial. But the rosy glow in Charlotte's cheeks reminds me what I'm missing.

"Are you ready to go?" My voice is uncharacteristically snippy. "I've got a fuck-ton of homework tonight."

Charlotte sighs and stands up, oblivious to my tone. "Is a fuck-ton more or less than a shitload?"

"Oh, *way* more. A fuck-ton more."

She nods blandly, accepting my expertise on expletive measurements without question. "Do you need a ride home tomorrow, too?" she asks, dreamily.

"Nice try." I laugh. "But I've got a kid after him tomorrow."

Zenn, I want to tell her. Zenn, Zenn, Zenn.

I bite my tongue and follow her out to the car.

CHAPTER 8

ALL DAY ON TUESDAY I FEEL RESTLESS and fizzy inside. It's not like I've never had a little crush on a guy before, but somehow this is different. I feel anticipation (and a little bit of fear) pooling in my stomach and then overflowing to every other part of my body. Why, I'm not sure. It's not like Zenn has shown any hint of interest in me. He remembered my face. He smiled at me *maybe* two times. He made a couple of corny sheep jokes. He has been cordial at best.

But those hands, those eyelashes, that charming smirk … and something about that haunting fractal. That vision is probably why I feel a little bit of fear mixed with the infatuation.

I assume the quiet knock on the door before Josh and I are finished with our lesson is Charlotte, trying to make a love connection. But when the door opens this time, it's Zenn. A few minutes early, even.

Josh looks up. He seems disappointed. I am not.

"Sorry," Zenn says. "I'll just wait out here."

Josh stands and gathers up his things. "It's cool, bro. We're done."

It might be my imagination, but I think Zenn cringes a little at being called bro. Can't say I blame him.

"I'll see you tomorrow, Eva." Josh pronounces my name *Eve-ah*, like the robot in *WALL-E* . My turn to cringe a little. I mean, it's a nice name. It's just not *my* name.

Josh gives Zenn a manly nod as he leaves. Zenn crosses the room and sits down, shaking his head. "We have three classes together and he still doesn't know my name."

"Apparently, he doesn't really know mine, either."

Zenn smirks and then produces a calculator from the pocket of his coat. "Not only on time but *with* my calculator."

"Nice work," I say, and I take the calculator to give the algo time to brew. Zenn flips through his math book to find the appropriate section. He's not paying for this session, but I realize that I'd probably pay *him* to sit here and study his hands. They are fascinating. My pastor dad's hands are soft, for holding and praying and serving. Zenn's are a working-man's hands, for hard, outdoor, physical work, not office work at a computer. I wonder what he does to make them look that way. Can't just be putting away carts at the Piggly Wiggly.

I tear my eyes away and look down at the calculator. I'm not getting anything. Not a tingle or a whisper. Just like when I held his math book. Nada.

I try to hide my confusion and have him start on a sample problem from his homework. He works on it, slowly but correctly, without my help. Does he even need me at all?

Well, crap.

I want to ask him why he's here. But tutoring is good for my college applications and what do I care if he wants to waste a little extra time doing math? So I just keep my mouth shut and we go through his homework problem by problem. I give him hints when he gets stuck. In our half hour, he nearly finishes it.

When we're done he closes his book and I slide his calculator, useless as it was, back across the table. He stands up, remembering his jacket this time.

"Hey," he says, his voice a little hesitant, gravelly, intimate. "I was thinking ..."

My hands start to tingle and I wonder if I've accidentally touched something to trigger a vision, but no: they are resting safely on my lap. I feel my heart beating in the soles of my feet.

"If your church wanted to repaint that van, I do that sort of thing."

Oh. Okay. Not what I was expecting — or hoping for — at *all*.

"You ... paint vans?"

He nods, kind of wagging his head side to side. "Well, other things, too. But I've done some motorcycles and, like, logos on cars for businesses." He digs a slightly crumpled business card out of his pocket and sets it on the table. "I work out of a body shop on Powers Street. If they're interested, have them give me a call."

I study the card but don't pick it up. Don't want to risk having a fractal while he's standing right here. "You can get rid of the headless sheep?"

"Absolutely. We can do something more subtle. Like ... bright purple with unicorns. Maybe some rainbows." He says this stone-faced but his eyes flick with the first real bit of humor I've seen in him today.

I laugh. "Okay. I'll let them know."

After he leaves I carefully pick up the card while I'm still seated. I have bruises on my knees from my fall on Friday, so I'm erring on the side of caution. But the card doesn't trigger anything. The more disposable the item, the less it seems to absorb fractals. The card says *Port Dalton Body Shop* with his name, *Zenn Bennett*, handwritten beneath the logo.

Well. He wants to paint my van. And unfortunately that's not a euphemism for anything.

CHAPTER 9

I MENTION ZENN'S OFFER TO MY DAD at dinner, while I'm cutting up bites of overcooked chicken for four preschoolers who, frankly, act like they would rather eat poop.

"Hey, Dad," I start, making sure I don't act too invested in the idea yet. "I meant to tell you. I'm tutoring a kid at school who paints vans —"

"Libby. Stop putting peas in your milk," my mom says.

Libby looks up at my mom, a handful of peas poised over her cup. She puts the peas back onto her plate and then sticks her hand into her milk, trying to fish out the few floaters she dropped in before she got caught. To no one's surprise she knocks the whole thing over and starts to cry. I grab my rag.

My dad doesn't miss a beat. "He paints vans?"

"Yeah. Well, other stuff, too, I guess. But he said he could help ... update the church van."

I try to be gentle about the van around my dad. Although he has never admitted to it, I wonder if he might have been the artist of the headless sheep.

"Ethan, eat your chicken." My mom is inching toward madness tonight. I hear it in her voice.

"But I don't *like* chicken!"

"You like chicken nuggets," my mom points out, her teeth clenched.

"*These* not chicken nuggets."

My mom shoots my dad a look of exasperation, but he's looking at me.

"How much would this updating cost?" My dad has an amazing ability to tune out chaos. I'm guessing that comes from enduring a decade of church council meetings.

"I don't know," I admit. "But I could ask him?"

Eli dips a piece of chicken into his bowl of applesauce, probably trying to moisten it up, and accidentally bumps his cup, sending it over.

"Oh, for the *love of God*!" my mom yells, which makes Essie start to cry now. "We're going back to the flipping sippy cups. I *swear*!"

I don't know who my mom thinks she is threatening. We'd all be *thrilled* to go back to the sippy cups.

Probably sensing that his gift for tuning out chaos is contributing to my mom's drift toward madness, my dad grabs the rag and starts mopping up the second cup of milk. My mom is tossing dishes into the kitchen sink. I probably should just let it go ... but ...

"So ... the van?"

"Fine, Eva," my dad says, more curtly than usual. "Ask him."

Before he can overthink his sentimental feelings about the Loser Cruiser, I hop up and start making myself useful.

∞

After another round of bath time and bedtime times four, I finish my homework and commandeer the one computer in our house. My mom and dad are watching *Revenge*, their television guilty pleasure.

I stare at the online application to MIT, although I know it nearly by heart. I know them all by heart: Northwestern, University of Chicago, Stanford. But I never get much farther than staring. It's not the essays that overwhelm me; my strengths are math and science, but I can write a mean essay if I have to. My ACT and SAT scores are more than respectable and if I do an interview, I should be fine once I get past the initial handshake. What makes me stumble is the biographical information, where I have to talk about my family. I mean, it took me years to even tell *Charlotte* that my mom and dad are not actually my mom and dad, so I don't know how I'm going to spill it all out to strangers in a succinct paragraph.

I don't *have* to put it on my application. I could just pretend that my family is traditional and leave it at that. But I also know that my situation is unique, and it might be the thing that makes me stand out in a sea of overachieving eighteen-year-olds. I'd feel guilty using my family's tragedy to give me a boost, but my real parents are dead. I never got to know them. If getting into college is one tiny good thing that comes out of their death … so be it. Right?

I just don't know how to present myself as the appropriate mix of orphan and overachiever to an admissions board. And even if my grades and test scores and dead parents were enough to get me in, there's the cost. Holy good God, the cost.

It costs $62,946 for *one* year at MIT. Pretty similar costs for any place I want to go. (Gotta wonder where they get that extra $46.) Four years would cost $251,784. Our house isn't even worth that much.

The university websites are wonderful, all the text written in an informal, laid-back voice that makes you fall in love with them. They say things like, *If you are admitted to *insert school name here*, we will make sure that you can afford to come to *school name* and We will help meet every single cent of your family's demonstrated need.* Um, yeah. Right. Maybe if I sell my soul. How can they possibly promise that?

The websites say that, after all that free money they can't wait to throw at you is doled out, the average cost for a student is closer to twenty-five thousand dollars. As if that lessens the sting. It's still a hundred grand for four years. My dad only makes about seventy-five thousand per year, and he supports a family of seven!

If I apply to all these schools — and I really, *really* want to apply — and I get in ... how can I put that pressure on my parents? How would I ever pay them back? First they rescue me from orphanhood and then finance a completely overpriced education when they still have four more kids to raise?

In my fantasies, I go off to one of these prestigious universities, solve a medical mystery, cure myself, and make my first million before I'm thirty. Then I pay for the quads to go wherever they want for college so they don't have to deal with this kind of stress. Reality is that I've been researching scholarships, which is depressing because they come mostly in chunks of less than a thousand dollars. And the amount of work you have to do just to *apply* for the scholarships would be overwhelming if that's *all* you did. But when you go to school and tutor and do things like student council so you have something "leadershippy" on your college applications *and* help take care of four three-year-olds, it's enough to make you weep into your spilled milk.

I have found one scholarship through a big corporation in Madison that gives out twenty-five thousand dollars per year for four years. That's most of what I might realistically expect to pay at MIT or a school like that, given the "needs-based" aid they hand out to families like mine. The scholarship is extremely competitive, probably more competitive than even getting into MIT in the first place. But as far as I can figure, it might be the only way for me to bankroll my education.

The key to that scholarship — the Ingenuity Scholarship — is having something that sets you apart. Some unique talent or skill that makes you one in a million. They are vague in their description and I'm not sure if my math talent, or my visions for that matter, would qualify me. I know it's worth a shot, but I just haven't been able to get up the nerve.

Tonight I stare at the application again.

Please tell us about the skill, talent or aptitude that makes you unique.

Well, where do I start? With just one touch, I can tell if you are stressed out or happy. With two touches, I can determine if you had a good childhood or a dysfunctional one. And if you let me hold on to your arm for a half hour or so, even though it might make me pass out, I could probably outline the top ten ways you are messed up. How's that for an aptitude?

I'm tempted to write this, but instead I focus on my math skills. I write about how I was doing long division in preschool, how I rarely have to be "taught" anything when it comes to math: all you have to do is show me a problem and maybe give me an example and I get it. Not like I *learn* it. Not like I *memorize* it. I just understand it inherently and completely. I try to blend confidence and modesty with a sense of humor. I write about how when I was in grade school and most of my friends kept diaries or made scrapbooks of pop stars, I kept a notebook of math jokes and riddles: *What geometric shape is like a lost parrot? A Polygon!* or *Why was the math book sad? It had too many problems.* I talk about how, in a world of shades of gray, sometimes it's nice to have black-and-white answers.

I write a brief, pared-down summary of my family history — parents died, Mom's sister dropped out of college to take care of me. I leave out a lot: how she met and married the young pastor at her church, how they adopted me, their struggle with infertility, the quadruplet siblings that were the end result. That might all seem too unbelievable, like I'm just making stuff up for attention. So I give them the basics but try to downplay the drama of being an orphan. Don't want to seem like I'm milking it for sympathy.

I read over my application and decide it's about as good as it's going to get. I impulsively hit Send before I can overthink it or delay any further. I'm exhausted from the effort and shut down the computer. The big scholarship application is done. The college applications will have to wait for another night.

CHAPTER 10

ON WEDNESDAY CHARLOTTE STOPS BY to pick me up, once again conveniently showing up a few minutes early. Today her hair is attractively messy in a way that screams Jessica has struck again. Lip gloss and eyeliner seem to be Charlotte's new best friends.

Josh remembers her name (and its correct pronunciation) without any help. We all walk out of the room together, Josh politely holding the door for us. Charlotte giggles at something he says. I'm not sure I've ever heard Charlotte giggle quite like this before. Or at least not since middle school.

Instead of having her drive me home, I fake that I need to get my dad's car from church so she drops me off there. But rather than my dad's car, I pick up the Loser Cruiser. I pull out the business card Zenn gave me, and head up the hill to the body shop.

I suppose I could call first, but the number on the card is clearly the shop's number and he probably wouldn't answer. The truth is I just want to see him again. I've been keeping my eyes peeled at school, but either he's never there, or he's some kind of phantom that apparates at will.

I pull the van into the parking lot and briefly check myself in the rearview mirror. Some days I don't look in the mirror at all between when I get ready in the morning and wash my face at night. I just don't think about it that much, which is unfortunate when your face is dusted with flecks of glitter from some three-year-old's princess crown. Then, an occasional glance in the mirror might be a good idea.

But today there is no glitter. Just my pale but clear skin, relatively pretty blue eyes that tend to get lost behind my glasses, and a mouth that's most interesting (and pitiful) feature is that it has never been kissed.

I climb out of the van and head into the shop. One of the garage doors is open and two guys are inspecting some damage on a car that appears to have hit a deer. A small tuft of fur is still stuck by the license plate frame. This unexpectedly makes my throat close up. I swallow to try to clear it.

The men look at me and one of them nods an informal greeting. Then they look past me at the Loser Cruiser and smile, nudging each other and making comments that I can't make out. Funny that my van elicits more lingering glances than anything about me.

The shop is dingy and 100 percent man — from the three mismatched, dirty chairs that line one wall to last year's sexy-tool-girl calendar attached to the top of the counter with tape, now curling up at the edges. No one has taken the time to just peel it off. My fingers itch to do it, but I know better. Even old tape can sometimes hold memories.

"Can I help you?" One of the guys from the garage has come in to see what I need. The name patch on the chest of his dirty shirt reads *Dave*.

"Um ... I'm looking for Zenn?" I hold up the business card, maybe trying to prove that I'm here for official car business and am not just some girl stalking him. He might get a lot of those.

Dave nods and looks at the clock on the wall. "Calder, is Zenn comin' in today?" he calls out to the other guy.

Calder yells back, "What is it, Wednesday? I think he's at the mansion today."

Mansion? Wait, he lives in a mansion?

"Right," Dave says, more to himself than to me. "He'll be in tomorrow. After four, four thirty, probably. Can I help you with something?"

I clear my throat. "He said he could paint our church van? With something a little less ... butt ugly?"

Dave smiles and looks past me at my van again. "Yeah, I'm sure he can help you with that. We can paint it a solid color for ... probably two grand? Anything Zenn does would be extra. He'd have to give you a quote on that himself." Already I feel the pointlessness of this endeavor. Two grand just to paint it a solid color. Bible quotes and rainbows extra. Crap.

"Okay. I'll see him tomorrow after school — I'll just ask him then."

"Right," Dave says again. "Sounds good."

"Thanks for your help." I nod and turn toward the door.

"No problem."

I decide to drive the scenic way back to the church,

through the historic part of town. The houses along the main drag are huge and old, and I suppose there are a few you'd consider mansions. I wonder if Zenn lives here. He doesn't strike me as the type of kid who comes from money — he doesn't have that preppy, soft, spoiled look about him. But of course I don't know anything about him, really.

At the church I go in to see my dad, whose car is still in the parking lot. Maybe if he's heading home soon I can catch a ride.

"Any luck with the van?" he asks when I plop down on a chair in his office.

I shrug. "The guy I tutor wasn't there. I'll talk to him tomorrow." I pull the sleeves of my sweatshirt down over my hands. "Is there any kind of ... budget ... for that kind of thing?"

"Budget? For the van?" He thinks for a second. "I suppose there is something for maintenance. I'm not sure how much. I can have Joanne check."

"Could you?"

My dad looks at me kind of funny, like he senses there is more to this story than just my desire to get rid of the sheep. "I could."

I nod and change the subject. "Are you going home soon? Or should I walk?"

"I can run you home. I told Mom I'd pick up KFC for dinner."

"Sweet. Ethan will be stoked."

Hopefully chicken strips will lull the kids into submission and we'll have a peaceful, spill-free dinner.

Stranger things have happened.

CHAPTER 11

"DOES YOUR FRIEND CHARLOTTE have a thing with anyone?"

The question comes while I'm in the middle of explaining the Gudermannian function to Josh, so it catches me off guard.

"Have a thing? Like I have a thing with trig?"

He laughs a little self-consciously. "Yeah, I mean, does she have a boyfriend or ... whatever?"

I put down my pencil. "No. She doesn't. Not right now." I add that last part, trying to make it seem like Charlotte is in a very rare and brief window of opportunity between love interests.

"Cool." Josh leans back in his chair and taps his hands on the tabletop. "Cool."

I look at him for a moment and before I think better of it, I reach over and pick up his cell phone.

"Is this that new one?" I ask vaguely. I don't know much about phones. I'm sure his phone is the newest and greatest model — I couldn't care less. I'm just making small talk while I peek into his life for a second. I want to see if I can sense his motivations because I'm not sure I trust him yet. Not with my best friend.

"Yeah," he says. He starts to explain how awesome his phone is, but I don't hear him because the fractal is already sweeping over me. It's only slightly milder than the one from Zenn's coat, which surprises me because I wouldn't think a guy like Josh struggles with much. But this one makes my palms sweat, my ears ring, my throat tighten. I set the phone down quickly, before full-blown dizziness or nausea sets in. I steady myself, taking a deep breath to try to shake off the surprising weight of rejection and insecurity and loneliness.

"Are you okay?" Josh's voice is concerned and I realize I've ignored him since I picked up the phone. I'm probably a little pale and sweaty, too.

"Sorry. Low blood sugar, I think."

Josh digs in his pocket and pulls out a half-eaten bag of Skittles. For some reason the fact that he has a bag of opened Skittles in his pocket and is not too embarrassed to offer me some makes me instantly trust him more. That, and the fact that his fractal is nothing like what I expected.

Although my blood sugar has nothing to do with why I'm pale and sweaty, I take a few Skittles to play along. They are slightly soft.

"Thanks," I say, and he smiles, happy to help.

He reaches for his phone and presses the button to check the time. I already regret touching it because now when I look at him all I can think of is that fractal. I get the feeling of watching someone kick an adorable puppy.

There is a tap at the door and Zenn peeks his head into the room. He lifts his hand in a small wave. Josh stands up and pronounces my name correctly as he says goodbye. I wonder if someone — maybe Charlotte? — tipped him off on that.

Josh leaves and Zenn takes his chair. I quietly inhale the fresh air he brings with him. In what I realize is becoming a habit, I study his hands. Today he has medical tape wrapped around two of his fingers and a bandage across one of his knuckles. I wonder, briefly, if he was in a fight. As if teenage boys are getting into fistfights every day. What is this, *West Side Story*?

"I stopped by the body shop yesterday with the van," I tell him.

He looks up at me. Wow, his eyes are truly gray. Like ... number 2 lead pencil gray. I'm probably the only girl in the world who would notice that, and also find it a little sexy. "Really?" he asks, his voice almost hopeful.

"Yeah. But I'm not sure the church can afford two or three grand."

He waves his hand, dismissing my argument. "It won't be that much."

"It won't?"

"I can get Dave to write some of it off as a charitable donation since it's for a church. I'll talk to him."

"Really?"

Zenn nods. "Do you want me to meet with the priest or whoever to talk about some ideas?"

"Well ... that would be my dad. The pastor."

"Oh!" he says. "Your dad?"

Yeah. I suppose that's pretty sexy — having your dad be a man of the cloth. "But he's delegated this to me, since I'm the one who thinks we should paint it."

"Oh," he says again. "Great. So ... what were you thinking?"

I shrug. I haven't put a lot of thought into anything but getting rid of the sheep. "Just something ... *less.*"

He nods and takes out his phone. He touches the screen and opens his camera roll. "Maybe something like this?" He finds what he is looking for and he holds the phone out to me. I hesitate. If touching his jacket was any indication, holding his phone could be a nightmare, just like Josh's. To my relief, he sets it on the table and slides it toward me.

I look at the screen and there is a picture of a motorcycle fuel tank painted with a very busty woman in a tiny black bikini top. Her hair is made of snakes, like Medusa's. Fire is shooting out of her eyes.

I grin and look at Zenn, who is deadpan.

"You know," he says, shrugging. "Something classy."

"Could you make her with, like, devil horns? And maybe paint the lyrics to 'Stairway to Heaven' along the running board?"

Zenn nods, smiling finally. He takes the phone and flips to another picture.

"You could just do the name of the church. Something basic. Or you could do something like this." He shows me another picture, this one of a mural painted on a school wall, a simple silhouette of children backlit by sunshine.

"Oooh, that's nice. I like that." This time I cautiously take the phone from him to study the picture and I brace myself for a fractal. But ... there's nothing.

"You could put a cross in the background or something. To make it more ... churchy."

"Is this a new phone?" I ask, grasping it more firmly.

"Huh?" He looks up, confused. "Oh. No ... not really."

Maybe he's not an Instagram-selfie-overtexting sort of guy, not attached to his phone at every waking moment.

Zenn takes out a pencil and opens his notebook and starts drawing. In just minutes he scribbles an amazing sketch, something I couldn't have done if you gave me weeks *and* something to trace.

"Holy shit." I watch his pencil fly across the page, like it's magic.

Zenn looks down at his sketch and shades in a little more. "I could come up with a couple of options for you to run by your dad." For the first time since I met him, he seems relaxed. His jaw is unclenched, his face calm and less weighed down with worry.

"Sure. That'd be great." I pick up the scrap-of-paper masterpiece. "Or I could just show him this. This should be more than enough."

I'm surprised to find Charlotte waiting in the parking lot when I come out of school. I guess it shouldn't surprise me. She's been lingering after school more often, planting herself wherever she might cross paths with Josh.

She sees me and starts hopping in her lanky, goofy way, like a baby giraffe on a hot asphalt sidewalk. I've rarely seen her so animated. She's usually all chill and yoga-ish. But she runs up to me and grabs my arm, bouncing on her toes. She's like a six-foot-tall version of Libby.

"He asked me! He asked me to homecoming!"

"Who?" I ask, although I already know the answer and maybe don't want to admit it to myself. "Josh?"

"Yes! Oh, my *God*! Can you even believe it?!"

We get in the car and she lets out a small squeal when the doors close.

"Josh. Freaking. *Mooney*!" She bangs her hands against the steering wheel with each word. It takes her several minutes to calm down enough to put her seat belt on.

"Will you go shopping with me on Saturday? I need a dress! Oh, crap, and *shoes*!"

Oh, man, I forgot about her shoe issues. Finding cute ones for her huge feet is always a challenge.

Before I can answer, she's babbling again. "I have a Pinterest board. Look it up on your phone and tell me which ones you like."

Charlotte has a Pinterest board of homecoming dress ideas? When did this happen?

I open up the Pinterest app on my phone and click onto Charlotte's boards and, sure enough, there is one for homecoming. I scroll through the dresses, all of them more subdued and sophisticated than any teenager in her right mind would wear. None have sparkles, none are strapless and not one of them is shorter than knee-length.

"Maybe you should get the shoes first and work backward from there."

She groans in agreement. "Uggh. I *hate* my feet!"

I nod in fake sympathy at her ridiculous problem: being

tall and gorgeous, trying to find something to wear for her date with the hot football player. Sucks to be her.

I agree to go shopping on Saturday, though I can't think of many worse forms of torture. But she's my best friend and it's our senior homecoming. Her first high-school dance with a date. For Charlotte, I will endure a day of searching for granny shoes and a dress that won't make her look like a politician's wife. It's the least I can do.

$$\bigcirc\!\bigcirc$$

And it really isn't so bad, after all, considering both Charlotte and I seem to be missing the gene that makes most women love shopping. We kind of wander around aimlessly, laughing a lot. We finally get down to business at DSW and find her a pair of low, strappy black heels that don't look too matronly. The large-size boxes are helpfully labeled with bright yellow stickers. ELEVEN! they scream at us. TWELVE!!! BIG-FOOT GIRL, HERE'S YOUR TWELVE!

"I know I should be offended by this," Charlotte says as she points to one of the hard-to-miss stickers, "but it really does make it easier. I can't even get attached to a pair of shoes if I don't see a box with that freaking number of shame. Saves me a lot of heartache."

I nod and think of how helpful it would be if boys had stickers like that. If they had a girlfriend, their sticker would say TAKEN, or maybe if they were gay, their sticker would say, OTHER TEAM. Would make life a lot easier for most teenage girls.

I wonder what Zenn's sticker would say. Maybe DAMAGED GOODS, based on his fractal.

After we get her shoes, we head to Macy's and browse the racks in the juniors department. Charlotte has a hard time hiding her disgust.

"They're all so ... shiny and bright."

"And *small*," I add. "They're like, Las Vegas doll dresses."

"Let's try some on," she says, and grabs a bubblegum-pink dress and another one the color of the inside of a lime.

"I'm not trying anything on." I doubt I'll get any fractals from the dresses — no one has worn them for more than a minute or two. Especially this hideous one, which I doubt has ever been taken off the hanger. But even without fractals, there's something depressing about trying on dresses for a dance you won't be going to. She grabs my arm and drags me to the dressing room. "C'mon. If I have to, you have to."

I find myself in a dressing room next to her, pulling off my yoga pants and pulling on the lime-colored dress.

"On the count of three we both come out, okay?"

I glance in the mirror and cringe. "Sure. On three."

"One ..." she says, her voice high and excited. "Two ..."

I wonder if I should take off my socks, then decide that they add to the comedy.

"Three!" And we both fling open our dressing room doors and step out into the aisle. I'm ready to laugh at how stupid we both look, but one glance at Charlotte and my laugh dies before it starts.

"Look at me!" she says, spinning awkwardly in the small space. "I'm like a piece of Hubba Bubba! But with sequins!"

"I hate you."

"What?" She stops spinning.

"You actually look good in that stupid dress."

"Shut up. This is hideous."

Yes, the dress is certifiably butt ugly. But Charlotte, with her long, shapely legs, her narrow hips and smooth skin, is still beautiful. The dress fits her perfectly.

My dress is about three sizes too big and hangs off me. It's the color of snot and as itchy as a wool sweater. It has no redeeming qualities.

I love Charlotte, I really do, but sometimes it's hard to be friends with a freaking supermodel.

CO

Eventually we give up on the Technicolor juniors section and look at the dresses for grown-ups. Charlotte gravitates toward things that Princess Kate or someone who goes to Princeton might wear. I have to talk her into something above her knees, something without long sleeves and a drop waist. We settle on a tight, asymmetrical black sheath that has one long sleeve and one bare arm. It shows one smooth shoulder and one peek of collarbone, but leaves the other side fully covered. It's a great compromise between slutty and nun.

After we settle on the dress, we splurge and eat at the Cheesecake Factory. Charlotte treats. But eventually the talk of all things Josh wears on me and I develop a dull headache. I'm excited for her. I am. I swear I am.

"I'm going to get my nails done tomorrow. Do you want to come?"

I don't say no, but I avoid giving her an answer right away. All day our conversations have been dominated by Josh and homecoming and … Josh. The two of them have been texting back and forth the whole time like they are getting paid by the word, which means I can hardly finish a sentence without her phone buzzing and her looking down and smiling at something he "said." At one point she offers to set me up with one of his friends, some rich-kid football player. I politely decline. ("Hell, no" is polite, right?) I have nothing against football players, per se. I just have a problem with pity.

So in the end, even though I know it's shitty of me, I tell Charlotte that my parents have to go to a wedding and I have to babysit the whole day. No pedicure for me.

I don't know why I lie.

Or, maybe I do.

CHAPTER 12

I SETTLE IN AT JAVA DOCK on my favorite couch. The place is empty tonight. Every teenager in town (except the very coolest, like me) is either at the homecoming dance, or at some very anti-homecoming homecoming party. I've decided that tonight will be the night I tackle my MIT and Northwestern applications. I've borrowed my dad's church laptop and have hunkered down with a pumpkin spice latte, a sugar cookie the size of a dinner plate and as much enthusiasm as I can muster.

Before I start the applications I make the mistake of going on Instagram. I usually check it from my phone, but the computer is handy and I am rewarded by nearly life-size pictures from various pre-dance get-togethers. Some are just a couple of friends hanging out while others are groups of thirty or forty popular kids meeting at the park or someone's house for a professional-grade photo shoot. Charlotte and I used to make fun of these parties. All the kids lined up, looking eerily the same, like some kind of cloning experiment gone wrong. Tonight the girls stand slightly angled toward one another with a hand on a hip, their dresses all equally short and sparkly, their hair curled in stiff ringlets. (Last year everyone's hair was flat-ironed.) The boys have dark shirts and colorful ties. Whatever one does, they all do, like overly coiffed meerkats. I see a picture of Josh and Charlotte, their arms around each other, looking about as model-like as you can get. Between the tasteful dress that I helped her pick out, the hair and the makeup, Charlotte is almost unrecognizable. But rather than looking like she doesn't belong, or like she's one of the clones, Charlotte stands out in an amazing way. She literally and figuratively towers over all the girls and some of the boys, stunning.

And her smile is glorious. She seems to be having the time of her life.

Maybe those parties only seem lame when you're not invited.

I close the Instagram window with a forceful click and sign in to the MIT application site. Time to get down to business. I hear the door of the shop open and close, but I don't look up. Won't let myself get distracted every time someone walks in. Must focus.

"Tall black drip," is the guy's coffee order, and for some reason I find this funny. *Drip* is an insult I've heard my non-swearing, too-polite dad use. I'm not even sure what it means, but I assume it's a nerd? Or maybe a jerk? Who knows. It's kind of like when my mom used to tell me I was being a pill when I was little. What is that supposed to even mean? I lose my focus and let my gaze drift up to the counter.

Aaaand of course it's Zenn. Why wouldn't it be? He has a talent for catching me at my worst moments.

While he waits for his coffee, I snuggle deeper into the couch, hoping he won't notice me. The only thing worse than filling out college applications the night of the homecoming dance is your crush seeing you fill out college applications the night of the homecoming dance. I guess it should make me feel better that he's not at the dance either, but it doesn't. When guys don't go to homecoming it seems like a conscious choice. When girls don't go, it just seems like they didn't get asked.

I study him from behind the screen of my laptop. I haven't seen him since our tutoring session on Tuesday, when I gave him the go-ahead to paint the van. He's in his usual army jacket but tonight he has on a knit hat that would look intentionally trendy if Josh were wearing it. On Zenn it just looks functional, like he's using the hat for its intended purpose: to keep warm. He stands with his hands in his pockets, looking at the bulletin board covered with business cards and flyers advertising band gigs, dog-walking services, tutoring. My own ad was up there until my schedule got so filled up.

"Tall black drip!" the barista calls out, like she's calling out his name and not the drink. Zenn is tall and dark, but there is nothing drippy about him. He is most definitely non-drippy, whatever that means. He takes his coffee and I think I am home free until he steps away from the counter.

Crap. He sees me. I am equal parts mortified and thrilled.

He raises his cup in a silent greeting and comes a few steps closer. He opens the lid and I try not to stare at his mouth as he blows on his coffee to cool it.

"Hey, Zenn." My voice sounds goofy in my own ears. Too loud in this small, cozy space.

He takes a tentative sip from his cup. Straight black coffee, no cream, no sugar, no chocolate syrup. What a badass.

"No homecoming for you either?" he asks.

I close my laptop and press my hands against the warm surface. I shrug. "I'm not much of a dancer."

Zenn nods in agreement. "Yeah. Me neither."

He comes even closer and sits down on the arm of the sofa across from me. His knees are spread wide, his forearms resting on his inner thighs, his hypnotizing hands holding his coffee in the triangle between his legs. He looks so comfortable, so at ease in his own skin. How does one get that way? You wouldn't think it would be hard — I mean, we're *born* in our skin. It *should* be pretty comfortable by the time you hit seventeen, eighteen. But for me ... not so much.

"Homework?" he asks, nodding at my laptop.

"Hmmm?" I drum my fingers against the cover. "Oh. Not really. Just ... surfing the web."

Surfing the web? Do people even say that anymore?

He nods and takes another small sip of his coffee. Swallows.

"Lots of people posting pictures?" he asks.

I shrug and feel my throat tighten. Oh, my God. What is wrong with me? I don't even care about homecoming! At least I never did before. Pull it together, Eva! I look down at the closed laptop until I feel more in control of my emotions, leaving a long, dead moment of silence.

"So ... I'm on my way to work on your van."

"Oh, yeah?"

"Do you … want to come with? See how it's going?"

I look up. This must be a trick question. Hang out alone at the coffee shop filling out college applications on homecoming night or accompany a hot guy … anywhere? No-brainer.

"Um. Sure?"

He nods and gives me a small, satisfied smile. "Cool."

I pack up the laptop, shoving my cookie into the case. When I stand up, juggling my coffee and trying to hoist the bag onto my shoulder, Zenn reaches for the strap. "Here. I'll take it."

"Oh. Thanks."

I never offer to help people with their things and I envy the way he can just take my bag from me like that. I envy how touch is, for most people, as easy as breathing.

He lifts his arm in a ladies-first kind of move, and I lead the way out of the coffee shop.

"Did you drive here?" he asks.

I shake my head. "I walked."

"Okay. I'm just across the street."

He gestures with his coffee cup to a pickup truck, old, but old in a rounded, classic, vintage sort of way. Not in a dumpy-piece-of-shit way. It's a deep maroon, the color of my mom's beloved merlot.

"Wow. That's a great truck," I say, thinking maybe he does have money after all. It looks mint — shiny and rust-free.

"Thanks."

It suddenly occurs to me that maybe I shouldn't be getting into his truck, at night, to go to a deserted body shop. I don't know him that well and I haven't had enough experience with boys to develop a radar about these sorts of things. But my fears subside slightly when he opens the passenger-side door for me. Once I'm in, he hands over my laptop case and makes sure I'm settled before closing the door carefully behind me. It's an old-fashioned gesture that, right or wrong, makes me feel safe.

Plus, I've got my dad's number on speed dial and there's a Taco Bell that's open until midnight right next to the body shop. It's not like we'll be in the middle of nowhere.

The truck has a vintage smell to it: a little musty, like my grandpa's attic. The faint 1960s scent of cigarettes and Aqua Net is embedded in the leather upholstery.

In the absence of cup holders, Zenn balances his coffee between his knees and starts the engine.

"Here, I'll hold it." I reach out. "That looks like a recipe for disaster."

Zenn laughs a little and hands me his cup. I'm careful to make sure our fingers don't touch in the hand off.

"Yeah, I guess stick shifts and hot coffee don't mix," he says.

"Unless you want a third-degree burn to the groin."

Oh. My. God. What is *wrong* with me? Just the mention of his groin has made my cheeks burn. I'm so grateful for the dark.

"I definitely do *not* want that."

His coffee cup is fractal-free, as I figured it would be. He's only held it for a few minutes, and nothing traumatic has happened during our walk to his truck. He drives us to the body shop, making small talk along the way.

"Did your friend go to the dance? The tall one?"

"Charlotte?" I try to remember whether Zenn and Charlotte have crossed paths, but I can't think of when they were both at the same place at the same time. She comes to see

Josh and Josh alone. She and Zenn have never actually met, as far as I know.

"I don't know her name. I've just seen you guys at lunch."

Ah. So he doesn't apparate. I wonder how he sees me but I don't see him. Then it occurs to me that maybe he just sees Charlotte.

"You have lunch fifth period?"

He shakes his head. "Sixth. But I've seen you leaving."

"Oh. Right. I guess Charlotte is hard to miss." He opens his mouth to say something — probably to comment on her increasing beauty and popularity — but I cut him off. "Yeah, she went. With Pepé Le Pew."

He smiles. "Mooney, huh? She'll come home with clear sinuses, anyway."

"Yeah. I hope that's all she comes home with."

Zenn glances in my direction. I hadn't realized I'd sound so bitter.

I wave my hand, dismissing my comment. "I shouldn't have said that. Sorry. He seems like a nice enough guy."

"You don't have to be sorry. I'm not going to defend Mooney."

"I just worry about her. She's not used to that sort of crowd."

"They do take some getting used to." Zenn pulls into the parking lot of the body shop. "I'm sure she'll be fine."

"Yeah," I agree, though the thought of what Josh might expect after his senior homecoming dance, and what Charlotte might be willing to do to keep him interested, worries me.

We both climb out of the truck. I leave my laptop on the seat and Zenn uses his key to open the shop. He leads me through the dark to the garage, where he flips on a few lights. The van is there, though it is almost unrecognizable. Gone are the blue skies and headless sheep. It looks fantastic already.

I tell him that.

He nods. "Amazing what a coat of paint will do."

The van is now a blank white canvas. He has already sketched the artwork on the side, and the lettering. It looks amazing, and he hasn't even started painting yet.

He moves a pile of rags off a chair and rolls it toward me. I sit while he starts getting his equipment ready: airbrush pen, compressor and various small vials of paint. He takes off his jacket and his hat and tosses them on a tool bench. His hair is so short it isn't even messed up, though he seems like he wouldn't care if it were. I imagine Josh might have spent more time on his hair tonight than Charlotte did.

It's cold in the garage so Zenn pulls on a paint-stained hoodie. When he reaches up to tug it on over his head, his T-shirt creeps up and I get a glimpse of the smooth, surprisingly tan skin just above the waistband of his jeans. My fingers ache to know what his skin — what *any* boy's skin — feels like. It makes me incredibly sad that I may never find out. Or at least without releasing a shit storm of childhood trauma and who-knows-what.

I fold up in the chair, wrapping my arms around my bent legs, resting my chin on my knees.

"Sorry it's so cold," he says as he scrolls through his phone and starts some music. "I don't like to turn on the space heater because of the paint fumes."

"It's fine," I say. "Better cold and alive than warm and blown to pieces."

Zenn gives me one of his rare, full smiles, and gets to work. He applies the paint in short, quick strokes that look like mistakes, at first. In fact, I almost say something, cringing at how he's so bold and decisive with *permanent* paint. But each added layer, each color, each stroke of his hand adds a new dimension. If he actually does make mistakes, I don't see them.

"How'd you learn to do this?"

He shrugs. "I don't know. It's just my thing. Like … you and math."

I don't remember learning math, although I'm sure I did. It feels more like I uncovered it, like the math knowledge was always there inside me and it was just a matter of peeling away other stuff to get to it. Michelangelo said that every block of stone has a statue inside and that the sculptor's job is to discover it. Maybe everyone has a gift like that: something that is there already, waiting to be discovered.

"This is so much cooler than math, though."

Zenn pauses and raises one eyebrow at me. "I'm not sure there is anything remotely cool about airbrushing church vans."

This makes me laugh. "Not airbrushing vans, exactly. Just … art. In general."

He changes the color cup on his gun, his hands moving like he could do it in his sleep. He tests it out on a piece of cardboard, then turns to the van and starts spraying.

"Do you ever make mistakes?" I ask.

"Never." His answer is immediate, purposefully serious, sarcastic.

I laugh.

"You make a 'mistake,' you figure out a way to work with it. It is what it is. You can't let it ruin everything," he says.

"That sounds kind of like a whole life philosophy."

"Well. It's a lot easier to do with art than it is with life."

I nod. "It's so different from math. Math is concrete. Right. Wrong. You make a mistake, you get the wrong answer. A calculation error can be ... catastrophic."

"That's why I stick with art."

I watch him work for over two hours, asking questions once in a while but mostly just watching, listening to his eclectic playlist, studying the way his shoulders move under his sweatshirt. It's nearly ten thirty when he sets down his airbrush kit and stretches.

"I'm starving," he says. "Wanna make a run for the border?"

"*Si,*" I answer.

"*Bueno,*" he says. "*Vamos, chica guapa.*"

I don't speak Spanish — I'm a French girl — but I think he called me either pretty or fat. I'm going to go with pretty.

◯◯

After we inhale eight of Taco Bell's finest tacos between us (Zenn: five, me: three), Zenn drives me home. He pulls up in front of my house and I try to see it through his eyes. It's not a very cute house: a split-level from the seventies. My parents would rather have one of the historic homes nearby, but anything with vintage details like crown molding is out of my parents' price range. My mom has made efforts to add some charm — window boxes and shutters and such. But as my grandpa always said, *It's like putting lipstick on a pig.*

Almost all the lights are out; it's hours past the quads' bedtime, and by now I'm sure my mom and dad have passed out as well. Insomnia is rarely a problem when you're taking care of a bunch of little kids. Sleep always trumps waiting up for your teenage daughter.

"Thanks for rescuing me tonight," I say.

Zenn tilts his head. In the dim light his skin looks even darker than usual. I wonder about his heritage, if he has some Native American in him or something.

"Rescuing you?"

"I was going to fill out college applications."

"Oh, yeah? To where?"

Now I've done it. Saying out loud that I want to go to the schools I want to go to always sounds pretentious and a little bit insane. Like I'm some sort of "beautiful mind." I shrug. "A couple different places."

"Don't be modest. I already know you're a genius."

I usually don't like being teased about being smart, but he says it almost affectionately. I still don't answer.

"Harvard? Yale?" He nudges me with his elbow. "Oxford?" He says it with a high-brow British accent.

I smile and shake my head.

"Come on. Where?"

I give him a squinty, stubborn look. He gives me one back.

"Fine. Stanford. MIT. Northwestern. Nowhere I can afford, but whatever."

He nods, impressed. "Well. At least you'll probably get in."

It's true, my chances of getting in are better than most. I should appreciate that fact at least. Whether or not it's actually affordable is a luxury that most kids don't even get to worry about. But to me it seems it would be worse to get in and then not be able to go. It would be like ... having a boyfriend but not being able to touch him.

"What kind of scholarships are you applying for?"

"All of them, pretty much. But there's one through this company that gives out a hundred thousand dollars. It's called the Ingenuity Scholarship. That's the one I really need."

"You'll get it. Aren't you, like, valedictorian?"

I roll my eyes. "No. Daniel Kim, that AP bastard." I've always finished *just* behind Daniel Kim in everything — test scores, class rank, you name it — which would be infuriating if he weren't such a super nice guy.

"Ah. Kim. Figures. That kid has even less of a social life than me."

"Besides, it's not really an academic scholarship."

He looks confused. "It's not?"

"They look for someone with a unique story and some kind of special talent or gift. Could be anything, really."

"Huh," he says.

"What about you? What do you want to do after graduation?" I've learned to be careful with this question because not everyone plans on going to college.

Zenn hesitates, still looking out the windshield. His profile is perfect: straight nose, slightly pouty lips, eyelashes, eyelashes, eyelashes. Damn. He could major in eyelashes. Get a full ride.

"Hopefully college. But ... I'm not holding my breath."

I sense that I shouldn't push, so I don't. "So, thanks again. For tonight. I didn't think I cared about homecoming but I guess I did. A little bit."

"Yeah," he says, still staring out the front window. "Everyone cares about this high school shit a little bit." He glances over at me. "Thanks for keeping me company."

I put my hand on the door handle but am hesitant to get out of his warm, comforting truck. I wonder, if I sat here long enough, if he'd kiss me. You know, just for something to do, not because he likes me or anything. Just to fill an awkward silence. Teenagers do that sometimes — just hook up out of curiosity or boredom. I could kiss him back — my mouth doesn't transmit fractals at least. But I couldn't touch him. I couldn't rub my hands down his back, slide my fingers through his hair. I could kiss him, but my hands would have to stay away from his body. It's too depressing to think about.

"See you on Monday," I tell him.

He lifts his hand in a small wave as I close the door.

CHAPTER 13

ON SUNDAY I GET TO SLEEP IN. *Sleep in* is a relative concept with four preschoolers in the house, but miraculously I
make it until eight and my mom doesn't even make me go to
church. I'm guessing she feels a little sorry for me, thinking
that I stayed out so late working on my college applications
instead of going to the dance. I don't tell her that I was with
a boy, not because she'd be upset or mad, but because she'd
have a thousand questions for me and I'm not in the mood to
deal with her trying to relive her youth through my experi-
ences. My story would be a bit of a letdown, anyway.

The morning is sunny, bright and cool, the kind of fall
morning that makes you feel guilty to be inside, so I decide
to go for a run while my parents and the kids are at church.

I run past Charlotte's house, but it doesn't tell me anything about her night. Her car is in the driveway. The curtains in her bedroom are still shut, but she doesn't have little

brothers or sisters so that's not unusual. I imagine her curled up in bed, her hair still stiff from last night's styling products, Josh's scent lingering ... well ... everywhere. I wonder how it went, if she had fun, if Josh kissed her goodnight and, if so, what it felt like to run her hands over his shoulders. I wonder what guys' shoulders feel like. I wonder if they held hands. God, the thought of holding hands with a guy is almost more of a turn-on to me than a kiss. Interlocking warm fingers, the brush of fingertips against a palm. It seems like such a tame and G-rated gesture, but to me it would be everything.

I wonder if Charlotte will call me later today with the details, or if she'll call Jessica first since the two of them seem pretty tight lately. Maybe because Jessica actually seems excited about Josh where I just seem ... skeptical.

I run slowly down Oak Street, admiring the big houses. Josh Mooney's old girlfriend lives in one of them, but I can't remember which. I can't even remember her name. I look up and down the street and guess it's the big Victorian with the complicated color scheme and gingerbread trim. It looks like her: frilly and high maintenance. In the way that jealous girls do, Charlotte used to call her Bucky because the girlfriend had slightly prominent front teeth. She wasn't bucktoothed by any means, but when you hate a girl because she gets to kiss the boy you like, any little imperfection can become a spiteful nickname. I don't even remember her real name. Rebecca? Bucky Becky? I think about texting Charlotte to ask her, but I don't.

Down the street there's a guy raking leaves in front of my favorite house: an Arts and Crafts–style with a huge front porch. I slow my pace when I realize the guy is wearing a green army jacket.

Holy crap. Could Zenn live in my very favorite house in the whole town? What are the odds? *And* he's up at eight thirty — what are the odds of *that*?

I cross over to the other side of the street because, although I would love to see him, I don't really want him to see me.

His back is to me, he is wearing headphones and he is focused on his task. He doesn't notice me today.

I circle back toward home and spend the rest of the day raking our leaves, helping my mom with laundry, doing homework, playing with the kids. Charlotte finally texts me back at nearly three o'clock.

Charlotte: Hey!
Me: Hey! How was it?
Charlotte: Totally on fleek!!!

Oh, Charlotte. Her attempt to use slang that is already outdated, and use it just slightly incorrectly, is why I love her. But the fact that she's saying *on fleek* at all makes me sad. This is the kind of language and enthusiasm that she has picked up since hanging out with Josh and his gang.

Me: That's good. It was fun, huh?
Charlotte: SOOOOO fun. I wish u were there.
I missed u!

I'm sure she was all broken up about me not going while she and Josh were making out.

Charlotte: What did u do?

I debate just telling her I hung out at the coffee shop. Something in me wants her to feel bad about abandoning our tradition of skipping homecoming and making ourselves feel okay about it with chocolaty coffee and muffins. But instead I decide to tell her the truth.

Me: I hung out with Zenn

There is a slight pause before she replies.

Charlotte: Wait … tutoring guy?
Me: Yep
Charlotte: Oh! Cool. Did u have fun
Charlotte: ?
Me: Yep
Charlotte: Cool
Me: Yeah.
Me: I saw your pictures on Insta. You looked really pretty.

I hate that I do this. I don't want to be one of those girls who gives empty compliments. But she did look pretty. She always looks pretty. And I know this is proper girl etiquette — to tell each other how pretty we are.

Charlotte: Thnx!!

I want to ask her more. I want to hear every detail of her night, but it feels too strange. It's like I'm a younger sibling she used to play Barbies with, but now she's outgrown them and only plays to humor me.

> **Me: Maybe we can go to Java Dock later and you can tell me about it?**

Another longish pause.

> **Charlotte: Shoot. Sorry. Jessica and I are going to *$.**

Starbucks. No more Java Dock.

> **Me: That's fine. I'll just talk to you tomorrow or something.**
> **Charlotte: K.**
> **Charlotte: Sorry ...**

It's that last sorry, like an afterthought, that does it. I feel tears well in my eyes. I don't want her feeling sorry for me.

> **Me: TTYL**

I wonder if she'll sense my disdain. We used to make fun of texting abbreviations like that: LOL, TTYL, BRB, GTG. But she's speaking a new language now because she texts back:

> **2DLoo**

I think I've lost her. She's becoming one of them.

CHAPTER 14

MY MOM AND I MAKE OUR WEEKLY TRIP to the grocery store late Sunday afternoon. My dad stays home with the kids and we tackle the shopping, stretching it out as if it were an afternoon at the spa. We enjoy our time together, our time without four little people asking for cereal or candy or cheese or soda.

I worry (and simultaneously hope) that I'll see Zenn at the Piggly Wiggly, but he's nowhere to be found. Another guy takes our cart; his name tag says *Brian*.

On the way home my mom drives down Oak Street and I'm not too proud to admit that I scope out the Arts and Crafts house again, wondering if Zenn might be around. I'm amazed how you can go from not knowing someone exists to thinking about him around the clock in just a couple of weeks. There is no sign of him until we pass Bucky Becky's Victorian, and I spot him raking her yard. I do a double take to make sure. Yes, there is his green jacket and his truck in the driveway. Could he be dating Bucky? Then I realize if that were the case she would have chomped down on his collar with her big buck teeth and dragged him to homecoming, whether he wanted to go or not. As we get closer to his truck I see a sign on the driver's-side door, one of those magnets that you can just stick on there, advertising *Eden Landscaping Service*. I think back to his scraped-up knuckles and the bandages and realize that blisters from yard work probably make more sense than injuries from fighting.

So. He works at the Piggly Wiggly. And the body shop. And some kind of landscaping place.

I'm starting to suspect that he is not rich after all, which makes me feel slightly more hopeful about the prospect of any kind of anything with him. As long as he's okay with, you know, no touching.

Right.

"You know him?" My mom has followed my lingering gaze.

I look back out the front window, trying to play it cool. "Who?" I'm as bad an actress as Charlotte. Maybe worse.

"That guy back there? You were totally checking him out."

"I was not."

"You kinda were."

I shrug and pick some lint off my black coat. "I think it was one of the guys I tutor."

"The one who went to homecoming with Charlotte?"

I shake my head.

"Oh." My mom slows the minivan. "Should we stop and say hi?" I can hear the teasing in her voice. She turns up the goofy children's music CD that plays in a never-ending loop, whether the kids are present or not. "Maybe we should roll down the windows so he can hear our tunes."

This makes me laugh. "Please don't."

She slows even more and starts to roll down her window. She sings along loudly with the CD:

"Harry the silly platypus
Has fur like a bear but a nose like a duck!"

"Mom!"

I look in the rearview mirror and see Zenn glance up at us. I'm sure he can't tell it's me, but I feel panicky and sweaty anyway.

My mom rolls up her window and presses on the gas. She turns the radio back down.

"What's his name?"

"Harry." If she's going to be difficult, then so am I. "The platypus."

My mom slows the car again, rolls down the window and turns the radio even louder.

"Zenn," I yell, laughing. "His name is Zenn." I turn down the volume.

"Ben?"

"Zenn. With a *Z*."

"Oh. Unusual."

I nod. I know she's just trying to make conversation, to get me to include her in my life, but it feels weird. Moms want to talk to their daughters about boys, but daughters do *not* want to talk to their moms about boys. I don't know why. It's one of the rules of teenager-parent interaction.

She is raising her eyebrows in a hopeful way. Oh, God, what the hell. It will make her so happy.

"He's the one painting the church van."

"Oh! In that case I should turn around and give him a hug."
She starts to brake again and I whine, *"Mom!"*

"I'm *kidding*. Jeez, lighten up, Ev."

I don't offer anything else right away, maybe to punish her. When my mom tries too hard to be chummy, I clam up. I am the gatekeeper of information and if she wants any of it, she has to limit her embarrassing behavior.

Now she sighs, and the melancholy sound of it makes me want to offer her more.

"We hung out last night."

Joy flashes briefly in her eyes, and I want to tell her not to get her hopes up. I think she's just thrilled that I wasn't alone on homecoming night. Must be hard to watch your kid be such a loner.

"I thought you were at Java Dock?"

"I was. But he stopped by to get coffee and then I hung out with him while he worked on the van. We went to Taco Hell. No biggie."

She keeps it low-key. "Cool," she says. "Is he cute? I didn't get a good look."

I want to be cool, indifferent, blasé ... but against my will I admit: "He's not bad."

Understatement. Of. The. Year.

CHAPTER 15

ON MONDAY IN AP LITERATURE we have to work in groups and, for the first time ever, Charlotte allows herself to make immediate will-you-be-my-partner eye contact with someone besides me. By the time she looks my way, she has already committed to working with a cheerleader and a basketball player. She gives me an apologetic look. I can tell she feels bad, but not bad enough to ditch them. Instead, I ask the two boys in the class who are least likely to get laid before their twenty-fifth birthdays. They graciously accept my offer.

At least I'm still appreciated in some circles.

The same sort of subtle abandonment is happening at lunch. A group of Josh's friends is trying to lure Charlotte to their table, but there is only one open seat. Charlotte stays with me, but glances longingly at the empty chair that is meant for her.

"Soooo," I say, trying to start up a conversation. "Are you going to do Science Fair again this year?"

"Hmmm?" Charlotte looks up from her phone.

"Science Fair? Are you doing it this year?"

"Maybe. I don't know. Are you?"

"Yeah. Carlson says I should. Since I want to major in something STEM related, he says it looks good to do it all four years."

She nods and takes a bite of her sandwich. "I might not. I'm not majoring in science so … you know."

"Right."

Someone laughs loudly at the other table and Charlotte glances over again. What am I doing? She's like a dog who wants to run and I'm standing on her leash.

This is so hard.

I toss my garbage in the trash can and feel like I'm about to do the same with our friendship.

"Char, I'm going to be tutoring at lunchtime, you know, before midterms. So … I probably won't be here much."

"You won't?" She sounds sad, but I don't know what to believe anymore.

"Probably not until after Christmas break. So if you want to find someone else to sit with, go ahead. Since I'm not going to be here anyway."

"Are you sure?"

I nod, not trusting myself to speak. Letting someone go is hard.

I guess I get it. It's exciting to have new friends. I remember when we first met in sixth grade and we couldn't get enough of each other. We liked the same TV shows, laughed at the same things, had the same sort of disdain for the cool crowd that comes from knowing you'll never be a part of it. Charlotte was all elbows and knees with puffy blond hair and braces. If you really looked at her, you could see that she'd be pretty one day. But at twelve, she wasn't there yet.

Up until fifth grade, my friendships were unaffected by my "gift." But after Lauren, all hell broke loose. Every rejection and insecurity and drama-filled adolescent moment left kids scarred, and when I touched anyone or anything, I became scarred, too. But Charlotte's fractals were surprisingly pure. Where touching most thirteen-year-old kids left me feeling woozy and exhausted, Charlotte's fractal still managed to be pink and sunny, hopeful and warm. Charlotte and I became connected at the hip, and eventually I told her all the secrets (well, the two main secrets) that I kept from everyone else: about my "parents" and my "condition." She's never shared any deep, dark secrets with me, but I suspect that's because she doesn't have any. Most of her secrets have been about which boy she likes at the moment. So I guess it's not surprising that we've gotten to this point, where she'd have to choose between a boy — that one special boy — and me. I guess I just thought that once we made it through middle school we'd be past this sort of thing.

I don't really have any lunchtime tutoring to do, so I'll have to find somewhere to hang out during fifth period. The other people we sit with at lunch are okay, but I don't want to hang out with them without Charlotte. She may be quiet and slightly awkward, but she is Miss Congeniality compared to me. How do I get closer to people when one touch tells me far too much about them? How do I ever erase that stuff from my mind and just be normal teenage friends?

Sometimes Charlotte has cello-group lessons during lunch, and I go to the library or to Mr. Haase's room. Guess I'll be doing that every day now.

$$\infty$$

When I check Josh's algo, I can tell that he's finally starting to get bits and pieces of trig. Sure enough he reports that he's gotten his grade up to a low C. He'll be going back to football practice starting tomorrow, just checking in with me weekly for maintenance. He seems happy and proud of himself and I'm not sure how much of that has to do with his math grade and how much has to do with Charlotte.

I have to admit he's not a bad guy, really, but I worry that his attention span won't last past Christmas. When you're as good-looking and popular as he is, there is always a line of potential girlfriends waiting in the wings.

I covertly touch his letterman's jacket while he's packing up his stuff. I'm not proud of the fact, but I can't help it. I want to see if there is anything going on that I need to worry about, but his fractal doesn't give me the kind of information I'm looking for. All I get is the same navy-blue sadness — a complex network of arteries branching off forever. There is the same puppy-kicking heartache, the same heavy weight of disappointment, and a slight fuzzy, dizzy feeling. I don't know what any of it means, exactly, but I doubt it has anything to do with Charlotte.

Zenn doesn't come for tutoring on Mondays and Charlotte left right after school, so I walk home by myself. I think about heading up the hill to the body shop to see how they're doing on the van, but I don't want to seem like some kind of stalker. I mean, it's a van I've seen a million times. They're putting the clear coat of paint on soon. There is literally nothing new to see.

Out of ideas, I take a detour to the cemetery. I don't go all that often because, frankly, I don't have much of a connection to my real parents, much less to the random place where they are buried. But I find cemeteries oddly soothing, and maybe I still come occasionally out of survivor's guilt. My mom brought me when I was little and I would make crayon rubbings of the headstones while she tidied up my parents' — her sister's and her brother-in-law's — grave. I can tell she visits without me now because their grave is still weedless and green compared to the ones around it. I'm not sure what the proper frequency is for visiting the grave of parents you never really knew.

I step carefully down the rows between headstones until I find theirs: Lynn and Thomas Scheurich. Once again, a smooth, round stone sits on the top of the marker. The first time I found one I thought it was just a weird coincidence — that a rock had been kicked up by a lawnmower and landed on the gravestone — so I brushed it back to the ground with my hand. But the next time I visited, I found another one, same place. The third time, I pocketed the rock and went home to Google *stones on graves*. It had to be intentional.

My Google results showed it is a Jewish tradition to place a stone or pebble on a headstone, indicating that you have visited. Unlike flowers, stones don't die, so stones are better suited to the "permanence of memory." I also learned that shepherds used to keep pebbles in a sling, one for each of their sheep, to keep track of their flock when they would take them out to pasture. Placing a pebble on the grave is a way to ask God to keep watch over your departed loved one. So it's a show of respect. And a symbol. Mystery solved.

Today, there is another one: nearly white, and speckled, about the size of an egg, but flat. I hold it in my palm and note it's the kind I find when Charlotte and I walk South Beach, made smooth and round by the sand and waves. Someone brought it here on purpose, and I suspect it's my mom. Even though we are clearly not Jewish, she loves religious traditions and tokens of any kind. We're not Catholic, but she lights candles for people who have died and uses a rosary when she prays sometimes. Leaving a stone on the grave would be right up her alley.

I reach into my jacket pocket and pull out my own stone — an almost square reddish one that I picked up the last time Charlotte and I were at the beach — and I swap hers for mine.

My mom and I don't talk much about my parents and she no longer feels obligated to drag me along to the cemetery with her, but I know she'll be happy to see this evidence that I am visiting on my own. If she notices the different rock and realizes I'm the one who left it, that is. I could leave hers there and add mine, or I could leave her a note or something, but I kind of like the idea that we're having an unspoken conversation, back and forth, with just our stones.

CO

On Tuesday I put on mascara, telling myself it's not that unusual; I do it sometimes. But then I also blow-dry my hair a little and put on some lip balm. It's lip *balm*, not lip gloss, but I know it's a fine line — just a slight variation of shimmer — between the two. When I look in the mirror the difference is so subtle no one would even notice. But I notice. I know it's all for Zenn, and my high-and-mighty stance about beauty now feels fake. Maybe it's normal to want to make yourself stand out around the guy you like, I tell myself. It's nature. I mean, that's why peacocks have fancy feathers and why baboons flaunt their rosy-pink asses. It's all a mating ritual and we humans are just animals when it comes down to it. Maybe Charlotte, with her lip gloss and eyeliner, is more normal and natural than I am. Maybe I'm the ridiculous one, destined for a life alone because I refuse to flash my pink ass. So to speak.

Frustrated and confused, I throw on my glasses and my favorite unflattering hoodie and head to school.

During fifth period I take my lunch to the library. You're not supposed to eat in there, but Mrs. Lanham loves me and won't say a word. Besides, it's not like kids hang out in the library at lunchtime, much less any who will be tempted down the road to delinquency by me, their nerd ringleader. The place is deserted.

In my hurry to blend back in with the normal kids when the bell rings, I take a corner too fast and crash straight into Zenn. Like, smack into him so hard that my glasses nearly fly off my face. Figures. I have never actually seen him during the school day before and yet now, at a vulnerable moment, here he is. I grab his jacket to keep from falling, but the fractal hits so fast I let go like he's on fire. Zenn steadies me by holding my shoulders.

"Whoa. Sorry," he says.

"Totally my fault. I just" — I gesture a curve — "took that turn a bit fast."

His hands are still on my upper arms, holding tight. His firm grip feels amazing and I wish I could grab on to him for balance (or under the guise of needing balance). But ... touching is a one-way street. I can be touched, I can't touch back. Not with my hands, anyway.

He looks down at the empty lunch bag clutched in my hand. "Did you eat in the library?"

Busted. What a loser. I adjust my glasses.

"Um ..."

Unexpected tears of self-pity sting my eyes and I blink quickly to keep them at bay. I don't think I fool Zenn. Still holding my shoulders, he steers me back into the library and pushes me gently to sit on a table. He drops his hands from my arms and leans down to make eye contact.

His direct gaze is unnerving.

"What's going on?"

I shrug and look away, a little uncomfortable with his concern. "Nothing. Just ... catching up on some homework."

I can tell he doesn't believe me.

"It's just ... my friend Charlotte." I hesitate to go into too much detail. "She's just ... different since she started dating Pepé."

Zenn smiles a little at my nickname for Josh. He straightens up and nods. "You've been friends for a long time?"

I nod. "I mean, she's happy. That's good. I just thought ..." I thought she'd never abandon me. I thought we'd be BFFs forever. No matter how I finish that sentence, it sounds vulnerable and whiny, so I just let it hang out there. I wave my hand dismissively. "I don't care. I'm fine."

"So fine you're eating lunch in the library?"

"I like the library."

"Obviously."

"I do. I like it better than I like most people. It's quiet. It has substance."

He laughs and sits next to me on the table. "I have study hall fifth period but my teacher always lets me go to the art room instead," he says. He nudges me lightly with his shoulder. "Come eat with me there."

"No, it's fine."

"Come on. Keep me company. I'll let you help me with math." He says this in a singsong voice, the voice my mom might use to bribe the quads with candy.

"You don't even need my help."

"Yes, I do."

"No. You don't."

"I do," he insists. "Come on. It'll be fun."

I'm sure he's just feeling sorry for me, but it feels nice to have someone care about me being lonely. Besides my mom, I mean.

"Okay," I tell him. "But only because you're kind of new here and I wouldn't want you to feel like a loser."

"It'll be, like, your public-service project. You could put it on your college applications."

I laugh at his joke, but also at the idea that spending time with him would be any sort of hardship on my part. Plus, at the very least eating with him might lessen the ache of losing Charlotte.

CHAPTER 16

BEFORE DINNER MY MOM DROPS ME OFF at the body shop to pick up the van. I suspect her eager offer has more to do with her wanting to get a glimpse of Zenn than it does with anything else. I say a silent prayer that maybe he won't be there, that maybe after our tutoring session this afternoon he went to work at the Piggly Wiggly. Not that I don't want to see him again. I'm just trying to avoid my mom's nosiness and the whole circus that four preschoolers bring with them everywhere they go. When I see his truck in the lot, I know my prayer, like many, has not been answered. My mom always says that God answers all prayers, it's just that sometimes the answer is not what you want. I think that's a convenient excuse for radio silence from heaven. I must have gotten the skeptic gene from my real dad's side of the family.

I hop out of the minivan quickly, trying to head off a scene, but it's too late. The church van is parked in the lot and my mom gets out to admire it, which makes all four kids clamor to get out as well. They are all old enough and savvy enough to slither out of their car seats, so in a matter of seconds my mom and all four of my siblings are out of the car and examining the van. I'm trying to corral them when Zenn comes out of the shop. He looks highly amused.

"Hey," I say, embarrassed.

"Hey." He smiles at the squirts, who have migrated toward him immediately. They look up at him with undisguised interest. My mom tries to be slightly more subtle, but she creeps over, too.

"These are my brothers and sisters," I tell him. I touch each of their heads as I say their names. "Eli, Ethan, Essie and Libby. And my mom."

Now my mom steps closer and lifts her hand in a small wave. I'm grateful she doesn't shake his hand. Even watching other people shake hands makes me a little nervous. It's like when you watch *America's Funniest Home Videos* and someone falls off a roof or gets hit in the crotch by a baseball bat: it doesn't hurt you, but you cringe in sympathy, imagining pain you can't feel.

"Nice to meet you, Mrs. Walker," Zenn says to my mom. Then he looks down. The little ones are still staring at him with blatant curiosity. "What's going on, small people?"

Now that she has his attention, Libby laughs and starts bouncing. "Hihihihi!!!"

Ethan is more focused. "Did you paint our van?"

"I helped paint it, yep."

Eli's eyes are big, impressed. "How?" he asks. I imagine he's amazed at how Zenn got such impressive results with finger paints or some big clumsy brush, the only kinds of painting implements three-year-olds know anything about.

"I use a special tool called an airbrush. It's like a little pen that sprays out paint. Do you want to see?"

Four pairs of eyes grow big and four small heads nod in unison. Zenn looks to my mom for permission.

"You sure?" she asks, like he might be a little bit insane.

"Sure," he says. I have to keep my jaw from hanging open. He has no idea what he's getting himself into. Should I warn him?

But my mom has already started preparations. "E's," she says firmly. Sometimes we call them that rather than saying each of their names. "Look at me."

They all turn in a unified motion of obedience and look up at my mom.

"Mr. Zenn is going to take us into his work area." She speaks slowly, her voice demanding attention. "We do not touch *anything*. We stay together. If you do not behave, we will not get to see how Mr. Zenn painted the van." Her speech has a military quality to it and I expect them all to salute when she's done. "Do you all understand?" she asks.

Four heads nod earnestly.

"Hold hands, please," she adds.

Zenn leads us to the garage, which is empty of cars at the moment. He lines the kids up and sits them down on four upside-down crates. Then he gets out an airbrush and explains how it works. He even lets them all feel the compressed air with their hands. When they start to get riled up, wanting him to spray them again and again, he moves on calmly and hooks the pen to the hose. He grabs a piece of cardboard and, in the blink of an eye, paints a simple dog on it — floppy ears, tongue hanging out — so cute and perfect that the girls start to bounce and want him to do more, like he's making balloon animals or doing magic tricks. Frankly, it *is* magical the way he can paint so perfectly from some vision in his head. He cuts a new clean sheet of cardboard into four smaller pieces and turns to Essie.

"Essie, right?" he asks her. "What's your favorite animal?"

"Koala bears."

He doesn't even look to me for translation, which is amazing because Essie can't say her *l*'s or her *r*'s and it comes out like "kowawa beaws." The hiss of the airbrush fills the garage and he paints a little koala bear in less than a minute, along with Essie's name in beautiful script. Then he turns to Libby. After he's drawn and personalized a cat, an elephant and a platypus — how he knows what a platypus looks like without referring to a picture is amazing in itself — he tells them that the paintings have to dry but he'll give them to me tomorrow at school and I'll bring them home. Not one of the kids argues or whines. My mom and I stand in awe.

Then he leads them back to the minivan and all four kids pile in. I'm not sure I've ever seen them so docile and obedient. It's like he has them in some kind of trance, like the freaking Pied Piper. I credit his hypnotic eyelashes.

My mom thanks him and climbs back in the van herself. When he turns his back she mouths, *Wow!*

I roll my eyes.

Zenn gives me the keys to the church van when they leave. I wait for questions about the age gap between the quads and me, about what it's like to have *four* three-year-old siblings, but he doesn't make me feel like a freak show. In fact, he doesn't act surprised at all.

"You were, like, the rug rat whisperer there," I tell him. "I don't think I've ever seen them sit that still for that long."

"Kids are all about paint. And animals."

"Right," I say sarcastically. "I'm sure that's all it is."

I climb into the van and Zenn closes the door behind me. I roll down the window.

"I'll see you tomorrow, fifth period?" he asks. "Art room?"

I hesitate before answering. "I guess so." I'm still not sure about this plan, but I'm finding it hard to resist the idea of an extra hour with him. Every day. I reach into my coat pocket for the envelope with the check. As Zenn promised, Dave did the work for only twelve hundred dollars, and Zenn worked his magic for only five hundred, so the whole thing cost less than two thousand, which my dad found in the church transportation budget. And it was worth every penny.

At least to me.

CHAPTER 17

I CAN BARELY CONCENTRATE during fourth-period French class. I feel like I've made a huge mistake, agreeing to meet Zenn *every day* for lunch. What the hell will we talk about? Why not just live in the fantasy of possibility instead of the reality of what this is: a dead end?

Usually French draaaags on forever, Monsieur Sullivan's constant *"En français, s'il vous plaît"* a metronome counting off the slow passage of time. But today the clock ticks at a frightening pace and before I know it, the bell rings. My stomach lurches.

Oh, God. Here goes nothing.

I take my time getting to the art room so that Zenn will already be there when I walk in. Seems like the better option than being there first. I swing by the bathroom, wiggle my way through a sea of girls taking selfies and then study my face in a tiny corner of the mirror while I wash my hands. I don't carry makeup with me so I pinch my cheeks, feeling like a grandma as the girl next to me gives me an odd look. I slap on a coat of ChapStick. I tuck a loose strand of hair back into my braid. Good enough.

I head to the art room slowly, doubling numbers in my mind every other step: 1, step, 2, step, 4, step, 8, step, 16. I get there by 16,777,216. When I open the art room door, Zenn is already inside, standing by a light table.

"Hey!" he greets me, more enthusiastically than I could have hoped for.

I try to look relaxed.

He brushes his hands together (I realize, now, that the light table is covered in a fine layer of sand) and waves me in. I set my backpack on a nearby chair and stand awkwardly, not sure if I should sit, not sure what to do with my hands. Oh, God. Whose horrible idea was this?

But then he smiles and says, "I'm glad you came."

Something releases its grip on my insides. I smile back. "Hopefully Mrs. Lanham won't feel rejected." I step closer to the light table. "What is that? Sand?"

He nods and runs a finger through it, leaving a curvy path.

"What are you doing with it?"

"Drawing."

"In sand?"

He nods.

"Show me."

Maybe I shouldn't be so demanding. But at least the sand gives us something to focus on besides the awkwardness of being alone together without a math book between us.

He rubs the edge of his pinkie against the surface and

clears an oblong shape in the sand. He fine-tunes the shape with his thumb and middle finger, but I still can't tell what it's meant to be. He reaches to the side and grabs a handful of the fine sand from a container next to the light table, then trickles more back onto the shape. His hands move so quickly to add and erase that I have a hard time focusing. But after a moment I realize what he's drawing.

"The Loser Cruiser!" I laugh.

He finishes up the puffy white sheep clouds with a flourish.

"Oh, my God, that's perfect." It is perfect. The perspective, the detail, the sheep clouds. He drew it in *sand*. With his *fingers*!

He looks at it for a moment and then, before I think to take a picture with my phone, he reaches into the sand container again to obliterate his work of art.

"Don't!" Without thinking, I reach for his arm to stop him, nearly touching his bare skin. I stop my hand just in time.

"What?" he asks.

"Don't ruin it!"

"That's the thing about sand pictures," he says. "They're only temporary."

"Well, that's sad."

"Not really." And just like that, he draws the same thing again, not identical to the first one but pretty close. To this one he adds the head of a driver, a girl with a braid. Then before I have time to say anything, his hand swoops in and clears a section and the Loser Cruiser transforms into Albert Einstein. Same sand, same table, completely different picture in seconds. I can't stop staring.

"Holy crap, that's amazing."

"*That's* a bit of an overstatement."

"No, it's not. How did you learn to do that?"

He wipes his hands together.

"And don't tell me it's just your thing."

"I didn't grow up with a lot of art supplies. I had to be creative."

I must look at him sadly, thinking of the fuck-ton of crayons we have at home, because he says, "I know. It sounds pitiful."

"No!"

He's doubtful.

"Okay. Well, a little. But look what amazing thing came out of your sorry childhood! I've never seen anyone do that before."

"I do have some odd talents."

Something about this comment makes my insides clench in a not unpleasant way.

"Do you ever think about going to college for art? Like, the art institute or something?"

Zenn scoffs. "Yeah, right."

"I'm serious. You could."

"It's, like, forty grand a year."

I laugh triumphantly. "I thought you hadn't thought about it!"

He gives me a look. "Thinking about it and actually doing it are two different things."

I think about my own battle with college applications and I know he's right. Dreams are one thing. Reality is something else.

"You could apply for a scholarship."

Zenn sighs. "I'm no straight-A student, Eva."

I do that sometimes: assume that everything is easy for

other people compared to the stuff I have to deal with. But I forget that academics are easy for me and that's something, at least.

"You should eat," he says, "or Mr. Haase is going to blame me when your stomach is grumbling all through AP Calculus. Or whatever genius-level class you're in." He looks at me for a second. "What math *are* you in, anyway?"

I feel my cheeks go red. The truth is by sophomore year I had finished or tested out of all the math classes the high school offers. Now I do an independent study with the local community college. I sit down at a table, unpack my lunch and change the subject back to him.

"You know, there are *lots* of scholarships out there —"

He cuts me off. "Eva, I'll be lucky to get an associate's degree and paint motorcycle fuel tanks for the rest of my life." His voice is calm but he flips off the switch for the light table a little roughly. I sense that I've hit a nerve.

"Sorry," I say quietly. "It's none of my business. It's just that you're so ... talented."

"Everybody's talented at something. Doesn't mean we all get to do what we want."

He's right. I know he's right. Only one person wins *American Idol* each season. Most of those really talented singers are never heard from again. But Zenn's fatalistic attitude makes me question my own dreams. Am I destined to get a community college degree and find some office accounting job that will keep me isolated from other people? Is that my future if I don't get a scholarship? If I can't cure myself somehow? No. It can't be. Zenn may settle for something like that because he can still have a normal life in other ways. He can get married and have kids and have relationships without secrets. But me ... my only hope is to go to a school with an amazing neuroscience-research facility and then guinea pig myself into some sort of cure. There is no *good enough* job that I'll settle for. It's all or nothing at this point.

CHAPTER 18

LATELY IT SEEMS LIKE THE MOST CONTACT I have with Charlotte is through Josh. She and I text a couple of times a week, but it's mostly Hey — hey — what's up — not much, you?, and considering we used to be in constant contact, we might as well not even bother. We haven't spent a Saturday night together since before homecoming.

Josh and I, however, have some quality time once a week to make sure his math grade doesn't slip. So I may be tighter with him than I am with Charlotte now. Besides Zenn, he might be my closest friend.

Weird.

Unfortunately, when we do spend time together, all he does is talk about Charlotte. Maybe he doesn't know we're not hanging out much anymore. I can tell by the way he talks that he really likes her, and that is a relief. He tells me about all her quirks: that she stands on one foot a lot, her other foot resting up by her knee like the tree pose in yoga, that she still sleeps with her baby blanket (which is so threadbare it's practically translucent), that she named her cello (Chelsey, obviously). I know all these things already, but I approve when he rattles them off.

I'm a little ashamed to admit that I've used our time together, while he's talking, to check his fractal. Just once. Okay ... more than once. I actually check it every time I see him. I touch his jacket or his phone and once I even placed my hand lightly on his arm, because skin-on-skin fractals are the strongest and clearest. Slowly I've started to put together his puzzle.

His fractal is tightly wound, like the rings of a tree trunk, which makes me think he's being controlled, likely by a parent. Based on the masculine colors — blue and army green — I suspect the controller is his dad, probably a type A personality who dictates most of Josh's decisions. I've gotten the sense, not so much through his fractals, but through spending time with him, that Josh is a bit of a closet nerd. He knows way more about superheroes and *Star Wars* and video games than most jocks would ever admit. But the intense structure of his fractal, combined with his expensive clothes and his Colgate smile, make me think that nerdiness is not acceptable for a Mooney. I get the feeling that nothing Josh does is quite good enough and, as a result (and maybe in rebellion), Josh may drink a bit. Maybe more than a bit, if the fuzzy, floaty feeling beneath everything is any indication. His whole vibe is less beaten down and lonely than it once was, and for that I credit Charlotte. Still, there's a lot brewing beneath his happy-go-lucky exterior.

I wonder if Charlotte knows any of that. I wonder if I should warn her. But I'm afraid that anything negative I say about Josh will come across as sour grapes. I mean, Josh's fractals are pretty intense, but so are Zenn's. I'd be kind of a hypocrite if I was trying to protect her while not heeding my own advice. So I keep my mouth shut.

She'll be fine.

We'll both be fine.

CHAPTER 19

I AM SOAKING WET DOWN TO MY SOCKS and underwear. The rain drips off my nose and runs in rivers down my backpack. My mom reminded me to bring an umbrella today but since the one by the front door was hers and I didn't want to walk home from school battling fractals, I left it behind. Along with my cell phone. And my house keys.

It was one of those mornings.

At some point during the school day the skies opened up. I watched out the window while I was tutoring Josh after school, praying it would stop. Hoping that maybe Charlotte would be somewhere to offer me a ride. But ... no luck. So now I'm walking home in a monsoon. I've given up on trying to keep anything dry. I head toward home even though I doubt I'll be able to get in the house. My mom is with the kids at their Fun to Be Three class until around five. My dad is at church, which is even farther away. Basically, I'm screwed.

And really, really cold.

I hear a car coming and I walk on the edge of the sidewalk as far from the street as possible. I can hear the spray from the car's tires, a fan of dirty brown water that will surely add filth to my soggy hell. The car slows politely. Then it slows more, pulling up next to me. My stomach drops and I wonder if anyone will hear me scream when the rapist yanks me into his car. The rain is so loud, and no smart person is out in this weather.

I sneak a peek from the corner of my eye and see *Eden Landscaping Service* on the maroon door. Holy crap. Maybe God does answer prayers sometimes! And sometimes the answer is, *Why, yes, Eva! I will send a handsome man to rescue you!*

"Nice day," Zenn calls cheerfully through his open window.

I look up at the sky. Rain pelts my face. "Gorgeous."

"Want a ride?"

I pretend to think about it for a moment.

"Come on. Get in."

I walk around to the passenger side, but hesitate after opening the door. I see his lovingly restored leather seats. "I'm soaked."

Zenn reaches in back for an old blanket, spreads it on the seat and pats it. I climb in.

I start shivering immediately. Or maybe I had already been shivering and hadn't noticed because I was alone. But now I realize I am shaking like a Chihuahua on the Fourth of July. Zenn cranks up the heat.

He turns toward my house but I explain, with chattering teeth, that I don't have my key. "You c-c-c-could t-t-t-take me to my ch-ch-ch-church. My d-d-d-dad is there."

He glances over and turns the car onto Oak Street. "Your lips are blue."

"Wh-wh-where are we g-g-g-going?"

"My place."

Goodness. God really is feeling generous today!

A few minutes later he pulls up to the Arts and Crafts house and I'm stunned. I had talked myself out of him being rich, especially since he said he didn't even have crayons as a kid.

"Y-y-y-you live here?" I stammer.

"Kind of."

I don't understand what he means until he pulls the truck around back. We get out and I follow him up some stairs to a loft above the detached three-car garage. It has been converted to a tiny apartment: one bedroom and a kitchenette–living space. I can see the sink of the microscopic bathroom just off the kitchen.

"You l-l-l-live here by yours-s-s-self?"

"My mom, too. Sometimes."

"S-s-s-sometimes?"

"She likes to party. I don't see her much."

I try to imagine what it would be like to have a mom who likes to party. Awful, I decide.

"Your dad's not in the picture?" I ask.

He shakes his head.

Wow. I don't know why, but I didn't expect that. I always think of my family as the exception, that everyone else's family has a mom, a dad and 2.5 teenage kids in a 3-bedroom house. My family is happy and healthy, but not exactly normal in the sense that I am technically an orphan being raised by my aunt and uncle, and I have quadruplet sibling-cousins who are fourteen years younger than me. But Zenn: no dad, party-girl mom, lives above someone's garage. I mean, I know people with divorced parents, but even that is not as common as statistics would suggest.

The apartment is pretty clean for a teenage boy who basically lives alone. Not a lot of personal or welcoming touches, but it's tidy and functional. He disappears into the bedroom and comes out with a folded towel, a sweatshirt and a pair of sweatpants. He holds them out to me.

"You can get dried off and then I can take you to your church or wherever."

I hesitate before taking the clothing. I have no idea what kind of fractals they might trigger, but once I get them on my body I should be fine.

I disappear into the bathroom to change. I touch the clothing with my hands as little as possible and even still I get little bursts here and there. Most feel purple and sad, loose and flowy. A little drunk. His mom likes more than the occasional glass of wine. And maybe she's drinking to forget something awful.

The clothes smell clean, though, and I'm grateful for their warmth and mere dryness. The pink sweatpants barely skim my ankles and say *Juicy* across the butt, and the sweatshirt is emblazoned with *Keep Calm and Kill Zombies*. I debate leaving on my soaked underwear, trying to decide which would be worse: seeing the outline of wet underwear through the dry clothes or going commando in Zenn's mom's sweatpants. I decide on the latter, so I tuck my panties into one pocket of my drenched jeans, my bra into the other. I carefully stack my shirt and jacket on top to hide the evidence. Then I finger-comb my hair and dry off my glasses.

When I come out of the bathroom, Zenn offers me a mug of something steamy. Again, I hesitate, then force myself to take it. It's a mug, not a cell phone. Shouldn't be too bad unless his mom cradles it every morning while she nurses a hangover and regrets with her coffee. When no fractal comes, I wrap my hands more tightly around it, happy for its warmth. I don't even ask what's in the mug — I just drink. Which is pretty stupid when I think about it. I still don't know Zenn that well, we're alone in his apartment, I'm not wearing underwear. This tea could be laced with some date-rape drug and here I am, just sucking it down. But like when he politely opened his truck door for me the night of homecoming, he now hands me a pair of dry socks and a plastic grocery bag for my wet clothes and my fears are allayed. Or ignored, at least.

I think I'm safe.

"Thanks," I tell him.

"I can't really help you with shoes. Sadly, my mom's are mostly fuck-me heels."

His tone is light, but I can't laugh. I think I'm right about his mom's drinking. Plus, any mom our moms' age wearing fuck-me heels, or Juicy sweatpants, is a disturbing visual. I try to imagine my mom wearing either and it does not compute. Just last year I got her to give up her Crocs.

"That's okay," I tell him. "I'm already one hundred percent better than I was." He gestures for me to sit down at the tiny kitchen table. I sit and study my mug, still surprised that it doesn't trigger anything. It says *Pritzer Insurance* on it, and

I realize it's probably just a spare promotional mug that no one ever uses. Just sits in the cabinet in case some drowned rat needs a hot cup of tea. Nothing personal about it.

"Have you lived here long?" I ask.

He shakes his head. "Just since June. We lived in Spellman before that."

I don't ask why they moved to Port Dalton from just one town over — I know that would be rude — but I'm guessing they got evicted. His mom lost her job. His dad left them. One of many tragedies that my dad hears about on a daily basis from his parishioners.

"It's cute," I say, looking around, and I mean it. It lacks a feminine touch, but the coziness of the slanted ceilings makes it feel like a cottage or a tree house.

"It's cheap," he says. "Which is key since my mom's not that gifted at staying employed."

I feel suddenly ridiculous that my biggest financial worry is how I'm going to pay for my snooty and expensive college education when he's working three jobs just to keep a roof over his head. The words are out of my mouth before I think them through: "Zenn, if you need anything, my church could help. We have a food pantry and —"

He cuts me off. "We're fine."

Crap. Now I've offended him. Smooth move, Eva.

I wonder how long Zenn's life has been like this. He's eighteen now, or at least close to it, and is safe from Child Protective Services, but I wonder how close he's come to being taken from his mom. I wonder how hard he's worked to keep their family of two together, how much he's had to be the parent instead of the son.

"Sorry," I tell him. "It's the do-gooder gene in me. I didn't mean to offend you."

"Takes a lot more than that to offend me. And it's nice of you to offer. But we're good."

I nod and sip my tea. He watches me for a moment and then looks down, his eyelashes making long shadows on his cheeks. I imagine leaning toward him and pressing my hand against his face. I haven't touched the face of anyone older than twelve in years and I can't even imagine what it feels like, the roughness of someone who shaves, against my palm.

"I remember this one time ... I was maybe eleven or twelve. We went to Target to get school supplies, like, the day before school started." He stares at his hands while he talks. "Everything was picked over and they didn't have some of the stuff I needed. I was giving my mom a hard time for waiting until the last minute. Like always. And then when we were checking out I could tell she didn't have enough money. She got this panicky look and started going through her wallet like she thought there was more hidden in there somewhere. I'm sure any credit card she had was maxed out. I was like, 'Come on, Mom.'" Zenn rubs his forehead with one hand like he has a headache.

"The woman behind us saw what was going on and offered to help. She had her Target REDcard in her hand." He's quiet for a second, remembering. "The bill was maybe sixty bucks, which felt like so much at the time, and she didn't even bat an eye."

"Did your mom let her pay?" I ask.

Zenn nods. "Oh, yeah." He traces the wood grain of the table with his finger. "I hated that she did. I hated that feeling of *needing* help."

I think of the homecoming date Charlotte tried to set me up on. Pity sucks. "Probably made that woman feel good, though."

"Yeah." He looks up at me. "But I'd rather work three jobs than feel like that again."

I get it. There is a lot to be said for self-reliance.

I break his gaze and glance around in embarrassment.

And that's when I notice the painting in the corner across the room. At first I don't realize what it is, but then I feel my stomach seize up and I stare at it, stunned.

"Fractal," I blurt out involuntarily.

He follows my gaze across the room. "Oh," he says, and looks back at me. Something in his eyes looks surprised and worried. He probably thinks something is wrong, with my word-blurting. "Yeah. You know fractal art?"

I can't exactly explain that he has painted what I "see" in my head. The detail, the pattern. The colors and organized chaos. I get up and cross the room to stand in front of the painting, which sits on a makeshift easel. Other paintings lean against the wall, but this is the one that has caught my eye. Close up, the intricate detail is amazing.

"You know *fractal* means *broken*?" he asks.

I nod. Yes, I know. That's my brain: broken, shattered.

"Why did you paint this?" I ask.

"Why do I paint anything?"

He still thinks I'm making polite conversation about his art. He doesn't realize that I'm freaking out on the inside. His hobby is painting the very images that haunt me.

"I don't know. It's kind of ... therapeutic."

I'm a little creeped out. It's like he got into my brain somehow and found the worst and most disturbing part and then painted it and put it on display.

He shrugs. "When you get into airbrushing anything, that's what people usually want. Weird shit that looks like it could be on an album cover or something. But actual fractals — they're really interesting to me."

"Have you heard of Benoit Mandelbrot?" I ask. Just on the off chance.

Zenn shakes his head.

"He's, like, the father of fractal geometry. He once said, 'The goal of science is starting with a mess, and explaining it with a simple formula.'" I don't tell him that's what I'm hoping to do some day: use my math and science skills to figure out my defective, chaotic brain. Reduce it to a simple formula and come up with some sort of cure.

"I don't know much about math. Or science. But that's pretty cool."

"He died in 2010." I don't tell Zenn this, either, but Mandelbrot's death breaks my heart because I hadn't even heard of him, or fractal geometry for that matter, until I was in ninth grade, and he died that fall. I think if I had known about him sooner, I would have hunted him down and picked his beautiful brain for a theory on why mine is such a disaster.

I turn away from the painting and nearly bump into Zenn. I hadn't realized he was right behind me. Tea sloshes out of my mug and onto the floor.

"Sorry," I mumble.

"It's okay," he says. "It's a rental."

His chest is just inches away from my face and I can smell the laundry detergent from his T-shirt. He lingers for a moment, and then steps around me to look through the stack of small paintings on the floor.

"I was going to give you this one, to thank you for your help with trig."

I look down at the painting and exhale. This one is different. It is almost soothing in its repetition, like a lavender seashell that circles in on itself. It reminds me of the kind of peaceful, well-adjusted fractal I used to get from Charlotte. I take the painting in one hand and rub my thumb over the patterns. The fractal he painted me doesn't give me a fractal, and if that's not the definition of irony, I'm not sure what is. His hands didn't actually touch the paint or the expanse of canvas. Just the paintbrush.

"Thank you." My voice is nearly a whisper.

Zenn is standing so close to me that I can feel the soft exhale of his breath on my hair. I look up at him. Swallow. Force some words out of my mouth. "I should probably go. I usually start dinner on Fun to Be Three days."

Zenn nods and takes my mug from me. In my distraction I'm not careful and our fingers touch, just a gentle brush of my cold ones against his warm ones. I pull back immediately and brace myself. If touching his jacket almost made me vomit, I'm not sure of the havoc his actual hands might wreak.

But there is nothing.

The touch must have been too quick.

I'm glad. I don't want to know only the dark stuff about him, the fractal stuff. I want to get to know him like a normal girl gets to know a normal boy.

He has a surprised look on his face as well, probably because I flinched from his touch. Not an inviting vibe.

Oh, well. Chalk up another one for weird germaphobe girl.

I slip on my wet shoes, grab my plastic bag of soggy clothes, my backpack and my painting, and follow Zenn back out to his truck.

He drives me to church, where I pick up a spare house key. My dad gives me an odd look when I go into his office. I had forgotten about the Juicy sweatpants and uncharacteristically *Walking Dead*-themed sweatshirt. I'll have some explaining to do over dinner tonight. I don't give him time to ask many questions now, though. Zenn is waiting out in the truck.

When he drops me off at home I thank him for rescuing me. Again.

"Any time."

I hop out, protecting my painting from the rain.

⊂⊃

Sure enough my dad brings up my unusual outfit over dinner.

"What was with the getup today? Was it clash day at school or something?"

I explain that I forgot the umbrella, and my key, and my phone this morning and that Zenn gave me a lift after I got soaked in the pouring rain.

My dad looks skeptical. "Your sweatpants said *Juicy* on the butt."

"He loaned me some clothes."

"He had these extra clothes ... in his car?"

I understand why he's concerned — I mean, what kind of guy has extra women's clothing in his car? — but I am impatient nonetheless.

"I didn't have my key, so we went to his house and he gave me some of his ... sister's stuff."

They are white lies. Zenn's "house" is not a house, and his mom is not his sister, but I sense that if I admitted we went to an apartment above a garage where Zenn pretty much lives alone and that those clothes were his mother's, it would give my parents a bad impression of him.

My dad still looks doubtful about the whole thing, as a good dad should. But he knows me. Knows my issues with touch, knows that I have not had a boyfriend. Like, ever. He knows he doesn't have much to worry about.

CHAPTER 20

THE AIR IS ALMOST BALMY for Halloween, warm and moist and more like June than nearly November. All the cozy, insulated costumes that would be great on a cold day are making trick-or-treaters sweat bullets, but the girls my age who are dressed up as sexy nurses/pirates/police officers are happy: no need to cover up their carefully displayed boobs.

The quads are going as the Teletubbies, which I don't think my mom realizes are outrageously outdated costumes. In fact, I was a Teletubby back in 1999 or so: Po, the red one. My mom found the three other coordinating costumes online for a steal and so the kids are all lined up in their rainbow dorkiness: Laa-Laa, Po, Dipsy and Tinky Winky. Even though *Teletubbies* has been off the air for ages, the kids still watch old VHS videos and are too clueless to know that their costumes are a decade or two too late. Thank God they are only three.

We take the kids trick-or-treating down our street, my mom, dad and I following them with various cameras like paparazzi. When we turn onto Oak Street, my heart rate quickens. We approach the Arts and Crafts house, and I wonder if Zenn is around. We won't go trick-or-treating at the apartment above the garage, but I wonder if he might be somewhere nearby. Raking or ... whatever.

As we get closer I see a woman sitting on the front steps of the house with a big bowl of candy. I assume she's the owner of the Arts and Crafts house until I get closer and see she's wearing a sexy devil costume. She has an ashtray and a pack of cigarettes sitting next to her on the step.

Oh, wow. I have a sinking feeling we're about to meet Zenn's mom.

"Oh. My. God," she says, as we walk up the sidewalk. My dad visibly flinches at her saying *God* as if she had said *fuck* and by now he's noticed her horns and her cleavage and her cigarettes. But being an open-minded and forgiving type, he doesn't shuffle the kids away like I'm sure he wants to. I wonder what he'd say if I told him this is the woman I borrowed the Juicy sweatpants from.

"These four are a-*dor*-able!" she nearly yells. She has clearly partaken of some Halloween treats of the Jack Daniel's variety.

The kids walk up the steps hesitantly. With a little encouragement from my mom, they say, "Trick-or-treat."

Zenn's mom plops a handful of candy into each bag. "They're the TVtubbies, right?"

"Teletubbies," I correct her gently.

"Right! Teletubbies! My kid used to watch that when he

was little!"

I smile at her. Her kid! She's talking about Zenn! She looks like him. Not so much her coloring, but she has the same smile and the same eyelashes, though hers are enhanced by a couple coats of mascara.

I'd like to talk to her for longer but I'm terrified that her "kid" will come around the corner any minute and it will be this whole awkward meet-the-parents scenario. The slutty devil meets the man of God. Perfect.

So instead of engaging her, we wish her a happy Halloween and steer the kids on to the next house.

After about an hour the kids are sweaty and exhausted and we are only too glad to return home to hand out candy instead of gathering it up. My mom dumps most of the candy the kids got back into our bowl to give away.

They are barely in bed when my phone buzzes and at first I think it's some kind of Halloween prank when Zenn's name shows up. We exchanged cell numbers a while back in case he had any trig emergencies which, unfortunately, he hasn't. Until now, maybe.

Zenn: Hey

I smile and slide my fingers over the screen. Our first text. It's really him, right? I force myself to wait one full minute before responding, lest I look *way* overeager.

Me: Hey! What's up?
Zenn: See any good costumes today?

I had expected a question about trig, or maybe a follow-up about the van. But he's just making conversation.

> Me: I saw a slutty Nemo.
> Zenn: Nemo? Like, the clown fish?
> Me: Yeah.
> Zenn: That's so wrong.
> Me: Nothing is sacred anymore. How 'bout you?
> Zenn: I saw a slutty ketchup bottle. But that's not as good as Nemo.
> Me: How is ketchup remotely sexy? I don't get it. Am I missing something?
> Zenn: It goes on wieners? I have no idea …
> Me: Right! It's a condoment. ☺

There is a slight pause and I wonder if I've gone too far in our first texting conversation. But then he replies.

> Zenn: Sorry. You made me spit out my drink all over my phone.
> Me: Sorry. ☹
> Zenn: Don't be. That was good.

Another text comes through, this one from Charlotte.

> Charlotte: Hey!

Oh, look at that. It's my super popular friend, the one I have spent every Halloween with in recent memory. The one who ditched me this year to go to a party dressed in some kind of couples costume with her new boyfriend. But look! She has deigned to communicate with me! Hooray!

I ignore her text and send a goofy face to Zenn.

CHAPTER 21

THE ART ROOM IS LOCKED when I try the door. I wait for a couple of minutes but when Zenn doesn't show up I figure I have a choice: the library or the cafeteria. Alone by myself or alone in a crowd. I decide I'm tired of hiding out, so I head toward the cafeteria, determined to exude confidence.

I sit down in my old spot and say hi to all the people I used to eat lunch with, minus Charlotte. They are friendly, though not that excited to see me. Makes me realize I should focus on trying to make more than two friends.

I sneak a couple of glances in Charlotte's direction and on my third covert look, she looks back. Then someone calls her name and she turns and I've lost her attention. Again.

After school I wait for Zenn for fifteen minutes but he never shows. He might not be at school today since he wasn't at lunch, but I wait for him just in case. My ego is taking a bit of a smackdown because I thought he would have texted me now that our relationship has moved on to texting status.

I know I'm fooling myself about what our lunches and our texting could mean. But there is still a part of me that hopes we could have a normal relationship. I tested his jacket the other day when he stepped out of the room and it nearly flattened me again with that dark, almost violent fractal, implying something I'm not ready to face yet. It was deep crimson red and smoky black. It had the sensation of fighting, of battle. Plus a touch of the floaty, drunk feeling I got when I touched his mom's clothes, and when I touch Josh. He may have a lot of secrets we haven't talked about yet.

Oh, who am I kidding? We both have a lot of secrets we haven't talked about yet.

I eventually give up on waiting and head home, irritated with myself that I didn't catch the bus when I had the chance.

I'm crossing the school parking lot when I hear Charlotte calling my name.

I turn and there she is, lovely as always.

"Hey!" she says, slightly out of breath from running to catch up. "I saw you at lunch today! Are you done tutoring?"

Is she afraid I'll be back for good and she'll have to make a choice between the popular kids and me? If she'd have me back, would I go?

"Um, not yet. He just ... wasn't here today."

"Oh! Cool." She pulls her jacket more tightly closed and I realize it's because she's wearing a fairly low-cut shirt.

Not super low-cut — I mean, it's Charlotte — but it's more revealing than anything she usually wears. We're talking collarbones showing, not boobs. I wonder if she was fine with wearing the shirt today until she ran into me, the only one who would notice.

"So, how's it going?" I ask.

"Good!" she answers cheerfully. Too cheerfully. "Pretty good," she amends, and bites her lip.

"Great!" My voice has the same awkward quality. What the hell has happened to us? "How's Josh?" I ask politely. I assume this is what we're supposed to do: back and forth, keep it simple.

"Good. He's good."

"That's good." This is ridiculous. I remember texting her from the bathroom stall when I was thirteen and got my period for the first time. She once told me her dad used to apologize for her height, and that she would take cold baths and stack books on her head because she thought she could slow her growth. I used to tell her everything. I never thought we'd get to a point where we could barely have a conversation.

"Do you ... want a ride home?"

I wave my hand. "No, that's okay. I can walk."

She looks a little hurt. I know she knows how much I hate walking home. But God help me if I'm going to hop into her car like a dog desperate for a ride.

"I mean, I don't mind. It's nice out."

Charlotte looks up at the cloudy sky. She can see right through me. It is not that nice.

"Okay. Well ... I'll talk to you later, then?" she asks.

I want to say, *I don't know, will you?* But instead I just say, "Sounds good."

$$\infty$$

The next day Zenn still isn't at school and I don't bother waiting. I head for the bus but I'm barely out the door when Charlotte calls to me again.

Today her collarbones are covered by a T-shirt with garden gnomes on it and *Chillin' with my Gnomies* underneath. It's one of my favorites. I smile a little.

Better. Much better.

"Hey, Ev. You want a ride?" she asks. Something in her voice challenges me to say no again. Her chin is high, and she looks a little ... angry.

Why is she angry at me? *I'm* not the one who started dating a popular jock. *I'm* not the one who abandoned her for a new group of friends.

"Or is it so nice out that you want to walk?" Okay, I'm not imagining it. There is definitely some anger there.

I look down at my boots and wonder for the first time how much of the distance between us has been her, and how much has been me.

I hesitate. "I guess. If you don't mind."

"I wouldn't have asked if I minded."

There is a pause and then I say, "Yes, you would have."

"Yeah. I probably would have."

We walk away from the buses toward her car.

$$\infty$$

She talks me into swinging by Java Dock and before you know it we are pulled into the parking lot at the beach, sharing a muffin and watching the waves break against the sand, just like old times. I think of Zenn's sand art, how temporary and fleeting it is. Just like everything else.

We get out of Charlotte's car and walk for a bit, like we used to. I pick up a couple of pretty stones that I intend to leave on my parents' grave. My favorite one is a dark gray that looks black when it's wet, with a thread of white cutting right down the center. It has a yin-and-yang feel to it, and it reminds me of the two of them, buried side by side.

As we walk, I point out evidence of a bonfire to Charlotte, the charred remains of wood piled on the beach.

"Yeah," she says. "Halloween. I was here." I don't think she's telling me to make me jealous. Her voice sounds kind of sad. "I texted you that night. You didn't text me back."

Oh, right. Halloween. That was the first night Zenn texted me and when hers came through, I promptly ignored it. I don't even have a good excuse to give her. I was mad at her. And I was caught up with a boy.

Just like her.

"I thought you went to some kind of costume party," I say.

"Nah. Everything changes at the last minute. It was just a bonfire."

I nod, knowing that she probably hates that: plans changing at the last minute.

"In movies they always make those beach bonfires seem so cool."

"It wasn't?" I ask.

She shakes her head. "Josh disappeared with a couple

guys for a while and I kind of sat by myself. It was too hot for a bonfire, so I was sweating."

I laugh. Charlotte may be gorgeous, but she's also a sweater. She's almost never cold, especially on a night as warm as this Halloween.

"Sometimes it feels like ..." But she doesn't complete her thought. She seems sad, hurt by more than just my distance and half-assed friendship. I wait for her to continue, but she doesn't.

I reach out and touch her arm and she just looks down at my hand. I assume her new friends touch her all the time, in the way that all teenagers do, and that she's used to it. Maybe she won't realize I'm spying.

Her fractal is lavender, like a faded bruise, and dense like fog. It feels like a muffled argument, like a battle between someone with a megaphone and someone whose mouth is covered with duct tape. There is a giddiness there, but it's weighed down by something else ... a helium balloon tied to an anvil.

I don't know exactly what it means, yet, but I'm furious at myself for ever introducing Charlotte to Josh if this is what he's done to her fractal. If his fucked-upness has somehow rubbed off on her.

She looks up from my hand.

"What's it say?" she asks, though I'm sure she already knows.

"What's he doing to you?" I ask.

"Who?"

Her lying is getting better, but I give her my impatient look anyway.

"Josh?" she asks incredulously. "You think it's just Josh?" She shakes her head and pulls her arm away.

"What is it then?"

She looks out at the water again. We sit for a moment and eventually she offers her arm to me. Maybe it's easier to let me read her fractal than it is to talk about it.

I focus on the shapes and the feelings and the pattern and slowly I get a sense of isolation, of a huge lake an inch deep.

"They never talk about anything. Ever."

Ah. I get it. The new friends.

"I mean, they talk. They talk *a lot*. But it's about clothes and parties and cute boys and how many calories they had for lunch. But they don't know anything about me. I don't think they even want to. I can't stand it anymore."

And I can't help myself, but I smile before quickly covering my mouth.

She says, "I miss you."

"I miss you, too."

"Then why haven't you been calling me? Or texting me?"

"You seemed like you wanted to try out that group. Josh's friends. I didn't want to get in your way."

She looks down at her lap. "It felt like you were disappointed in me. Like ... like by dating Josh I was somehow one of them. It felt like you had written me off."

"Me?"

She nods.

It's probably true. That's what it felt like. An either/or situation: me or them. "You're sitting with them at lunch now," I remind her.

"Only because you left me stranded at that table with

Negative Nora and her whiny bunch. I'll take the calorie counters over the complainers any day."

Truth again. The girls we sit with can be truly miserable.

"Come back to lunch and we can sit together again," Charlotte offers. "We can both get away from the Glumsters. We'll sit somewhere else."

I think about it for a minute, weighing my friendship with her and my growing whatever it is with Zenn.

"It's that guy, isn't it?"

I must blush or something because I don't say a word and she still nods knowingly.

"Are you guys dating?"

"No. No. Nothing like that. Just ... friends."

"Right."

"Come on, Char. You know I can't touch anyone. And this guy ... man. I've touched his jacket and nearly passed out. I can't imagine what it would be like to touch *him*." I don't tell her that I have touched him, however briefly, once. I don't tell her that it didn't give me even a hint of a fractal.

"Well," she says, decisively. "He can touch *you*, can't he?" Her voice is suggestive and teasing. Man, I've missed hanging out with her.

"Well ... yeah."

She smiles. "So there you go."

I don't even know how to answer.

CHAPTER 22

ZENN HAS BEEN OUT FOR THREE DAYS in a row and I'm starting to worry. I decide that, as his friend, I should check up on him. That's what friends do, right? If it were Charlotte, I'd make sure she was okay. And since I only have two good friends, I have to look out for their welfare. This is what I tell myself.

I swing by the cemetery on my way to his house, dawdling so I don't seem so pitifully eager. It would be really sad for me to show up at his door only minutes after the final bell. So I stop by my parents' grave and swap the small, white stone that is there for the gray yin-and-yang one I picked up yesterday with Charlotte.

When I get to the Arts and Crafts house, Zenn's truck isn't in the driveway but I decide to try anyway. If he's home, I hope he's home alone. And I hope he's receptive to a surprise visit.

I take a deep breath and knock on the door and wait. And wait. When no one answers, I reluctantly turn back down the steps and am halfway to the bottom when Zenn's truck pulls in the driveway.

He parks and climbs out before he sees me waiting on the stairs.

"Oh, hey!" He is clearly surprised, but not disappointed. He might even be happy. I'm new at this whole boy-girl thing, so it's hard to tell.

"Hey." I hold up a yellow folder with his trig homework. "I just ... you weren't at school again so I got your homework from Mr. Haase." I hope my excuse doesn't sound as transparent to him as it does to me. "Didn't want you to get behind."

He comes up the steps and I get a better look at him. He is filthy. Dirt coats his jeans and his sweatshirt. It covers his skin in a fine layer making him appear even darker than he normally is. And hotter, if that's possible.

"Oh. Okay. Thanks." He takes the folder from me and opens the door. "Come on in."

Even though his voice is subdued, I hesitate only a second.

He drops the folder onto the tiny kitchen table. "I just ... have to get cleaned up."

"Oh, sure! Sorry! I'll go ..."

"No, you can hang out. I'll be quick."

"No, seriously. I just wanted to drop off your homework. See if you were okay."

"Eva," he says. "Stay."

His voice is kind but firm. I can tell he wants me to stay. I *want* to stay. "Okay."

He disappears into the bedroom, and then into the bathroom. After a moment I can hear music — something soulful with banjos and maybe harmonicas — and the shower running.

Holy God. He's in the shower. Right behind that door.

I nearly get up and leave, but then I realize I'm being ridiculous. I'm eighteen years old, for Pete's sake. The mere thought of a naked guy in close proximity should not send me running for cover.

The nosy part of me wants to slide my hands over everything in his apartment, learn as much as I can in these few minutes alone with his stuff. It's so tempting to snoop sometimes, out of curiosity or boredom. But with Zenn I'm too afraid of what I might learn, so I sit primly on a kitchen chair with my hands on my lap.

The kitchen is so tiny that I can almost reach out and touch every cabinet and appliance from my chair. The only thing that looks properly used is the coffeemaker. There are no curtains on the window, but a small ceramic cartoony-looking turtle sits facing outward on the windowsill, as if watching for guests to arrive. Next to the turtle is a row of small, round stones, lined up by gradient: light gray to almost black. I stand up to look at them, and smile. They are all about the same size, each one slightly darker than the one next to it. Leave it to an artist to organize his stones by color. Or maybe they're his mom's stones. Either way, seeing them lined up like that makes me happy.

True to his word, the shower goes off in just a couple of minutes, and after another few minutes I hear the turn of the doorknob and brace myself for ... I'm not sure what. Zenn in a towel?

But that would be too much like some soapy TV show. My real life isn't hot guys, fresh from the shower, roaming around in towels. My life is more staid and predictable than that, like a PBS documentary. Sure enough, he emerges in clean jeans and a fresh T-shirt, his hair damp and as messy as his short hair gets, like he towel dried it and that's about it.

And good lord he smells amazing.

"So ... are you sick?" I ask. He doesn't look sick. Just ... tired. "Can I get you, like, some ... soup or 7 Up or something?"

He smiles a little and shakes his head. "I'm fine," he says. "Just got a lot going on." He scrubs both hands over his hair in a gesture of frustration and helplessness and then slips them into the back pockets of his jeans. This might be my cue to butt out. But ... I'm choosing to ignore it because he seems so overwhelmed.

So alone.

In a moment of boldness or insanity, of uncharacteristic impulsiveness, I stand up and cross the few steps between us and slide my arms into the triangles his arms make with his body. I press myself up against him lightly in a tentative hug. He doesn't move and I almost pull away, but I've committed myself now and I think it would be worse to have him look at me with confusion than to stay pressed against him in my just-trying-to-be-comforting hug. At least this way we don't have to make eye contact. Besides, he feels so solid and warm. I carefully ball my hands into fists, keeping them away from his body, and allow the rest of me to linger, press, enjoy.

He hesitates for a second longer before pulling his hands from his pockets and I mentally prepare myself for the rejection of him pushing me away. But instead he wraps his arms around me, pulling my body more tightly against his. I nearly sigh from the feeling. We stand, my cheek pressed against his chest. I inhale the clean, simple smell of him.

"Are you sure you're okay?" I ask him again.

"A little better now."

There's something slightly flirtatious in the way he says it. It's a tone he hasn't used with me before and it makes me blush against his shirt. God, my fingers itch to be splayed across his back, to grasp at his T-shirt and slide through his hair. Instead, I tangle them together behind him so they won't go all rogue on me.

The music is still coming from the bathroom and it might be my imagination but it feels like we are swaying slightly as we hug. I feel Zenn's face near my hair, his breath on my ear, the rough brush of his chin against my temple. I look up slightly and his mouth is right there, just above mine. Neither of us moves. We hesitate in indecision, my breath catching in uneven hitches. His arms tighten around me just slightly.

"You sure it's nothing contagious?" I whisper.

He looks down at me, shakes his head, barely. We breathe the same air for a moment and I think maybe he'll kiss me. Maybe I'll kiss him. Maybe I'll open my hands and press them against his back with the rationalization that touching him, just once, will be worth whatever fractal he gives me.

But he doesn't kiss me and I don't kiss him. I don't unclench my hands.

What happens instead is the apartment door flies open with a pop. We drop our arms from each other quickly, guiltily, but not before the couple standing in the doorway sees us.

"Well, fuck me!" Zenn's mom exclaims, thumping a case of beer onto the kitchen table. "Zenn's got a girlfriend!"

Zenn's head falls in a gesture of irritation and embarrassment. They enter the apartment and set a bag of groceries down next to the beer. His mom has forgone her devil costume for a pair of jeans and a hooded sweatshirt that looks like it might be Zenn's. Some kind of clip — I think it's called a banana clip — holds back her hair, and her bangs are teased like it's 1990. She holds out her hand to me.

"Hey, Zenn's girlfriend. I'm Cinde."

Apparently she doesn't recognize me from Halloween. No surprise, I guess, since she was half in the bag that day.

"I'm not ..." I start, but then I figure what's the point. She's just teasing us anyway. I hesitate a second before grasping her hand quickly and letting go. It's enough to trigger a fractal, but I'm prepared and I take a deep breath. It stays small and manageable, just a small whirlpool of fuzzy darkness. "Eva," I tell her.

The man holds out his hand as well. "Mike," he says. I've barely even touched him when the army jacket fractal sweeps over me and I nearly lose my balance. I pull my hand away rather rudely and lean against the table. Zenn gives me a funny look.

Mike has the same thick, dark hair as Zenn, though slightly flecked with white at the temples. The same bronzy skin, same dark, vaguely Asian eyes. I put two and two together.

"Mike's my ... *dad.*" Zenn says the word like it's foreign and unfamiliar in his mouth.

"Oh," I say, and sway on my feet a little. "Nice to meet you."

"Are you okay, hon?" Cinde asks.

Zenn pulls out a chair and gently pushes me onto it. "Just a little warm," I say.

Cinde gives Zenn a teasing look and I realize she thinks I'm flustered from being wrapped around her son. But I've nearly forgotten about that in the fractal chaos.

Cinde pops open a beer. "How 'bout a cold one?" she says, and holds the can out to me.

Before I have a chance to answer, Zenn groans. "Jesus, Mom."

"I'm kidding! Shit, everyone's always so fucking serious!"

I have no doubt that she swears often, but it feels like she's doing it now to seem cool and young. She offers the beer to Mike and he declines as well. Instead he gets me a glass of water from the faucet. Cinde sips the beer and flips open the folder on the table, oblivious to the fact that I might pass out in her kitchen. "You guys having a study date?"

Zenn speaks for me. "Eva was just dropping off my homework."

"Mmmm hmmm," Cinde hums, like homework is a code word for *blow job*.

"I should go," I say, standing up so quickly I nearly topple over.

"I'll drive you home," Zenn offers.

I still feel weak and nauseated. I would love a ride. "It was nice meeting you both," I say even though I don't really mean it. I secretly wish they had never shown up.

"Likewise," Cinde says, and lifts her beer in a sort of toast.

Out in the truck Zenn starts the engine and leans back against the headrest. "Fuck," he says. "Sorry about that."

I pretend I'm not embarrassed at all. Like I get caught pressing my body against boys every day. "Don't worry about it."

He puts the truck in Reverse and rests his arm along the back of my seat as he turns to back out of the driveway. For some reason, the gesture feels almost as intimate as the hug.

"So ... your dad, huh?" I say.

Zenn nods tightly, not playing along.

I'm persistent if not subtle. "Is that what's been going on? Why you haven't been at school?"

Zenn sighs and stares out the window. Finally he says, "My mom has gone all ape-shit crazy now that he's here. Drinking too much, not working. When I'm home I have to babysit her."

"Do you need anything? Can I help?"

Zenn shakes his head. "I've been thinking about leaving school."

"What?! No."

"If I worked full-time we'd probably be okay. I wouldn't have to rely on her to be reliable."

"Zenn. You can't. That's not the answer."

He shrugs. "Maybe it is. Maybe this is all just a waste of time. School. Art. All of it."

"Education is never a waste of time." I realize how stupid and preachy it sounds as soon as it's out of my mouth. "Just ... give it until the end of the semester. Okay?"

His jaw clenches, his hands grip the steering wheel.

"Okay?" I ask again.

"Fine. But I really don't see the point."

I don't know how to argue with him. Maybe it is a waste of time. But what can I say? He can't quit. I won't let him. But I try to keep it light. "You wouldn't *miss* trig? What are you, crazy?"

He finally cracks a smile. "You are *such* a nerd."

It's like he just told me he loves me.

He parks in front of my house and I want to reach out and touch him again ... something. But self-doubt gets the better of me.

I just say, "Thanks for the ride," and climb out of the truck.

I'm halfway to the house when Zenn rolls down his window. He calls out, waving for me to come back.

"Hey," he says, "do you want to do something tonight?"

Oh, my God. Maybe that hug wasn't just a friendly hug for either of us. Maybe it was something more. Or maybe he just wants to get out of his apartment, away from his mom and dad.

"By some miracle, I don't have to work," he says, studying his hands on the steering wheel. "And I'd prefer to *not* be around those two."

He's nervous. Oh, my God, he's definitely nervous.

"And ... well ..."

My silence has gone on too long. I'm bordering on cruel now. "What do you want to do?" I ask coyly.

"I don't know. I haven't gotten that far."

"I'm just messing with you. It doesn't matter. I'm in."

CHAPTER 23

I TEXT CHARLOTTE AS SOON AS I GET INSIDE. She shows up ten minutes later with her brand-new makeup bag in hand, like a doctor making a house call. I feel horrible that I haven't been there for her the way she is here for me now.

I look in the mirror and figure she's got her work cut out for her. I take a quick shower while she pieces together an outfit from my closet, nothing crazy, but a combination that I would never think of. Then she uses some kind of paste and a hair dryer attachment to make my wavy hair as curly as possible. Then she forces me to sit still while she applies more makeup than my virgin skin has ever seen.

"Easy, Char. I don't want to look like a pageant contestant."

"You won't. You'll just look like you, only an HD-worthy version."

Sure enough, my pores become invisible, my eyes bigger, my mouth fuller. If I had known makeup could do this

I would have tried it sooner. Charlotte makes me wear my contacts, insisting that kissing is much easier without glasses. I take her word for it because, frankly, what do I know about kissing? And what are the odds of that happening anyway?

When I come out of my room, Libby wants to touch my hair. Normally it's in a braid or a bun or a barrette, so the fact that it is loose *and* curly is just too much. I must look like a fricking princess to her.

Maybe to my mom, too, because she looks at me almost longingly. "Oh, Ev. You look —"

I cut her off before she starts to sound like the gushing Instagram posts of my peers. I'm not going to the *prom*. It's just a date, if even that. I glance at my reflection in the microwave and do a double take.

Holy crap. I *am* a fricking princess! Makeup is amazing!

"It's not too much?" I ask.

My mom reaches out and touches my cheek lightly. "No. Just enough."

All my negative feelings about Jessica disappear and I'm grateful that she tutored Charlotte so she could help me in my moment of need. Charlotte hasn't met Zenn yet, but she rightfully senses that it would be weird for her to be waiting with me when he shows up, so she gives me a hug and whispers, "Text me later. I want details."

She pulls out of the driveway just moments before Zenn is supposed to arrive.

"Mom," I say quickly, "I don't really know if this is a date or what so I'm not going to have him come in, okay?"

She touches my hair. "You don't think it's a date?" Her

voice is skeptical and I understand why: the hair products suggest otherwise.

"Maybe. I don't know. But can we not make a big deal out of it?" I kiss her on the cheek. "I won't be too late."

"Okay." Her voice is disappointed. "Have fun. Be careful." It's what she says every time I leave the house.

"I will," I reassure her, though for the first time in my life I don't feel like being very careful at all.

I walk out just as Zenn pulls in the driveway.

I get in his truck and he smiles kind of shyly. If he notices a major transformation, he doesn't show any shock. "I was going to come to the door," he says.

He was going to come to the door! I add that to evidence that this may, in fact, be a date.

"We'd never get out of there. The E's are still up and they'd have you drawing animal pictures all night."

"The ease?"

"Oh. Yeah. E's, like the letter *E*. That's what we call them sometimes. 'Cause all their names start with *E*."

He nods, and then cocks his head. "Libby?"

"Elizabeth."

"Right."

Since neither of us has any money, or at least not any money we want to spend at a sit-down restaurant, we decide to pick up some pizza and take it up to the bluff that overlooks North Beach. The huge playground there is deserted — it's after seven on a Friday night in November — so we have our pick of places to hang out. I timidly point to a sign: PARK CLOSES AT DUSK.

"You nervous, Walker?" Zenn teases. "Not much of a rule breaker?"

I pretend I don't care. But I am nervous. Eva Walker doesn't break rules. And maybe that's not the only reason for my nerves.

Zenn takes a blanket from the back of his truck — I think the same one that I sat on that day I got drenched — and I carry the pizza box and we climb up the gigantic wooden play structure to a platform sheltered from the breeze by a low wall. We sit with our backs against the cedar planks, eat pizza and talk.

Zenn tells me his dad has been out of the picture for a long time, that he's only seen him a few times his whole life. He doesn't tell me what that's done to him, what it's like for a kid to grow up without his dad. But I can hear some of it in his voice.

He tells me his mom held it together pretty well when he was younger. She kept jobs for a while at least. He said he didn't need a math tutor back then.

"I wasn't ridiculously smart like you," Zenn says, "but I was an honor-roll kid until my mom went off the rails. I mean, I am a quarter Asian, after all."

"Your dad's side?" I ask, and he nods.

"My grandpa was in Vietnam. Brought home a wife."

"Like *Miss Saigon*," I say, "with a happier ending." I can't believe I said something so dumb. Clearly his life hasn't been that happy, and he's probably never heard of *Miss Saigon*. The only reason I know it is because my mom saw the musical in Chicago when she was a teenager and obsessively played the sound track my entire childhood.

He gets it, though. "Moderately happier than a prostitute who commits suicide, sure."

"When was that?" I ask. "That things went downhill with your mom?"

"I was probably twelve, thirteen? When I was old enough to stay home alone for longer, she started waitressing at night. Then working at bars. And then ... well. Yeah."

His life started unraveling at about the same time mine did, when everyone I touched became a minefield.

He's tearing apart a pizza crust, breaking it into a hundred little pieces.

"We started having serious money problems. Kept moving. I got my first job when I was fifteen and .... here we are."

Besides the time he told me about his back-to-school shopping trip, it's the most personal he's ever been with me, the most open. It could be the moonless dark, the unusual quiet of the park, the feeling that we are the only ones around for miles. It could be the hug that maybe broke down a wall between us. Whatever it is, I like it. I like sitting here, our shoulders pressing lightly against each other, hearing his deep, smooth voice giving me a new piece of his puzzle.

He peeks into the paper bag that holds the napkins and little packets of parmesan cheese and red pepper flakes that came with our pizza.

"Oh, man. Jackpot," he says, and pulls out a couple of mints, the chalky vanilla kind, wrapped in a tiny sleeve. We suck on our mints and he's quiet and I think maybe he's waiting for me to say something. Even though I'm secretly in awe of him, of his responsibility and his work ethic and just his overall toughness, I don't want to make a big deal of what he's just told me. Instead I admit that I've been avoiding finishing my college applications.

"Why?" he asks. "Are you afraid you won't get in?" I can tell by the tone of his voice that he thinks that's ridiculous.

"I'm almost more afraid that I *will* get in, but I won't be able to go and my parents will blame themselves. And that maybe I'll blame them a little, too."

It feels good to finally say it out loud, to admit that my fear is as basic and selfish as that. I don't tell him that the guilt feels worse because they didn't choose to have me. They rescued me and they owe me nothing, and yet I still feel like they've let me down somehow. Like, maybe I wasn't enough for them so they had to have four more of their *own* kids, sucking dry any hope for my college fund.

I look at his mouth, wondering if his mint is gone. And then I realize I've looked at his mouth and I feel my cheeks grow hot. But I think he's looking at my mouth, too, so maybe it's okay.

"Can I ..." he starts.

I nod quickly.

"You don't even know what I was going to ask." He's teasing.

"Doesn't matter." If he asked to shave my head and paint a fractal on it, I would let him.

He looks at me for a moment and then looks down.

So I look down.

And then we both look back up at the same moment, and he tilts his head ever so slightly before he leans in and presses his mouth against mine.

His lips are soft and barely parted, hesitating for a second, maybe waiting to see if I object. I most certainly don't. I kiss him back, hoping my mouth doesn't betray my eagerness. God, he tastes like peppermint and vanilla and hope.

Date, I think to myself. So this *is* a date.

My hands hover, clenched, just an inch from his chest. I fight the urge to touch him. Not just to touch him, to slide my hands over every inch of him. The kiss deepens a little more, his warm, rough hands finding their way to my neck, cradling my face, his thumbs tracing my jaw.

I can't take it anymore. Maybe ... maybe it'll be fine. Actually, I don't really care if it's fine or not. I want to touch him even if I have fractals. I *have* to touch him. I unclench my hands and press them against his chest, tentatively at first. I can feel the steady beat of his heart beneath my palm. I brace myself for the fractal that I hope will be worth it. I pause, waiting, and it seems like he hesitates, too, our mouths just barely apart, our breath mingling. I do feel light-headed and dizzy, but it's not a fractal. Just ... lust, maybe.

I forget about bracing myself. If it comes, it comes. He can scrape my sweaty, dizzy body off the playground equipment for all I care.

Without realizing it, I've grasped his jacket in both hands and I notice for the first time that the fabric feels different, softer. The army jacket is gone tonight and in its place is a soft, thick cotton hoodie with a fleecy lining. I don't know why I didn't notice before. Maybe the hoodie is new, maybe it's something else, but whatever it is seems to be negating my fractals.

The white steam of our breath swirls around us like a little passion cloud and even though it's cold, my body temperature has gone through the roof. I feel like I'm melting from the inside out, like lava might flow out of me at any moment.

When Zenn pulls away, I nearly follow, not wanting him to stop. He leans his forehead against mine and takes a breath.

I try to loosen my death grip on his sweatshirt.

"I have to tell you something," he says. His voice is serious and I swallow the lump that forms immediately in my throat.

Oh, God. No bad news. Nothing bad. This is a happy place.

I try to pull myself together.

"I applied for that scholarship you told me about."

My mind is still a little fuzzy from being so close to another human for so long. I'm having trouble processing his words.

"Scholarship?"

He nods. His thumb traces my cheekbone. "The big one."

"Oh," I say, trying to make sense of this news. "Okay."

He pulls back a little more and I want to grab him so he doesn't go far. "I applied right after you told me. That night of homecoming? I mean, I'm sure nothing will come of it — I've never won anything in my life — but it's been bothering me that I never said anything."

"A lot of people apply for that scholarship. The odds are against both of us, probably."

"You're not mad?" he asks.

"Why would I be mad?"

"I don't know. I mean, you told me about it and then I try to get all up in your action."

It's shameful how much I want him to get all up in my action.

"It's open to everyone, Zenn. There's no reason you shouldn't apply."

He looks relieved.

"You seriously thought I would be mad?"

"I don't know ... maybe?"

I'm more upset that he stopped kissing me.

It's getting late and we seem to have broken the spell. I want him to kiss me again, but I'm not sure how to get him to do it. I'm definitely not bold enough to grab him and pull him closer. So instead we talk a little more about school and his jobs and little things until he stands up, signaling it's time to go home. When he drops me off, he leans in and kisses me again, but this time it's a soft brush of his mouth against mine, light, sweet, crazily romantic.

I'm not sure how I got into the house. I'm sure I walked, but I don't remember at all. All I remember is the minty-vanilla taste of his mouth.

CHAPTER 24

ESSIE PRESSES HER TINY, COOL HANDS against my cheeks. I can tell it's Essie because she is gentle and quiet. If it were Libby she'd be bouncing on my mattress, screaming, *Wakeupwakeupwakeupwakeup!* I open my eyes to find the sun shining brightly through the crack in my curtains. Essie's hair is a tangle of fine blond curls. The night has slipped away. The world is still spinning. Nothing has changed.

Except everything.

I give Essie a piggyback to the kitchen and set her up with a bowl of Cheerios and slices of banana stacked in a cylinder. She likes it when I arrange her food in shapes. I'm sure she'll *love* it someday when I teach her how to calculate the volume of those shapes (cylinder = $\Pi r^2 h$). Once she's set up I study the contents of the fridge, exhausted by the effort of not spilling my heart to a three-year-old. It's tempting to gush to someone, anyone, about Zenn. About his mouth and his hands and his delicious smell. I shove a bagel in my yapper to keep myself from telling Essie something completely inappropriate, like how I wonder if anyone has ever lost their virginity on the play set she goes to every Friday morning.

Yeah. *So* not cool.

But, God, I want to touch him again. I want to feel his actual skin with my fingertips — its heat and probable silkiness. I want to see if the lack of fractals was a fluke. I want to run all sorts of experiments on him, touching every inch of his bare skin to see if all of him is safe. Wouldn't be a bad way to spend a Saturday afternoon.

And if he is safe ... then what? My breathing gets shallow at the thought of it.

I promised Charlotte details and she's a more appropriate audience than Essie. I grab my phone and text her.

Me: Hey!

I'm amazed and flattered by how quickly she texts me back, even after being sort of estranged. She's always been a better person than me.

Charlotte: Hey! How'd it go???
Me: So good. So so good.
Charlotte: AAAAAHHHHHHH! I want to hear but I have riding this morning.

(Did I mention that Charlotte is an equestrian? Ralph Lauren picture complete.)

Me: That's OK. We'll talk later.
Charlotte: OK, but ... was there ... lip action?

God, she's such a goofball.

Me: There was.
Charlotte: AAAAAHHHHHH!!!

I smile at my phone. God, I missed her.

Charlotte: Tongue??? Tongue action??!
Me: I'll text you later.
Charlotte: AHHHHHH! You better!

I set my phone down, smiling. He likes me. It seems hard to believe, but even I know that a kiss like that is evidence of *like*.

And if I'm thinking about him this morning, maybe he's thinking about me.

So, it wouldn't be that weird for me to ... say ... drive by his house. See if he's home.

Before I talk myself out of it, I shower and get dressed and head over to his apartment, telling my mom I'm running to the library. I'm such a nerd that she doesn't even question it on a Saturday morning. But when I get there, I see his truck is gone and I realize he's probably at one of his many jobs, trying to support his family. Stupid of me to think he'd be sleeping in on a Saturday morning. Silly to think he'd be lounging in bed, remembering what it felt like to kiss me. Guys don't do that anyway. Do they?

I sit in my car for a moment, knowing I should leave and text him later, like a normal person. But then I have the genius idea to leave him a note. How cute is that? A real note, like on paper. So I dig up a scrap of paper from the glove compartment — a preschool coloring worksheet of Ethan's where Jesus's face is a royal blue — and scribble a few casual words on the back.

Was driving by, wanted to see you. <3 Eva

I think the obviously unplanned quality of it is charming. I get out of the car and am heading up the driveway when the door to the apartment opens and I freeze in my tracks.

Crap, whose stupid idea was this? A *note*? On a Jesus coloring sheet? I quickly turn back down the driveway to get out of there fast.

"Hey." A voice rings out behind me. It's a woman's, rough and smoky.

I turn and see Cinde halfway down the stairs in her robe and a pair of UGG-style boots, her hair tucked under a baseball cap.

"Eva, right?" she greets me happily. "I was just coming out to get the paper."

The paper is sitting a few feet to my left. I pick it up and cross the distance between us to hand it to her.

"It's really their paper." She nods to the main house, her voice conspiratorial. "I read it real quick and put it back."

Her covert operations to get some local news make me a little sad, but I suppose a newspaper subscription is a luxury they can't afford.

"You looking for Zenn?"

"I —" I crumple up the note and tuck it in my pocket.

"He's at work."

"I figured. I saw his truck wasn't here."

"You wanna come up for a cup of coffee?"

"No, thanks," I say. "That's okay."

Her face droops and I realize she's not just being polite. I've seen the look on my own mom's face a hundred times, searching for connection only to be rebuffed. She shoves her hands deep into the pockets of her robe.

"I guess I don't blame you. I was awful yesterday. I'll tell him you stopped by."

Before I can talk myself out of it, I step closer. "Actually, coffee sounds good."

She smiles and, despite the mascara smudged under her eyes, I see she's actually quite pretty. Or she was once. She looks older than she probably is. Her skin isn't as smooth as my mom's, and she has deeper crow's-feet at the corners of her eyes, slight wrinkles around her mouth, probably from smoking. But she's thinner than my mom, too. I guess a mostly liquid-and-cigarette diet can do that.

I follow her up the stairs and she gestures for me to sit down. It feels really weird being here without Zenn and I wonder if I've made a big mistake.

"I'm just gonna throw some clothes on real quick."

I sit at the kitchen table and wait, like I did just yesterday. Was that just yesterday? My mind wanders back to his mouth, his lips, his hands ...

Cinde comes out of the bedroom in the Juicy sweatpants and I shake the thoughts of Zenn from my mind.

She takes the Pritzer Insurance mug from its spot on the shelf, pours me a cup of coffee and slides the mug across the table. She removes the lid from the sugar bowl and pushes that toward me as well. I scoop some into my mug. I can't tell her I don't care much for coffee, and I'm certainly not going to ask if she's got some chocolate syrup to make it better.

"I do want to apologize about yesterday," she says, sitting down. "I know I was obnoxious."

I shake my head. "No, I'm sorry. I was just ..."

"Embarrassed. I know. My fault." She bites at the edge of her fingernail. "Usually it's Zenn walking in on *me*. Poor kid."

I don't even know what to say to that.

"I mean, not with Mike. We're not together anymore." Her voice is tinged with a subtle regret.

She seems vulnerable this morning, all her bravado and teasing gone. I relax a bit and glance around the kitchen, my eyes coming to rest on that ceramic turtle by the window and the row of smooth, round stones.

She says, almost to herself, "Apparently we were *not* meant to be."

I stand up.

"What's wrong, hon? You need milk?"

I shake my head and take the two steps to the window. I study the stones, like I did yesterday. Yesterday there were eight. Today there are nine.

"Oh, those. Yeah, Zenn is always picking them up."

There were definitely eight yesterday. Part of my weird math thing is that I count everything. I don't even realize I do it, but I know how many fluorescent lights are in my lit class (twelve) and how many diapers I change most days (lately it's only six), and I know that yesterday there were eight rocks and today there are nine. I glance at each one, from light to dark, and the very last rock is the deepest gray, almost black, with a white streak down the middle.

The refrigerator buzzes, a dog barks outside. Cinde spins her mug slowly and it makes a quiet scraping sound against the table.

Is that my rock? The last one I left on the gravestone? There are thousands of rocks on the beach and I'm sure at least some of the others look like that.

"Did he tell you Mike just got outta jail?" Huh? I turn back and shake my head, trying to participate in the conversation. My stomach feels churny and tight. Zenn's dad was in jail?

"Yeah. I suppose that's not something Zenn blabs to everyone."

I shake my head and think of the fractal from Zenn's jacket — the darkness, the violence, the fear. The sensation of falling, or crashing, or ... colliding. Panic. Regret.

She opens her mouth to talk again and I realize I've got to leave. I shouldn't be here, and definitely shouldn't be hearing any of this from her. If Zenn wanted me to know about his dad, he would tell me. I'm confident that he will tell me, maybe some night in the not-so-distant future when we are curled around each other, catching our breath from kissing, and he feels so close to me that he tells the whole story. I shouldn't be hearing this from anyone but Zenn, when he's ready.

I look up at the wall clock in fake surprise. "Oh, wow. I didn't notice the time. I've got to go."

Cinde hangs her head. "Shit," she says quietly. "I shouldn't've told you about that. Zenn's gonna kill me."

"No, it's fine." I try to reassure her. "I just really have to go."

"Don't think bad of him, okay? It didn't have anything to do with him."

"Oh, I know. Of course it didn't." Now I sound falsely cheerful and patronizing.

"I'll tell him you stopped by."

"No!" I say. "You don't have to. I'll see him later. No big deal." For some reason it seems very important that Zenn *not* know that I stopped by and chatted with his mom. "Thanks for the coffee." Her smile back is sad and forced.

All morning I jump between thinking about what Cinde said about Mike, about kissing Zenn and about that gray rock on his windowsill. It's a weird stew of thoughts that leaves me feeling a bit horny and really confused.

Mike was in jail, possibly for years. Long enough, anyway, that Zenn never got to know him. What the hell did he do? Murder a few people? Run a drug ring? Sexually abuse some kid? Is that why Zenn never said anything about his dad?

My mind runs in circles. Zenn still doesn't text; he's probably working. Restless, I end up at the cemetery. I'm not exactly surprised to find that my rock is gone and a new one, orange and flat, sits in its place. I don't have one to leave today, but I take the orange one anyway. Could the rock in Zenn's kitchen be mine? Seems unlikely ... and yet ...

My curiosity gets the best of me. A part of me wants to wait for Zenn to tell me, and a part of me has to know now. I'm a problem solver, a puzzle puzzler, it's what I do. And I definitely need something to distract me from the fact that I can't stop thinking about his mouth.

So I do end up at the library after all, sitting at a computer. I type in *Bennett sentencing* with the eraser of my pencil (because, you know ... my hands). I get a couple of hits about a Milwaukee drug dealer named Julias Bennett being sentenced for cocaine possession, but after a quick glance, I know it's not him.

I try simply *Michael Bennett* and get results about a Michael Bennett who serves on the board of education in someplace called Evansville.

I know Zenn grew up in Spellman, so I try *Michael Bennett Spellman WI* and as I scroll down I find one article that makes my hands go numb, my temples throb, my throat tighten.

It's a headline I've seen before:

BABY SURVIVES CEDARBURG CRASH
THAT KILLED PARENTS

CHAPTER 25

HOW THE HELL DID THIS ARTICLE COME UP in a search for Michael Bennett?

My eraser hesitates above the computer mouse. Something heavy — a large, gray stone — settles in my stomach as I click on the link and continue reading the article.

> A young Port Dalton couple died in a two-car crash Sunday evening when their car was struck by a pickup truck that had crossed the center-line. Miraculously their infant in the backseat survived, with only minor injuries.

I press my hand to my forehead, feeling like I might be sick. I skim down, past the picture of my parents. And then I find it.

Police say the driver of the pickup truck, 25-year-old Michael Franklin of Spellman, was traveling home from a Super Bowl party southbound on Cedarburg Road when he crossed the centerline, clipping the back of the Toyota Corolla occupied by Thomas Scheurich, 26, Lynn Scheurich, 25, and their 4-month-old daughter. The Toyota was hit broadside by a third vehicle and then spun into a utility pole. Both husband and wife died at the scene. Their baby is now with family members. Franklin was unharmed, but the pregnant passenger in his car, Cinde Bennett, 23, was taken to Columbia St. Mary's for observation.

Police believe that alcohol was a factor in the crash and Michael Franklin faces two charges of DUI manslaughter.

⚭

I hold my breath for a moment as I try to process this information.

Cinde Bennett is Zenn's mom. She was in the car that hit my parents. She was pregnant with Zenn at the time.

And the driver ... Oh, my God.

The driver was Zenn's dad.

Michael Franklin.

I've known the name of the guy who killed my parents for ages — how could I not? I learned it as soon as I was old enough to ask, since the first time I Googled my parents' accident. If Zenn's last name had been Franklin, that would have set off all kinds of alarm bells for me. But his last name is not Franklin. It's Bennett, from his mom. I had no way of knowing.

And I realize that, just like I know the name of the guy who killed my parents, Zenn must know the names of the people his father killed. He's likely quite familiar with the whole story, knows they were from Port Dalton, suspects they are buried here. And I know, now, that the ninth stone on his windowsill is mine and the rocks I've been picking up are his. Not my mom's.

I don't know who he thinks he's exchanging rocks with, but I bet he doesn't suspect it is me. My name was kept out of the papers after the accident and unless he really looked, I don't think he'd be able to connect me to Thomas and Lynn Scheurich. I don't know why he'd think to try.

I feel something smoldering in my chest, hot and tight. I can't breathe right and I wonder if I could be having a panic attack. I take a few deep breaths to calm down, to try to figure out what I'm feeling. After a moment I realize it's not anger. It's not even sadness. It's ... fear, I think. Fear of what this discovery means and how it will change things.

No, he doesn't know. He couldn't know. He couldn't know and act like everything is normal. He couldn't look me in the eyes, *kiss* me like he kissed me, and have that big a secret.

He visits my parents' grave because he's a good guy. A kind, sweet guy who has no idea he's getting involved with that dead couple's daughter.

Oh, my God. This is nuts.

I stare at the computer screen, at a fuzzy mug shot of Zenn's father from 1997. I study the grainy photo and see once again the resemblance to Zenn. Michael Franklin's hair is longer and he has a thin, scruffy beard, but he looks enough like the Mike I met the other day for me to be sure that it is him.

I Google the correct name this time — Michael Franklin — and find other articles about the accident. One confirms that Michael was — or *is* — a Gulf War veteran, honorably discharged in 1994. I don't remember that from when I looked him up before. I might not have even known what the Gulf War was when I read about him for the first time. I think of Zenn's jacket, the spot where the name patch would be. I can guess the reasons why Zenn or his mom may have removed it. Our story was big local news back in 1997. I guess it's the same reason Zenn has her last name and not his dad's.

He pleaded guilty and was sentenced to twenty years. I wonder if he would've gotten such a strict sentence if I hadn't been in the car. I mean, he was a veteran with a clean record until that point. But you drive drunk and orphan a baby, they're going to throw the book at you. He didn't fight the charges. He didn't plea bargain. I check my Google search but there is no article about him getting out of jail. I guess that's how it goes these days. Unless you're famous, people lose interest. Plenty of new tragedies to focus on.

I'm grateful for people's short attention spans now. I'm grateful that my mom isn't reading that he's out of jail, then studying that eighteen-year-old photo and thinking how much the guy looks like Zenn.

I have to be grateful for the small things at the moment. Because the big things suck big-time.

CHAPTER 26

EVENTUALLY I LEAVE THE LIBRARY. I have to go home at some point. I'm sure I look normal on the outside. No one knows that a bomb just dropped on me and my fledgling love life. I certainly don't know what to do with the knowledge that Zenn's father killed my parents. It was an accident, an accident that he's paid for as best he can. Zenn had nothing to do with it.

But still. His father *killed* my parents.

It doesn't make me weepy or emotional. Stunned, yes. A little freaked-out, sure. But not weepy. I was only four months old when they died and I couldn't tell you one single thing about them that I haven't learned secondhand. But the *idea* of it? The idea that Zenn and I have had this connection since day one and had no clue? Yeah ... it's messed up.

I spend the day in a daze, going through the motions of making the kids hexagon-shaped peanut butter sandwiches and doing some homework, pretending everything is just peachy. I talk to my mom, though later I can't remember one thing we talked about. The whole time I'm with her, I'm just trying to figure out ways for her *not* to know what I know, yet I'm also shoving food in my mouth to keep myself from telling her. It's that weird battle between self-preservation and self-destruction: tempted to jump off a cliff while simultaneously clinging to the railing.

When Zenn texts me late Saturday afternoon — a text that I wanted so badly just this morning — my stomach lurches and my mouth dries up. I toss out a quick reply that I have a headache, heading off a get-together. Not because I don't want to see him because, God help me, there is a shamefully big part of me that *really* wants to see him. But there is another part of me that knows I need to think this through. I need to come up with some kind of plan because I'm convinced that Zenn does not know our connection. And I have a pretty good idea how he will take it. How anyone would take it.

Not well.

I spend Saturday night playing with the kids, and then struggling once again with the biographical section on my college applications. If my family history seemed complicated before, now it seems like an episode of *One Life to Live*. I go to bed late, hoping that exhaustion will help me sleep.

It doesn't.

⚭

Charlotte stops by on Sunday, anxious to hear details of my date with Zenn. I find that my giddiness is diminished by the discovery of our shared past. How do I gush about the soft lips of the son of the guy who killed my parents? But I do my best acting because I'm not ready to tell anyone the whole story just yet.

"So ..." she says, folding her long legs under her like a graceful insect.

"So ..." I say back.

"First of all, who is this Zenn guy? Do I know him?"

I shake my head. "Probably not. He's new." I find it strange that Charlotte and Zenn haven't crossed paths, but that's how the social structure of our high school is. Everyone travels in their own lane.

"What's he look like?"

"He's pretty tall. Taller than you. Short, dark hair. Eyelashes that make you want to bear his children."

She thinks about my description but appears to be coming up blank.

"He usually wears an old green army jacket? His hands are always kind of beat-up?"

She snaps her fingers and her eyes light up. "Ah! That guy?! He is *so* good-looking!"

"You think so?" I say this because even though I think he is gorgeous it's fun to hear her say it, too.

"God, yes! I know exactly who it is. He has gym the same hour as me. I think Coach Foster was trying to get him to play basketball. Did he try out?"

"I ... I don't know ..." We've never talked about basketball. Could that be why I've been tutoring him?

"Okay, so. You and tall, dark, mysterious army-jacket guy are ... hooking up?"

I bite my lip.

"You are! You totally are!"

"Well ... just the one time."

"And ... nothing happened? You didn't get any ..."

Like my parents, she doesn't like to name my visions out loud. As if not calling them what they are makes any difference.

I shake my head. "I didn't. Isn't that weird?"

"I mean, you *did* touch him, right? Like, with your hands?"

"Yeah. I mean, not his bare skin or anything." I feel myself blush. "But that usually doesn't matter."

"But you touched his clothes?"

"Yeah."

"Oh, my God. This is *huge*! Like, where did you touch him?"

"At the park. On the play set."

"No. Like where on his *body*."

"Oh!" I feel myself blushing even more. What am I, twelve? "I don't know. His chest. Maybe his shoulders ..."

"Jeez, you were all over each other! And nothing? None of your ... fractals?"

I shake my head. I'll admit it: after we kissed the other night I had the romantic idea that maybe he didn't give me fractals because, well ... our feelings for each other are special. That he's "the one" or something equally corny, like some Disney fairy tale. But now I wonder if there's another explanation. Something to do with that night that changed both of our lives eighteen years ago.

"Oh, my God!" she exclaims again. "We should totally go on a double date!"

How her mind goes from my huge news that Zenn doesn't give me fractals to double dating, I have no idea. I guess she's been waiting for this moment since Josh first asked her out. But I try to imagine Zenn and Josh hanging out and it doesn't compute. I can't imagine anything moving forward after what I've learned.

"Maybe." I try to change the subject. "How's it going with you guys?"

It may be my imagination, but I think Charlotte's excitement dies down a tiny bit. "Good!"

I study her face and her eyes dart away.

"Is this a Katie Holmes–Tom Cruise kind of thing?"

Charlotte just looks at me blankly.

"You know. Like where she fantasized about marrying him when she was a kid but then did and found out he's a crazy Scientologist?"

"No!" Charlotte swats me and rolls her eyes.

"The shine hasn't worn off? Even a little?"

"No. Not like that."

"Then what?"

She picks at the skin around her fingernails. "I don't know. I guess it's just his friends. He acts different around them than he does around me."

I nod. I don't tell her that I already know this.

"I wish he would just ..." Her words drift off and she looks at me hopefully.

"Hey, don't look at me. I have absolutely *zero* relationship advice to give."

"What do you think, though? Do you think he's a good guy? Do you think I'm going to get my heart broken?"

I smile at her. "I think he's a very good guy."

And I realize I do. But I have no idea about the safety of her heart.

◯◯

Sunday night Zenn texts me again.

Zenn: Hey!

The exclamation point tells me he is still oblivious. Of course he is. He didn't try to stop by my house with a note on the back of a Jesus coloring sheet. He didn't have a heart-to-heart with my mom. He had no reason to Google my name and unravel our story. He's the smart one, the lucky one. Meanwhile, I have the unfortunate task of figuring out what to do next.

Me: Hey
Zenn: I want to see u. Can I see u?

My heart flutters and I cover my smile with my hand, though no one is around to see it. But I can't do this. Can I? Can I do this? I think for a second and text back.

Me: I have a lot of homework. Maybe another time?

There is a pause. I stare at my phone, waiting.

Zenn: Are you avoiding me?

> Me: No! No. Just … AP Lit is kicking. My. Ass.
> Zenn: OK.
> Zenn: That's what you get for being an overachiever.
> Me: haha
> Zenn: Tomorrow?

Nothing is going to have changed by tomorrow. His dad will still have killed my parents. My heart will still be in my throat when I hear his voice. And I still won't know what to do about any of it. But I text back:

> **Tomorrow.**

I skip our lunch together and hide out in the library instead. I know this is getting out of hand and that he is going to realize I'm blowing him off. But I still don't know how to handle this.

I think I've bought myself one more day when I make it out of school without seeing him, but then I hear him calling me across the parking lot.

He's walking toward me and I realize for real why I've been trying to put space between us: because I have zero willpower when it comes to him. I am pulling toward him like a magnet.

"Hey," he says, slightly out of breath. Like the first time we met.

"Hey," I say back.

He stands close to me now, closer than he did before we

kissed. He doesn't ask me where I was at lunch. He doesn't give me the third degree. He just looks down at me with those eyelashes and I fold like a paper airplane. He raises an eyebrow, lifts one corner of his mouth. He tugs at the shoulder strap of my backpack lightly. Oh, screw it. I'm doomed.

He glances at his phone. "I have to go to work," he says, and he doesn't even try to hide the regret in his voice. I want to reach out and touch him, but he's wearing that damn army jacket.

"Tonight?" I ask him, all resolve gone. "What time do you get off?"

"Seven."

I pick the first place that comes to mind, a place where I know we can be alone to talk. "Meet me at my church? Around eight?"

"At your church?" I nod and he doesn't question me further, just says, "Okay." There is no kiss, but there is this incredible moment where he looks at me — no, scratch that. He *sees* me, with those stormy eyes and those fantastic eyelashes and he tugs playfully at the end of my braid and I feel like I can barely breathe. "See you tonight."

CHAPTER 27

I TELL MY MOM THAT CHARLOTTE AND I are working on a group project and that the only time we could get together is tonight. She tells me not to stay up too late, but I know she'll be dead asleep by the time I get home, no matter when that might be. I head off with no idea what I'm going to say to him. I know I probably should end it. It's just too weird and soap opera-y and my mom would freak out if she ever found out that Zenn is Michael Franklin's son. I should end it and just focus on the task at hand: a college, a scholarship. In the long run, that's what really matters.

Right?

But it's not *fair*. I finally find someone amazing, and we like each other, and I can kiss him and touch him (and he actually seems to want to kiss and touch *me*), and I have to let him go because of something neither of us had anything to do with. This feels like my one chance. This feels like *it*.

What are the odds I'll ever find a guy like him again? What if I never figure out my condition and I'm alone for the rest of my life?

God, this *sucks*.

I don't let myself fuss in the mirror with my hair or makeup. I wear what I wore all day and the only vain thing I let myself do is brush my teeth. No sense in my breath smelling like my mom's mac and cheese. I head out, heartbroken but determined.

Zenn is sitting on the church steps when I get there, his long legs stretched out in front of him. He stands when I approach and raises an eyebrow when I open the door with my dad's keys.

"Are we going to get in trouble?" he asks quietly, even though we're completely alone.

"What's the matter, Bennett? Not much of a rule breaker?" It comes out a little flirtier than I intended. I'm supposed to be gearing up to end things, not flirting.

He shrugs. "Well ... it *is* a church. Isn't God watching us? Or something?"

"It's okay," I say, holding up my other hand with my fingers crossed. "God and I are like this."

I knew no one would be here tonight and that we'd have privacy to talk. But I may have also chosen this place because it feels safe. In spite of all my skepticism about God and religion, church has always been a safe place for me. I close the door and lock it behind us.

He follows me to the nursery, the playroom where the quads spend a good part of their Sunday mornings. I flick on the fluorescent lights overhead, but the sudden brightness is so jarring that Zenn reaches past me and flips them back off. For some reason, I find this incredibly sexy.

Pull it together, Eva!

When my eyes adjust, I gesture to one corner of the room that is stacked with pillows and we sit on the pile next to each other. He's being very polite and patient. I realize I need to speak first.

"So ..." I start, my voice quiet and serious. "I need to talk to you about something."

"It's the scholarship, isn't it? You *are* mad."

I shake my head quickly. "No! I'm not mad about that. At *all.*"

He looks so confused that I can't help smiling, which makes him grin back at me, relieved, his face lighting up like I'm sunshine or ... candy. Something that he can't resist. I've never had a guy look at me like that before.

I can't ruin this. I can't. And he's right there, just inches away and I still remember the soft vanilla taste of his mouth.

"I'm sorry I blew you off this weekend. And didn't meet you for lunch today," I say, pulling at a thread that has come loose from the pillow I'm sitting on. "I can see why you'd think I was mad. But I wasn't. I was just feeling ... a little overwhelmed."

He still looks confused.

"I'm kind of new at ... all this."

He places one of his hands on mine, stilling it, and I hold my breath, just in case. But no fractal.

"It's kind of new to me, too," he says.

I shake my head, wanting him to realize without me saying it. It's more than just the fact that I've never had a boyfriend.

I look at him but the words pile up in my throat. And before I can get them in order again, he leans closer and his mouth catches my lips. Gently at first, and then more firmly like he's making a statement with his kiss: *I missed you* and maybe *I want you.* Like he's telling me that he doesn't care if I'm virginal and inexperienced. Like he's telling me that no matter what secrets I've uncovered, he's willing to make this work. Though he can't make that promise. He has no idea what I've uncovered.

I try to resist. I really do, but he tastes and smells and feels so good that I quickly forget all about what I need to tell him and my lifelong aversion to touch and wrap my arms around him. I deserve this. Everyone deserves this: to love and to touch. Why should I deny myself what everyone else has?

It's funny how, after years of guarding my hands so carefully, they reach for him instinctively. It's also funny how, after years of getting fractals when I touch just about anyone or anything, this fractal actually startles me. For once in my life I'm not ready. I gasp a little, open my eyes and pull away. No. None of this shit, not from him. Not now.

Then I realize I'm touching his jacket again. That damn army jacket of his dad's.

Now that I know the fractals belong to his dad, I touch the jacket again out of curiosity, but the fractal is too strong, too dark. I realize that the terror and fear are maybe less from any war and more from the accident, because he must have been wearing it that night. The fractal is like the spiderweb of a shattered windshield. God, I can't think about that right now. I remove my hands from Zenn.

"What's wrong?" he asks.

"Can you take this off?" I ask. He looks surprised and more than a little intrigued by my request, but he obeys without question, sliding it off and tossing it aside. He kisses me again and now I can once again touch him with no consequences other than my own hammering heartbeat and liquefying insides.

Almost immediately Zenn pulls away. "Hey, I never asked you. What was that thing the first day we met?"

"What thing?"

"Remember? How I caught you picking my jacket up with your foot?"

Oh, crap. Yeah. How to explain that? How to explain any of this?

The truth? The truth about my fractals seems easy compared to the bigger, harder truth hanging over my head.

He's studying my face, his hand on my thigh, his thumb stroking gently. Fractal or no fractal, I can barely think when he's touching me.

"What is it?" he asks again. He probably expects my answer will be something silly, like I'm a peace activist and have an aversion to military clothing or something, but he sees from my expression it is not.

Well. I guess I have to tell him something.

"So ... I have this thing."

He nods, listening.

I clear my throat. "When I touch ... anything, really ... I have this ... reaction."

"Reaction?"

I nod.

"Like an allergic reaction?"

"Not exactly." I hesitate, thinking of how to best describe my fractals. "You know those paintings you do? The fractal art?"

He nods, barely following.

"It's kind of like that. But, like, in my brain."

"In your brain," he repeats. He sounds skeptical. "You see ... fractal art? When you touch things?"

I wag my head in a kinda-sorta motion. I've got to give him credit — he doesn't look entirely incredulous. I mean, I realize how crazy it sounds.

"*Seeing* is maybe too literal. It's hard to describe. I just get this ... sense? I guess it's kind of visual, but it's also a feeling? I don't know ... but I understand things."

"Wait. You get this when you touch *anything*?" He lets his hand drop, as if he's hurting me. This is what I was afraid of.

"Just about. Except ..." I hesitate to tell him, because it sounds weird and romantic and possibly a little creepy. "Well, except you."

"Except me?"

"Yeah."

"You can touch *me* and you don't get them?"

I nod.

He looks down at my hand and lets it sink in for a minute. "Well. Lucky me," he says. I think he thinks I'm joking.

"I'm serious," I tell him. "I've had them ever since I can remember. But with you ... I don't."

As if to try to prove it, I lift my hand and place it on his cheek, directly on his warm skin. Nothing, except for that fluttering in my stomach.

"I don't know why." My voice is almost a whisper. He stares at me for a minute and then he takes my hand from his face and holds it, palm up, in his hands.

"You're serious?" he asks.

I nod.

"Have you gone to a doctor?"

"Tons." I nod. "And psychiatrists. And even, like, an exorcist."

"What!"

I laugh a little. "Well, not an exorcist, exactly, but like a psychic healer? Don't tell my dad. He'd freak out. My mom took me one time. Didn't work."

"You don't know what causes it?"

I shake my head. "It might be something I was born with or ..." I plant the seed for a future conversation: "I was in an accident when I was little and I had, like, a minor head injury or something. But I've had MRIs and CT scans and all that stuff since then. They haven't been able to find anything unusual. At this point my only hope may be to figure it out myself. At MIT, Northwestern, Stanford ..."

Zenn is still looking at my hand, his fingers now tracing up and down mine like he's feeling for the reason. "It's like my paintings?"

I nod and close my eyes, enjoying his touch. Simple, innocent stroking of his fingertips along my palm. It's even better than I imagined. "I call them fractals because ... there are, like, patterns? Repeating patterns. Remember how we talked about Mandelbrot? The mathematician?"

"Mmmm hmmm." Now he lines up our hands, our fingers, palms pressing against each other. I open my eyes and see that his fingers are longer than mine by nearly a whole segment. He could almost bend the tips of his fingers over the tops of mine.

"Mandelbrot had this idea that things that typically appear as rough or chaotic, like waves or shorelines, actually have a degree of order. There is a geometric repetition on all scales." I realize I'm sounding a little technical and nerdy, but I'm not sure how else to explain it. "No matter how close you look, the patterns never get simpler." I let this sink in for a second. I can tell he's listening because he's looking at me now, focused and intent.

I continue. "When I touch people or their stuff, I get these glimpses into their shit. The stuff that they struggle with. Which, in some ways could probably make me a great therapist or something someday. But the problem is, the patterns never get simpler. In fact, in some ways they get more intense each time. And when I start to think I can solve it, that I can help or *do* something, the pattern is always there. Like Russian nesting dolls that go on forever. Perfect little miniatures of one another that never end."

I close my eyes again.

"They make me feel useless. I want to help but I can't. And then I know this stuff about people — these very private problems — and I can't unknow any of it. So I've always just avoided touching people. And stuff in general. It's why people think I'm, like, a germ freak."

Now his fingers slide between mine and we make a little prayer of sorts with our two hands.

"You get it from touching *things*, too? Not just people?"

I nod. "It's why I want people to bring their calculators when I start tutoring. Because the calculators soak up all their math frustrations. And ... well ... it's just math, so I can figure it out pretty quick and it helps me get to the core of what they're struggling with."

"Seriously? That's the secret to your tutoring genius? You cheat?"

He's kidding. "I prefer, 'use my God-given gift.'"

"Did you get anything from my calculator?"

I shake my head. "Nothing."

Maybe he's proud that he stymied me?

"Do you think you're a math prodigy because of the fractals? Like, maybe your brain works differently in general?"

I shrug. "I don't really know. Since we don't understand why I have them, it's hard to know which came first, the math stuff or the fractals. I sort of think" — I bite my lip, hoping this won't sound too weird — "that the fractals are the way they are because that's just how my brain works. Maybe if I were a creative person, like you, they'd be different. But math is my language so they are kind of like math. With patterns and stuff. Of course, if the fractals came first, then maybe I'm good at math because of that. Or maybe they're both related." I sigh and shrug again. "Short answer is, I really have no idea."

"But wait. If you don't get these fractals from me, why do you get them from my jacket?"

"Because it was your dad's jacket. Right?"

"How did you know?"

"Um ... well ... they're clearly his fractals."

A look of mild terror crosses his face. "No wonder you wanted me to take it off."

"I suppose if I got fractals from you, then the jacket would eventually take on your own personal shit from you wearing it. But since you seem to be sort of neutral, all your dad's shit is still right there. And maybe ... some of your mom's?"

He still looks worried. He hasn't told me anything about his dad and I suppose he's wondering what I might have learned.

"It's, like, nothing specific," I reassure him. "At first. My fractals, I mean. The more I touch one person, or their stuff, the more I can see over time. But at first it's all just kind of a mess."

He looks relieved. Can't say that I blame him. I think of how complicated my mom's fractals can be — laden with all her guilty regret for the things she gave up when she quit school to raise me, with her intense grief, with her constant exhaustion — and they are nothing compared to his dad's.

"Can you show me?"

I'm confused. "Show you?"

"Like, touch something and tell me what it feels like?"

I hesitate. Do I really want to prove what a freak I am? But how else do I make him believe me?

"Yeah. I guess so." I look around. "But not in here. It's all kid stuff in here and I don't get them from kids." I catch myself. "Well, sometimes I do, but they're different. Happier. And the younger they are, the fewer I get."

I get up and he stands, too.

"Maybe you don't get them from me because I'm some sort of stunted three-year-old," he suggests.

He's already heading out of the room to the sanctuary. I follow him to the front of the church and he picks up a hymnal from one of the seats.

I shake my head. "That won't work."

"Why not?"

"It's too generic. Like a shopping cart or a doorknob. Too many different people hold it for too short a time. Plus, it's paper."

"Oh." Like that makes perfect sense. I see a square of white fabric on the floor near the communion rail. I pick it up and find it's a crisp white handkerchief. Here we go.

He watches me closely. I'm not sure what I look like when a fractal strikes. I've never sat and looked in a mirror while I had one, and I'm too distracted by the colors and patterns and feelings anyway. But I don't *think* there are any outward physical signs, except for when a bad one makes me sweaty and nauseated. It's too late to worry about appearances now because the fractal is already sweeping over me. It's not a horrible one. I can still think, still talk.

"It belongs to a woman," I say. "An older woman —"

He cuts me off. "How do you know?"

"Well, it's a handkerchief, and no one younger than sixty carries a handkerchief."

"How do you know it's a woman?"

I refocus. "I don't know. The colors are ... muted? Like, mauve and light blue? They're not young colors, not masculine colors."

"You see colors?"

"Usually."

"What else?" He leans against the communion rail and crosses his arms.

"She's divorced? Or widowed, I think? The patterns are ... I don't know ... slanted? Sad? Lonely."

He's watching me closely, maybe believing. Maybe not.

"But there's something more recent. Some kind of a health issue."

"How do you know?"

I shake my head. I struggle to verbalize it. "The patterns are ... growing? Spreading? Like an oil spill in water." Now I know. "Cancer. She's got cancer."

He hasn't taken his eyes off me.

"I think I know who it is," I say sadly. "It's Mrs. Larkin."

"Mrs. Larkin?"

"Ellen Larkin. It's hers. I didn't know she was sick. I wonder if my dad knows." I'm talking more to myself, now, feeling raw and helpless, as I often do afterward.

He takes the handkerchief from my hands and unfolds it. There's a monogram on the corner: *HL*.

"Herb Larkin. That was her husband."

Zenn is floored. Without any proof, he still believes me. Maybe that's why I really brought him here: to a place of belief without proof.

"You're psychic," he says.

I shake my head. "No."

"Kinda."

"I can't see the future. Or even the past, exactly. I just ... feel all the feelings."

"That's ... wow."

I feel a little vulnerable and embarrassed, like I just read him a poem I wrote in fifth grade. But he doesn't seem to be too freaked out. He reaches for the bottom edge of my hoodie and tugs me closer.

"You don't know how good it is. To be able to ... touch

someone." My voice cracks a little. "I mean, without all that noise. I guess that's why I'm feeling so —"

"Overwhelmed," he finishes for me.

"Yeah."

"I can imagine." He studies me and then looks down at my hands. "Well," he says, his voice lighter, "I'm glad to help out any way I can." There's that flirtatious tone again.

I gather up a handful of his T-shirt and pull myself closer to him. He rests one hand on my waist.

"You don't get these fractals when other people touch you?" he asks. His mouth is now close to my temple, his breath loosening something inside me.

I shake my head. "Well," I say, my voice kind of sticking in my throat. "Not fractals. But I didn't realize I didn't get them from you *right* away because ..."

His head dips and his mouth is by my ear.

"Because ...?" he says. His breath against my skin makes me shiver.

"Because when I touch you ... or you touch me ... something just as crazy goes on in my brain."

"Oh, yeah?" His fingers press lightly against my lower back, pulling me even closer.

I nod.

"Mine, too," he says.

Well. That about does it for me. He presses his lips against my jaw and now we communicate with our hands and our mouths and our warm, moist breath.

I slide my hands down his back on top of his shirt and feel the slope where his spine runs in the valley of his rib cage, the surprisingly hard angles of muscle and bone that lead down to his hips.

I feel greedy. I want to touch everything: his hair, his skin, his muscles, his bones, his soul if that's possible. All these years I've kept my hands carefully tucked away and until now I don't think I ever truly realized what I was missing. The velvet of his earlobe, the slight roughness of his cheek, the tender skin on his neck, the firm solidness of everything else. Good lord, it's so *much*. And I haven't even ventured under his clothes.

His kiss is soft and searching and gentle, except when it builds and crests and breaks like a wave, and then it becomes more urgent and less gentle. I feel like I can't get close enough to him. I want less space between us. No space between us.

So, this is how teenagers get caught up, forget birth control, and end up pregnant. I always thought that practicality would win out and that no matter what the situation, cooler heads would prevail, especially in my case. But that was before I'd ever kissed … well, anyone. Now that Zenn's mouth is on the sensitive skin just under my ear, now that his lean, warm body is pressed up against me, now that my hands can enjoy the topography of his chest … now I see what all the fuss is about.

Our breathing speeds up, our bodies press more tightly. My hands grip his shoulders with a recklessness I didn't know I had in me —

Bong, bong, bong …

We both startle when the church bells ring.

Bong, bong, bong …

I realize he is still leaning against the communion rail so that our heights are more even and I'm literally wedged between his legs. In the middle of my church sanctuary. Wow.

I take a step backward and he straightens up, reaching out to adjust a fabric banner that got shifted in our frenzy.

Bong, bong, bong!

"Wow," he says, as if realizing for the first time where we are. "We are going *straight* to hell, aren't we?"

I laugh, but something vaguely Cinderella-ish about the clock striking reminds me that this is all an illusion. Even though my powerful attraction to him can eclipse our strange shared history, that may not be the case for him. It's not fair to either of us to let this go further without telling him what I know.

I will tell him now, while we are feeling close and vulnerable, in the peaceful and forgiving quiet of the church. Another reason I may have brought him here.

But Zenn's cell phone buzzes and before I can censor my big mouth I say, "Is that a cell phone in your pocket or are you happy to see me?" Oh God, what is wrong with me? Nervousness brings out the worst in me.

Zenn just laughs. He's not easily embarrassed. "Um ... both?"

He fishes the phone out of his pocket and looks at it for a moment. His face changes from happy and relaxed to tense and serious.

"Ev, I have to go. I'm sorry."

But I still haven't told him!

"It's my mom."

"Oh. Okay. Sure."

"She gets weird sometimes. When she drinks ... I just need to check on her."

"Of course." I walk with him back to the nursery to get his

jacket, even though my legs still feel like jelly. We go through the narthex and I follow him out to his truck. He kisses me goodbye, distracted, and hops inside.

"I'll talk to you later?"

I nod and watch him drive away.

⊕

Before I go to bed, I have to know if everything is okay.

Zenn: Yep. Fine. Sorry for running out. Gtg — see you tomorrow?

His lack of enthusiasm freaks me out. Could his mom have said something to him? Could she know what I know?

To make it worse, I don't see him at school the next day, and my phone is dead silent. I text him again and he doesn't respond. Maybe the Camelot period of our brief relationship is over. Maybe the whole relationship is over.

The next day I wonder if he really is dropping out. But then I go to the art room and he is there.

He smiles at me but there is tension in his mouth. He has faint circles under his eyes.

"You okay?" I ask.

He nods. He's not mixing paints today, just sitting at a desk doodling on what appears to be his literature assignment.

"No painting today?"

He shrugs. I notice his hair is getting a little bit longer in the front and it sticks up when he runs his hand through it.

"Everything okay with your mom?"

"I don't really want to talk about it here," he says.

Even though I get it — school is not the place for deep conversations — my feelings are hurt a little. But then he says, "I have to work after school, but do you want to come over tonight?"

I wonder if he's inviting me over just to break up with me, if he found out about my parents. I can't even think about that. I can't lose all this now that I've finally found it. I can't go back to my isolation and self-imposed loneliness. He wants me to come over and I know I won't say no.

I wonder if his mom will be there and I'll have to figure out what to say. I wonder a million things in a second but my answer is a simple, "Yeah."

CHAPTER 28

AT EIGHT I PULL UP IN FRONT of the Arts and Crafts house in my mom's minivan. In exchange for using the car, I helped her get the kids to bed before I left. I can tell my mom is torn between being happy for me that I finally have some kind of social life, being resentful that I have other things to do now and being worried about me. She gave up what should have been her carefree twenties to be my mom and I wonder if she's jealous of me sometimes, too. Not that there's been much to be jealous of up to this point. She's made it eighteen years without having to think about me having a boyfriend. Now some big fears — of me getting hurt or pregnant or damaged in some way — are probably hitting her like bricks.

Zenn lets me inside and gestures to the couch, asks me if I want something to drink. Things feel kind of stiff between us, especially considering the last time we were alone together I was basically a puddle of confessions and lust. I know I have to tell him the rest tonight, before things go any further.

I take him up on a glass of water for my dry throat. He hands it to me but I drop it almost immediately, startled by the fractal.

"Sorry!" I bend to pick up the glass, to stop the spill, but the fractal makes me drop it again. I leave it on the floor this time. Zenn grabs a towel from the kitchen and mops up the water. He raises his eyebrows in a *what-was-that-about* look.

I feel like I peed on the carpet instead of just spilling water on it. "The glass ..." I say.

He picks it up and studies it a second. Based on the fractal, I suspect it's a glass that his mom drinks from often.

"I didn't even think," he says. "I'm sorry."

He goes to the kitchen and looks at the shelf, probably for the least offensive glass.

"I used the Pritzer Insurance mug that one time," I remind him. "That was fine."

He takes the mug, fills it with water and brings it to me.

"Are they painful?" he asks.

"No," I reassure him. "Not physically. Sometimes they give me a headache, or make me a little queasy, but that's all. They just ... surprise me sometimes. Especially when I let my guard down."

He sits next to me on the couch.

I make small talk to distract him from the fact that I'm kind of a major freak. "How was work?"

"Fine," he says. He's still studying the glass that I dropped. "My mom uses this one all the time."

I nod.

"So what's it like? Her ... fractal?" he asks.

I silently debate about what to tell him. "Um ... Fuzzy. Swirly. Kind of sad. Lots of blues and purples, like a bruise."

He nods. I don't think I'm surprising him.

"What's my dad's like?"

He looks at me, his gray eyes searching, but hinting that they already know what his dad's fractal might feel like. I look away.

"He was in jail," Zenn tells me. He sets his mom's glass on the battered coffee table. "For almost eighteen years. He just got out."

Here it comes. I probably should act surprised but I realize that not being honest will only come back to bite me, so I just stay quiet instead. I nod nonjudgmentally.

"Vehicular manslaughter. Drunk driving. After the Packers-Patriots Super Bowl."

I take a deep breath.

"The Packers won, so ... you know. Reason to celebrate."

His voice is ironic, not making a joke, exactly, but trying to lighten things up.

"My mom had me right after the accident." He leans back against the couch and stares at the ceiling. I see his Adam's apple rise and fall. "Messed her up pretty good."

"We're all messed up," I say.

"True. But she's at a whole different level." He shakes his head and closes his eyes. He looks exhausted. "Last night she was wasted. She gets kind of manic and just ... I worry about her. That's why I had to leave."

I reach for his hand, sliding my fingers between his. I realize for the first time that his family has been affected at least as much as mine has by that accident. Who knows where we all would be if things had been different that night. The difference of a few minutes, a drink or two, a missed light at an intersection ... Even eighteen years later, that night is still threatening to take things from me.

"Your family is so normal." He shakes his head. "You sure you want to get involved in all my shit? Jailbird dad. Slutty drunk mom. Me ..."

I turn his face toward mine. I plan on saying *yes, I'm sure, I'll take all your shit and then some if I get to be with you.* But what comes out is: "My family is not as normal as you think."

I take a deep breath. I have to tell him. He's going to find out eventually. "I knew about your dad. About the accident and jail and all that."

His eyebrows go up in surprise, surprise at my change in topic, surprise that I know.

"Your mom told me," I explain.

"My mom? When?"

"Saturday. I came by to see you and had coffee with her."

"Oh, God." He moans.

"But that's not ..."

Something in my voice makes him sit up. His full attention is always disconcerting. I have no idea how to do this.

"I don't know how to say this. It may seem like I'm all over the place, but bear with me." I clear my throat, take a sip of water, clear my throat again. "My parents are not my real parents," I blurt out. "They are my aunt and uncle."

He nods slowly, looking confused, but he stays quiet.

"My brothers and sisters are actually my cousins."

"Okay ..."

"My parents died."

He inhales. Exhales. "Oh," he says. "I'm sorry." His voice is sincere, sad, not even a little bit suspicious.

I don't mean to diminish their death, but I wave my hand in a way that probably does. "I was just a baby. I don't remember them. So although it's tragic in theory, it's all I've ever known."

I hope maybe this is enough for him to make the connection, but why would it? He nods, still clueless. He thinks that's all there is: dead parents. I reach into my pocket and pull out the flat, rectangular orange stone that I found when I visited their grave on Saturday. I take his hand and press the stone into his palm.

He looks down at it, confused at first, but then something clicks.

"They died in an accident." I pause before delivering the final punch. "Eighteen years ago."

He recoils, like I've actually punched him with my fist. He shakes his head again. I let it sit for a minute, not wanting to overstate it or spell it out if I don't have to. But I don't have to. He knows.

I fill the silence with words.

"I know it's insane and bizarre that somehow we met and didn't know any of this. It is. But I think that connection also has something to do with why you don't give me fractals."

I think I've already lost him. He's pulled his hand away from mine.

"We were both there that night. It must have something to do with that."

He's not really listening anymore. "My dad killed your parents?"

I nod. "But, Zenn ... I'm okay. I know it was an accident."

"But your last name is Walker."

"Yeah. My aunt and uncle adopted me. Changed my name."

He stares at me for a minute, letting it sink in and then he looks away. I can tell he's shutting down, going numb.

"I'm *fine*, Zenn. I don't miss what I never had."

"You *are*? You *don't*?" I can tell he misses everything he's never had because of that accident: a dad, a normal childhood, a happy mom, money, a stable life.

"I mean —" I start, but he stands up and paces the room. I stand up, too, and never figure out how to finish my sentence. No matter what I say, it feels like I am downplaying being orphaned just so I can hold on to a boy. It sounds flippant even to me.

He stops by the small, high window seat that looks down over the driveway. He braces a hand on either side of the window. Finally he says, "This is just my fucking luck."

I step closer but I don't touch him.

"Just my luck that I meet someone like you, and this ... this fucked-up shit is the backstory."

"Zenn. It's okay. We can get past this."

"Maybe you can. But ..." He suddenly sees something, not out the window, but in the puzzles he's putting together. "Wait. When you hurt your head, when you were little, that was from the accident?"

I barely nod, and his head falls back. "Are you kidding me?"

"Zenn, I'm *fine* now."

"No, you're not. You have this fractal thing messing up your life. You never even knew your parents. You're not fine. How could you be *fine*?"

I am fine. Aren't I?

"You must *hate* him."

"I don't." And I must put some kind of undue stress on the word *I* because he looks at me. *"I don't,"* I repeat, changing the emphasis.

"Someone does, though. Your aunt? Your uncle?"

My silence is my answer.

He sighs heavily, his eyes on the floor.

"Don't you think it's a sign or something that I don't get the fractals from you? That you're the *only* person?" I don't tell him that it feels like we are *meant* to be together because that seems like too much, too soon. But I think it. And I feel it.

He shrugs. "It doesn't matter. When your family finds out who I am, how do they ever get past that? How does my dad? How does my mom? She was there, too, you know." He gasps, remembering something else. "Oh, my God. She *held* you! After the accident she held you until the cops came. Oh, man. This is just too ..."

I didn't know that part, didn't know that his mom held me that night. The knowledge leaves me with unsettling images that I don't often indulge: my mom and dad, bleeding, dead or close to dead in the mangled car. And now: a very pregnant Cinde cradling me in the cold. Zenn and I were just inches apart that night. I shake my head to push the thoughts from my mind.

I step in front of him, between him and the window, and force him to look at me. "Zenn. It's going to be okay. We'll figure it out." His whole body sags a little. He doesn't believe me. I don't know if I believe myself.

What if this is it? Oh, God, this can't be it. But he's shutting down and I don't have anything to say that will change anything. I know he needs some time.

"I'm gonna go. But don't ..." I struggle to find the right words. "Don't give up yet. Okay? There's a reason we found each other. There has to be."

CHAPTER 29

I SIT AT THE COMPUTER, my hands frozen on the keyboard. I can't concentrate. I can't do anything, lately, other than think about Zenn. It's been four days and I haven't heard a word from him. Maybe I was foolish to think we could somehow forget our dysfunctional history and be together. Maybe some obstacles are just too big.

Since I haven't been able to focus, I've distracted myself by hanging out with Josh and Charlotte. I tell Charlotte that Zenn has to work instead of telling her the truth: that our lives are like something out of a Mexican soap opera. She seems happy to have me with them, excited to share Josh with me away from his friends. Charlotte is right — he's different. When he's with his friends, he has to pretend to be something he's not, and it has left him lonely and exhausted.

The funny thing is, I learn this more from conversation than from his fractals.

When I actually do touch him, his fractal is better than it once was. Lighter, brighter, happier. The thing that I've always found so daunting about my visions is that I can't change the past. But maybe I underestimate how much people can change their own futures. Josh still looks like a popular kid on the outside, but just by being himself with Charlotte, something is changing on the inside.

Meanwhile, my outsides and my insides are equally a disaster.

I lean my head onto the desk and close my eyes. What makes everything worse is that I had pretty much gotten used to my isolation. Before, I mean. My family, Charlotte, and a couple of acquaintances who could loosely be categorized as friends were enough for me before I met Zenn. But now I don't know if I can go back to pretending I don't need connection or intimacy or deep and sometimes complicated feelings. I don't know if I can go back to being that lonely, that flat.

My phone buzzes and I peek at it halfheartedly. After four days of waiting for a text from Zenn, I'm trying not to get my hopes up. My parents took the kids to see the newest Disney movie and it's probably my mom reminding me to put the leftovers away, as if any of us will want to eat them again. But when I glance at the screen, I see it *is* from Zenn.

Zenn: Hey
Me: Hey
Zenn: I'm outside. Are you alone?
Me: Yes
Zenn: Can we talk?
Me: Yes

My replies are probably too quick and eager, but I don't care at this point. I glance at myself in the computer-screen reflection and figure it will have to do. I hop up and run to the front door.

He's standing there, hands in his pockets. My stomach feels like it's filled with helium.

"Hi," I squeak. My voice sounds helium-filled, too. I invite him to come in.

He studies his hands for a minute, rubbing his palms together. When he finally looks at me, I see in his eyes that something has changed. I open my mouth to ask him what he's decided but I probably should just let him speak first. I close my mouth again.

He reaches out and puts his hand on the back of my neck and pulls me closer. He dips his head down toward mine until our foreheads touch. I feel his desperation, his sadness, his need, so similar to mine. We stay that way for a long, intense moment. When he opens his eyes again, I can't help myself. I rise up on my tiptoes and kiss him.

He hesitates a moment and I start to pull away, thinking I've misread him. Maybe he was gearing up to say goodbye. But then he pulls me closer and kisses me back, almost apologetically, and then a little urgently, like we're making up from a fight. It tells me he has missed me. It tells me that he's willing to try to make this work.

My whole body sighs with relief.

I have a choice here: a choice to take what I want and maybe even *deserve*, after living most of my life in relative isolation. My mom's resentment is not my problem. His parents' guilt is not his problem. We can't control many things in life, but I can choose this. With him.

I know the couch is right behind me so I step backward until my legs hit it and I sit, pulling him down by the front of his shirt. There is no grace, no smooth moves. We are a frenzy of hungry mouths and tugging fingers. He leans me back against the couch so that he's half on top of me, and I press my whole body up toward his, as if I'm trying to meld us into one.

His mouth moves to my ear, to my neck, to my collarbone. I take off my glasses and toss them on the coffee table.

"I thought you wanted to talk," I tease him quietly. The helium is gone and now my voice is throaty.

He stops abruptly.

"Kidding," I say. "Totally kidding. We don't have to talk."

Stupid, stupid, stupid Eva. Shut your big fat mouth! I pull him down to kiss me again, but he resists.

"Sorry," he says, his voice apologetic. "Maybe we should talk." It seems like he's embarrassed or regretful for kissing me instead of using words, as if he's been rude. But I'm the one who started it. And if he knew that I've been waiting my whole teenage life for a boy to kiss me like this, he'd know he doesn't have to apologize for anything.

I shake my head a tiny bit, my voice more serious now. "We don't have to. Not ... right this minute. Or maybe ... ever." Nothing else really matters now. Just this.

So he kisses me again and then somehow I'm sliding my hands all over his torso until his shirt is just a barrier to my exploration. I'd like to slide my hands under it, but I've barely touched another human in six years. I can't imagine just putting my hands wherever I want, skin on skin. And it feels too personal, too presumptuous, like maybe I should ask first. Do normal people ask before they touch each other's bare skin?

"Can I ..." I start, not knowing exactly how I'm going to finish.

"Mmmm hmmm," Zenn breathes in my ear.

"You don't even know what I was going to ask," I whisper back, mimicking him.

"Doesn't matter," he says, mimicking me.

I don't say anything for a moment and Zenn nudges my ear. "What?"

"I was just going to ask if I can ... like ... feel your skin."

He pulls away to look at me, amused.

I cover my face with one hand. "God, that's weird, right? That I asked?"

Zenn pries my hand off my face and places it under the hem of his T-shirt and there it is: his smooth, hot, incredible skin and the taut muscle underneath, like a cotton sheet fresh from the dryer stretched over granite. I slide my fingertips up just an inch or two but I'm too timid and embarrassed to go much farther. Plus, Zenn is watching me, serious now.

Self-conscious, I lift my hand but he immediately places his hand on top of mine, pressing it back against his body.

"Sorry," he says quietly. "I forget about your ... that you can't ..." His voice trails off.

He forgets that I've been living in a self-made bubble, that I've never touched a boy's bare skin before. At least not the skin of a torso, a back, the intimate slopes of muscle and bone that have piqued my curiosity since I hit puberty.

He doesn't finish his sentence. He just kisses me again and I allow my hand to slide up, over his shoulder blade, down the valley of his spine. I feel myself blush when my fingers touch the waistband of his underwear poking slightly out of the back of his jeans. He doesn't seem to notice, or to care.

I toy again with the idea of pulling his T-shirt over his head, getting it out of the way so he can press his heated body down on me like an electric blanket. It creeps up higher and higher as my hands slide up his back, but I'm so new to all this that I can't even imagine removing my own clothing, much less someone else's. So I make do with exploring underneath, sliding my fingers over the ridges of his rib cage, letting my knuckles graze hip bones and stomach muscles.

One of Zenn's hands finds the buttons on my oh-so-sexy flannel shirt and undoes one, two, three of them. I swallow my fear and self-consciousness and let him open my shirt just a bit. He doesn't unbutton it all the way, just enough to reveal my collarbone, the edge of my pale pink bra.

I'm suddenly a little nervous about what I've started. Once hands start exploring under clothes, and then the clothes start coming off, I suppose things can move pretty quickly at our age. I've only just started playing ball and already I'm close to rounding second base. Even though I've never done anything remotely like this with a guy, for obvious reasons, Zenn is an attractive eighteen-year-old male. I seriously doubt this is his first time unbuttoning a girl's shirt.

"Zenn," I whisper, my voice sounding slightly frantic in my own ears.

"Mmmm?" he hums. His lips press lightly against the skin just at the edge of my bra.

"I just ..."

He must hear the panic in my voice because he raises himself up onto his elbow. He must be getting tired of all the interruptions.

"I'm just ..."

He doesn't let me finish. "It's okay," he says quietly. "We're just ... talking. Right?"

I nod and bite my lip.

"You've got, like, eighteen years of touch phobia to make up for."

"That's true," I say. I tentatively run my hands up his sides, climbing the gentle incline up from his hips.

"So, whatever. There's no rush." He kisses me once. Twice. "But, you know ... feel free to explore. Consider me, like, therapy."

I laugh. "Therapy?"

He nods. "Cheap, too." He kisses my neck. "No co-pay, even." He kisses my collarbone.

"And you're a qualified therapist?"

"Not even a little bit. But seeing as I'm the only person you can touch ..."

"You'll have to do."

He nods. "That's what I'm counting on."

I laugh, and then he kisses me and I don't feel like laughing anymore. We lose track of time, kissing so that we don't have to talk about dead parents and felon fathers and all the reasons we probably shouldn't be together. Eventually Zenn grants my silent wish and grabs his shirt at the back of the neck with one hand and pulls it off in the way that only guys do. Just like that, his bare chest is inches from my body, the ridges of his stomach muscles casting shadows in the dim light. Somehow the fact that his body has been defined by actual work — raking and shoveling and moving heavy boxes — rather than by long hours at the gym makes it that much sexier. I tentatively explore the bridge of his collarbone, the thick rounded muscles of his shoulders, the long lean lines of his arms. I didn't know skin could feel so soft and hard at the same time.

We kiss and touch and press until I vaguely hear, somewhere in the distance, the garage door open. I sit up in a panic.

"Shit." I fumble for my glasses with one hand, the buttons of my shirt with the other; somehow two more have come undone. Once I can see again, I toss Zenn his shirt. Wow. He looks even better when I can actually see.

Focus, Eva!

I run my hands over my hair, take a few deep breaths, make sure my pants haven't somehow become unbuttoned as well, hope you can't see any evidence of arousal on me or Zenn. He should have left before they got home — that would have been smart.

But I forgot they were coming home. I think I forgot they even existed.

Either way, it's too late now to do anything but try to look innocent. Luckily I have eighteen years of practice for that.

We make sure there is a good foot between us on the couch. I turn on the TV and search for something — anything — that we might be able to pretend we were watching. I settle on *Duck Dynasty*. It's a stretch.

Libby and Ethan bound in, still full of energy even though it's an hour past their bedtime. Eli is sleeping on my dad's shoulder, Essie on my mom's. My mom sees me on the couch. And then Zenn.

I focus my attention on Libby and Ethan.

"Hey, guys! How was the movie?"

"Goodgoodgoodgood!" Libby bounces for each *good.*

Ethan nods, surprisingly quiet for a change. I suspect he's infatuated with Zenn.

"C'mon, let's get your jammies on." I turn to Zenn. "I'll be back in a sec."

He nods, and gives Libby and Ethan a high five. He shakes his hand in pretend pain afterward.

In the girls' room my mom is carefully removing Essie's coat, trying not to wake her. I put my finger to my lips to remind Libby to be quiet, hoping my mom will take the hint, too. She doesn't.

"How long has Zenn been over?" she asks.

"Not too long," I lie. "He had to work tonight."

I wonder if she can sense my deception, smell the lingering lust on my skin. It feels like she is weighing saying something else, maybe reprimanding me for having a boy in the house when they aren't home. She must decide against it, figuring I should be allowed what simple pleasures I can find in a boy's company. Little does she know that the pleasures I can find with Zenn are more extensive than she imagines.

We get the girls in bed while my dad handles the boys. I'm hoping we've given Zenn ample time to catch his breath. When we return to the living room, he stands and says hi to my mom. I realize he has never met my dad.

"Dad, this is Zenn."

Zenn reaches out and they shake hands.

"Good to meet you, Zenn."

"You, too, sir."

The *sir* is a nice touch.

The moment is made so much more awkward by the knowledge that Zenn and I have and my parents don't. I feel like we are deceiving them, not just by pretending that we were watching *Duck Dynasty*, but by not telling them what we now know about each other.

"I should get going," Zenn says. "I have to work pretty early."

My parents tell him goodbye and I walk him out to the car, careful to maintain a safe distance between us.

At his truck, when I'm pretty sure my parents couldn't see us even if they tried, I lean in to feel his body against mine one more time. He wraps his arms around me.

"We can't do this forever," he says quietly. "Can we?"

"I don't see why not."

He smiles, but I can tell he's serious. Maybe I am, too. I think I'd be willing to do just about anything to keep this feeling, this closeness that I've never had before. Lying to my parents seems a small trade-off for what feels like love. "They might never find out," I argue.

"You did."

"That's because I'm freakishly persistent and love research. I *tried* to find out."

"Why? Because my mom said my dad was in jail?"

I nod, feeling a little guilty. "And I saw my stone in your kitchen."

He shakes his head, "I can't believe that was you."

"Who did you think it was?"

"I had no idea. The gardener? Some random relative of theirs? Not *you*." He looks back down at me. "Who did *you* think it was?"

"My mom."

He thinks about this for a minute and then says, "We watched *Schindler's List* in history last year — have you seen it?"

I shake my head. We never got to watch movies in my AP U.S. History class, unfortunately.

"There's a scene at the end when the people Oskar Schindler saved leave stones on his grave. Our teacher said that the stones are supposed to ..." He searches for the right words.

"Represent the permanence of memory," I finish for him, remembering the phrase from my own research.

He nods.

"I looked it up, too. When I found your stones."

We're quiet. He reaches up and tucks a loose hair behind my ear.

"It's just a matter of time before she figures it out," he says.

I take a deep breath. Exhale. "I know."

"She looked at me funny tonight."

"It's probably because your shirt is on backwards."

"It is?" He looks down, pulling the neck out to confirm. "Fuck."

I laugh. "That's not why she was looking at you funny. I think you look familiar to her."

He looks down at his shoes and says, "Fuck" again, more quietly.

"You're right. She's going to figure it out."

He nods. "Do you think we should tell her first?"

I shake my head. "I don't want to."

"Me neither." He kisses me lightly, then not so lightly.

CHAPTER 30

IT'S FRIDAY NIGHT and Charlotte has finally talked me into going on a double date with her and Josh. She sweetened the deal by offering to pay with her dad's credit card and who am I to turn down a free meal? Zenn and I are still in denial about the gravity of our situation, casually dating as if our backstory is normal and not about to blow up in our faces. We meet at the restaurant and when Josh and Charlotte walk in, I'm once again blown away by how stupidly good they look together. Zenn notices, too. "Hey, look. It's Barbie and Ken," he whispers.

I punch him in the arm.

Our hostess leads us to a table and we sit, adjusting our napkins and fidgeting with our water glasses. I have to give Josh credit; he makes the first effort. He has more social skills than the rest of us combined, so I suppose it's the least he can do.

"Char says you're a good basketball player," Josh says to Zenn. "Why didn't you try out for the team?"

Zenn takes a sip of his water. "Didn't think I'd have the time."

Josh dismisses him. "It's not that much. Just after school until five thirty or so. A couple of games a week. Maybe a tournament on the weekend."

"Zenn works every day," I say. I may sound defensive, but I'm actually proud.

"Every day?" asks Josh.

"Sometimes two jobs." I spit it out before Zenn can stop me.

"You have *two* jobs, dude?"

"Three, actually," I correct him.

"Eva." Zenn's voice is a warning, but his eyes are smiling.

"*Three* jobs? And school? How the hell do you do that?"

"Not very well. It's why I need a tutor."

"Shit," Josh says. "Then what's my excuse?"

We all order drinks — Zenn and I more water, Josh Coke, Charlotte iced tea — and there is another awkward silence before Charlotte makes some inane comment about tea and where it's grown and I know I'm going to need to do something to spice things up.

"Have you guys seen this blog post," I ask them, "where the author compared consent — like, sexual consent — to having a cup of tea?"

They all stare at me for a moment, shocked by my choice of topic. Zenn looks amused, Charlotte looks horrified, Josh looks confused. Does their reaction stop me? Oh, no. Not even a little bit. It's better than talking about how the Assam region of India is the largest tea-producing area in the world.

"It was ... well, it was brilliant, actually. She explained how it could apply to all sexual situations. Just imagine that, instead of initiating sex" — I feel myself blush a little at the word, but pretend I haven't — "you're making the person a cup of tea."

Josh looks doubtful. Perhaps he's never had to wonder about a girl's consent before. Maybe this is a new concept to him: girls not tearing off their underwear at the mere thought of him.

I continue. "Basically she says you ask them, 'Would you like a cup of tea?' and if they say, 'Fuck yes, I would fucking love a cup of tea!' then you know they really want a cup of tea."

Zenn laughs, and I realize that might be the only reason I'm telling this story: to make him laugh.

Charlotte, who as far as I know has never even *had* a cup of tea, sexually speaking, nods earnestly.

"If you ask if they want tea and they say, 'Um, I'm not really sure,' then you can make them a cup of tea but they may not drink it. And if they don't drink it, she says, don't make them drink it. Just because you made it doesn't mean they are obligated."

Zenn is grinning.

"If they say, 'No, thank you,' then don't make them tea at all. If they are unconscious, don't make them tea. If you make them tea and they start to drink it but fall asleep mid-cup, don't pour it down their throat."

Now finally Charlotte laughs, nearly spitting out her own iced tea. Josh looks at her adoringly and I wonder if maybe she has indeed had some variety of tea with Josh. If so, I'm guessing it was likely not the variety he had to pour down her throat.

"It's amazing, really," I say. "It works for every scenario."

Something about my goofy analogy loosens us all up and the rest of dinner is surprisingly relaxed. Josh and Zenn get along well enough. I'm actually having fun. This must be what it's like to be a "normal" teenager.

We make it through dinner and I am convinced, now, what attracted Charlotte to Josh way back in middle school. It wasn't his boy-band hair and chiseled body, which was all I ever saw before I got to know him. Charlotte always saw a kindness in him, a surprising humility. Charlotte saw the person he was, not the person he was trying to be. Once I let go of the stubborn stereotype I had of him, I saw it, too.

During dinner when Charlotte excuses herself to go to the restroom, Josh half rises out of his chair, like men do in old movies. He offers her a taste of his meal and then tries hers, even though he's already mentioned that he doesn't really like salmon. And despite Charlotte's offer to pay for dinner, Josh takes care of the check before any of us have a chance to even politely reach for our wallets.

And the way he looks at her. Well.

He's a good guy.

Granted, he's still no rocket scientist when it comes to trig, but I'm glad first impressions — and fractals — are sometimes wrong.

After dinner we walk across the street to the arcade. Video games are not my thing, but it's something for us to do.

I don't really want to play anything because I fear the fractals of a thousand geeky boys will lay me flat if I touch the controls. Unlike a shopping cart, these things are fondled by the same person for hours on end. Zenn and I settle on pinball, and he controls one paddle and I control the other, mostly by punching at the button with my fist. My technique is not very effective, to say the least, but we end up laughing a lot. We eventually leave to get some Dairy Queen and then we split up: Josh and Charlotte to his dad's Mercedes, Zenn and I to Zenn's truck.

"That wasn't so bad," Zenn says, adjusting his rearview mirror.

"Nope."

"Mooney seems like an okay guy."

"Yeah …"

"What? You don't think so?"

"No! He is. He's a good guy."

"Charlotte likes him, right?"

"Hmmm? Oh, yeah. She likes him a *lot*. Like, she'll probably have tea with him soon, she likes him so much."

Zenn smiles. "Then … what's the problem?"

I'm not even sure there is a problem. Maybe my fractals make me think there are problems when there aren't. Maybe there's just life. Messy, complicated life.

"Something about his … fractal?" Zenn asks.

"No. Well. Yes." I sigh and look out the window, a little embarrassed to be talking about my visions again. I wish he would just forget all about them. But, I mean, I am a freak of nature. "I'm not even sure what it is, honestly."

Zenn is good at asking, then waiting and not pushing too hard.

"Maybe I'm just being protective of Charlotte, or whatever. But I think maybe he drinks." It's like I'm looking for some reason to doubt their relationship.

"Drinking's not that unusual for his crowd."

He's right. We're seniors. Kids drink. I don't know why I'm so judgy all of a sudden. Am I really worried about Charlotte? Or looking for reasons they shouldn't be together because my own relationship is doomed?

"Has Charlotte said anything about him drinking?"

"No, not really." I brush away my concerns. "I'm sure it's fine."

Zenn says, "I guess I see what you mean about knowing stuff and wanting to help."

I sigh.

"But sometimes people just have to figure shit out on their own."

It's a new idea for me: that I'm not responsible for fixing Josh, or protecting Charlotte, or healing my mom, or erasing the past. It's a relief to realize that I'm not expected to repair everything that is broken. That even if I could do it, I don't have to.

Suddenly I am overcome with the wish that we could go back to my house and just sit on my couch together, watch a movie, make out a little. I wish I didn't have to hide him from my parents.

"Why do you think you don't get fractals from me?"

His question surprises me, although I've wondered it myself a million times. "I don't know," I answer honestly. "The only thing I can think of is that we have some different kind of connection? Maybe from the accident?" He smiles. "Does that sound really corny and overdramatic?" He squeezes my hand, his warm fingers linked with mine in a way no one's have ever been before. We do have a connection. We do.

I let those two words settle on me like a mantra: *we do.*

CHAPTER 31

I WONDER IF MY MOM SUSPECTS SOMETHING when she asks me Zenn's last name.

"Bennett," I tell her. It's the truth, but I don't tell her that Bennett is his mom's last name, that his parents were never married, that his mom chose to give him her name in the chaos after the accident because she didn't want her baby associated with the man that caused the tragic story on the front page of every local newspaper. It's probably the same reasoning my mom and dad used when they changed my name to Walker. Simplify. Erase. Start over.

I can't tell if she knows something or if she's just making conversation. Parents are good at being sneaky like that.

"Have you told him about ... your parents?" It's hard for her to call them that because they only parented me for four months while she has raised me for eighteen years. I know she's torn between wanting me to remember them somehow, and wanting me to think of her as my "real" mom.

"Yeah," I tell her. "We've talked about it."

She might have planned on giving me a little lecture about honesty being important in any relationship, but I've beaten her to the punch.

"What's his family like? Have you met them?"

I have to be careful. No lies, but not the whole truth yet either.

"Yeah. I've met them."

"Both his parents?"

If she suspects that Mike is Zenn's dad, maybe she doesn't think I would have met him, since (for all she knows) he's still in jail. Then again, she may not suspect anything. Maybe I'm reading into it.

"They nice?"

"Sure. Yeah."

"Any brothers or sisters?"

"No. He's an only child." As soon as it's out of my mouth, my stomach lurches a little. I suddenly remember telling my dad that the Juicy sweatpants and Zombie sweatshirt belonged to Zenn's non-existent sister. I doubt he mentioned that to my mom, but if he did, I'll be caught in a lie. I've never lied to my parents before like I have been lately.

I don't like it.

But my mom just nods. "What does his dad do?"

Here we go. The truth. Just the minimal truth. "He works at the same body shop where Zenn painted the van."

"Oh, yeah? Is it a family business?"

I shake my head. "No. They just work there. I think a friend of theirs owns it."

"Mmmm."

I don't tell her that his parents aren't married. I don't tell her that his mom drinks too much, or that Zenn has been supporting them for years. I certainly don't tell her anything more about Mike. But I know it's just a matter of time before the whole truth comes out.

"What are Zenn's plans after high school?"

Oh, so she wonders if he's good enough for me, I guess.

"He'd like to go to college but his family doesn't have much money."

My mom snorts ironically. I'm preaching to the choir.

Apparently I've shared enough now. "Well, he seems like a good kid."

"He is."

There is a pause in conversation and I think maybe we're done. But then she says, "You guys ...?" and trails off.

Oh, God. What is she fishing for?

I look at her blankly.

"It's just that ... he's your first boyfriend."

"He's not my *boyfriend*," I correct her. Is he? Is he my boy-friend?

"Whatever. He's the first guy you've dated. More seriously, I mean."

"More seriously than who? Sean Kirkdorf?" I throw out the name of my elementary-school boyfriend, the one boy I "dated" in fourth grade. The extent of our dating was leaving birthday gifts on each other's doorsteps so we didn't have to see each other or talk.

"Well ..."

I scoff. "Yeah, well. It's hard to date anyone when you can't touch anything."

"Eva!"

"Ew, Mom! I didn't mean *that*! I just meant, like, hold hands or whatever!"

My mom laughs and I start laughing, too.

"So ... he's okay with you not ... holding hands?"

"First of all, Mom, you're grossing me out."

"You're the one being gross. I'm seriously just asking how things are going."

Well, now she's done it. She's put me in a situation where I'm going to have to tell her that I don't get fractals from him. And that will open up a whole can of worms.

"He's been very patient," I tell her. How I can say this with a straight face is beyond me. The idea of him having to be patient with me is ridiculous. I'm like an eager puppy, pressing myself into his outstretched hand.

"Have you told him about your ... condition?"

I roll my eyes. She acts like my brain malfunction is as simple as a case of eczema. "Yes," I tell her. "He knows I have some issues."

"And ...?" She doesn't like to talk about it, doesn't like to call it anything because if she names it out loud it becomes more real. Not something minor. Not something that will go away on its own. My fractals are kind of like Voldemort — the things-that-must-not-be-named.

"I guess we wait and see."

"Maybe we should try another doctor," my mom suggests. "Take you to the Mayo Clinic or something?"

"It's fine, Mom," I say. "No sense in wasting more money."

"Maybe you'll still outgrow it." Her voice is suddenly too

bright.

"Maybe," I say.

I know she'd feel better if I told her that I can touch Zenn, that I can have a regular relationship with someone. Or maybe it would make her feel worse, especially if she knew who Zenn was. Who knows what she wants to hear.

"Are we done with the third degree for the evening?" I ask. "I've got some homework to do."

"Fine," my mom says. "If teenagers volunteered just a little information on their own, parents wouldn't have to dig so hard."

"If we did that, we would be pretty lousy teenagers."

CHAPTER 32

ZENN IS NOT AT SCHOOL AGAIN TODAY. Every time he skips I feel like he's drifting away from his college dreams, from his bright future. From me.

I check my phone to see if he's texted — he hasn't — but I do see that I have an email from a Stephanie Rayner. I don't know a Stephanie Rayner, but it's not labeled as spam, so I open it.

> *Dear Ms. Walker,*
>
> *Gemini Corporation is pleased to inform you that you have been selected as a finalist for the $100,000 Ingenuity Scholarship. Your application stood out among those of over 2,000 Wisconsin seniors and we would like to complete an interview before selecting the winner. Please contact me at your earliest convenience to set up a meeting ...*

There is more but I stop reading. My heart is hammering in my chest. I'm a finalist! I could actually get this!

And then I think of Zenn, who also applied. Oh, God, please let him be a finalist, too! Because it's not like our relationship needs another challenge. We've already got secrecy and fractals and messed-up parents. At least if we are both finalists, one of us has a shot. It would be proof that the world is not totally out to get us. And I want him to have a chance. Maybe this is what love feels like: wanting something for someone else as much as you want it for yourself. Of course, he has to graduate before he can even qualify for a scholarship.

I text him.

> Me: Where are you?
> Zenn: Working. Why? U OK?
> Me: Yeah. But I thought we had a deal?
> Zenn: What deal?
> Me: About school.
> Zenn: It's just one day. Have a big job to finish before it snows.

I don't text back right away. He is working to keep a roof over his head, to feed himself and his mom. He is not lazy or dumb or irresponsible. I want to ask him about the email, but if he didn't get one then I will feel horrible. So instead I just text.

> Me: OK.
> Zenn: I'll be done by 3. I'll pick you up.

He is waiting for me when the bell rings, filthy again. Funny how I'm finding the smell of soil kind of sexy.

"Do you, like, *roll* around in the dirt at work?"

Dirt is caked under his fingernails, ground into the creases of his knuckles.

"You need a manicure," I tell him.

He laughs. "Yeah. I'll drop twenty-five dollars to make my hands look pretty."

"I'll do it for you. C'mon. You'll love it."

He looks doubtful.

"It'll be part of my therapy." Just thinking about touching his hands makes me warm and soft inside.

"Fine. They'll just look shitty again tomorrow."

He drives us to his place and I offer to make him a sandwich while he showers. He points me in the direction of the bread and the fridge and I carefully assemble what I need, testing items around the kitchen for fractals before using them. I sense that Zenn's mom doesn't do a lot of cooking. By the time he comes back to the kitchen I have his sandwich ready, along with a bowl of warm, soapy water, a fingernail brush I found under the sink and a small bottle of hand lotion from my backpack. He picks up his sandwich with one hand while I plop his other hand into the bowl.

"You have to let it soak," I tell him. "Or ... at least I think you do. I've never actually had a manicure myself."

"Really? Isn't that, like, a mandatory rite of passage for girls?"

"Not for me." I hold up my pathetic, damaged hands with their short and unpolished nails.

"Oh, right," he says.

"But in the movies they always soak in some kind of liquid first. Right?"

"Some kind of liquid?" Zenn laughs. "This should be interesting."

"How hard could it be?"

"With *my* hands? Pretty fucking hard."

After he finishes his sandwich and his free hand has soaked for a few minutes, I lift it out of the water and tell him to put the other one in the bowl. I take the fingernail brush and scrub gently at the permanent dirt lines in his knuckles. My mind is spinning, trying to figure out how to bring up the email.

"You're gonna have to scrub harder than that, Ev. That dirt has been there for years."

I scrub a little harder. His fingers are relaxed, slippery, warm. I imagine them sliding along my skin and feel a blush creep up my neck. I clear my throat. "Your hands were the first thing I noticed about you," I tell him.

"My hands?" He lifts the hand that is still soaking and studies it. "They're not exactly my best feature."

"They're really ... manly."

He laughs.

"My dad's hands are so ... soft and clean. Yours are, like, weathered."

"That's just a nice word for beat-up."

"I like them. I guess I notice hands. Maybe because mine are so ..." I can't think of the right word. *Fucked up?*

He watches me for a moment and then says, "I got an email today."

My eyes meet his.

"Me, too."

He takes the fingernail brush from my hand and sets it on the table. He knits his fingers between mine, our palms together, knuckles toward the ceiling like we are going to play uncle. Our hands are slippery from the soapy water and there is something sensual about the way they slide against each other.

"So maybe at least one of us will win," I say.

He nods. There is a tension in the air, but not a bad tension. Not jealousy about the scholarship. It comes from where our hands are joined and it runs up my arm. I feel it in the thrumming of my heart. Zenn must feel it, too.

"We have maybe a half hour before my mom may or may not come stumbling through the door."

I swallow once before I croak out, "Yeah?"

"Do you want to spend it giving me a manicure that will be ruined tomorrow? Or should we do something more productive with our time?" His slippery thumb caresses mine.

"Like ... study?" I suggest, teasing. I squeeze his fingers between mine lightly. He squeezes back.

He shrugs and takes his left hand out of the bowl. He reaches for my other hand.

"We should study," I say, as he pulls me up from my chair. "You have to graduate to qualify for that scholarship, and guess what? I got your trig homework from Mr. Haase."

"Oh, yay," Zenn says. He tugs on my hands, leading me around the table toward him. He guides my hips so I'm sitting on him, facing him, straddling his lap. He takes off my glasses and sets them on the table. I have a feeling we're not going to be doing any studying.

I'm definitely okay with that.

"That would be pretty hot, huh?" he says, sliding his hand down my braid. His fingers catch in the rubber band and gently tug it out. "If I started talking trig?" He leans close and says, "Sine. Cosine." His lips touch my earlobe and I hold my breath. "Tangent."

"God, that is hot," I whisper, only half-joking. I slide my fingers into his hair and he closes his eyes in pleasure. He slowly untwines my braid. I close my eyes, too.

"Secant." He kisses me softly, his lips barely brushing against mine. "Chebyshev method."

"God, you make even Chebyshev method sound dirty."

"It's not me," he says innocently. "Chebyshev method just *sounds dirty.*"

I open my eyes and pull away from him slightly. I trace my fingers over his face: the tiny moon-shaped scar under the arch of his eyebrow, the slant of his straight and perfect nose, his cheekbones, his full lips. He didn't shave this morning and his jaw is slightly rough. My fingertips make a quiet rasping against his chin.

"Viète's infinite product," he says. Seriously, I'm not sure I've ever heard anything sound as sexy as he can make a simple math formula.

"I don't understand something."

"I can't help you with Viète's infinite product. That's your thing."

"No. I don't understand how you didn't become super-popular within minutes of transferring."

"Me?" He looks incredulous. "Popular?"

"Seriously. You are so ... *so* good-looking." I probably shouldn't be so open with my compliments. I'm sure there's some kind of coy game I should be playing, but I never learned.

He rolls his eyes. "Right."

"You are. And you're funny and artistic and smart and you have a kick-ass truck."

"I *do* have a kick-ass truck," he concedes.

"I would think those vulture girls would have swooped in at the first sniff of fresh meat when you showed up."

He tucks my loose hair behind my ears. "I'm poor. I dress for shit. I don't have time to play sports. And I couldn't care less about any of this high school bullshit."

"And ... you're kind of a rebel," I add, as if he's proven my point.

"Eva," he says, sliding his still-damp hands just under the edge of my shirt, pressing his fingers lightly against my lower back. "I don't have the time or patience for anyone whose biggest concern is kissing their friends' asses. You don't play their game, they don't want you in their circle. You know that."

I think of Josh, balancing on the fragile tightrope of popularity. He's right.

"I mean, you're smart and funny and pretty, and *you're* not popular."

"I'm not pretty."

"Why is *that* the compliment that you resist?"

I'm not sure. I enjoy being called smart and funny, but when he compliments my looks I feel funny in a different way.

"I don't know."

"It's because you are deeper than a puddle. But you are.

book

Very. Pretty."

I can feel my cheeks burning. I change the subject, but his talk of my good looks has made me warm inside. "How'd you get your cool truck anyway?" I lean down and press my lips against where his jaw nearly meets his ear.

"Dave — from the body shop? — he got it for a steal, we fixed it up. He gave it to me as an early graduation present."

"Wow." I catch his earlobe lightly between my lips. "That's pretty generous."

Zenn's breath hitches. His fingers press into my back. "I bring him a lot of work."

"Ah. So it's, like, commission."

"Kinda."

He squirms a little beneath me.

"Am I making your legs fall asleep?" I ask, trying to lift my weight off his lap slightly.

He shakes his head. "Nothing is falling asleep."

His suggestive tone makes me blush again. I look down without meaning to, and then blush more.

I kiss him, my hands on either side of his face, holding him like he might run away if I let go. He pulls lightly on my hips, pressing me down against him more firmly. We kiss, and kiss, and his hands wander up and around, exploring. If I thought we had more time, I'd take off my shirt and his shirt and anything else that's getting in the way. But we only have minutes before his mom could walk in.

"This is crazy," I whisper. "What are we doing?"

"Therapy, I thought," he whispers back.

I pull away. "Seriously. What are we going to do?"

"About ... the scholarship?" he asks.

"About everything."

Zenn smooths my hair. He bites his lip in a way that makes my insides tangle. But he doesn't answer.

CHAPTER 33

I DON'T TELL MY PARENTS about the scholarship. I'm not sure why, exactly. Maybe it's because I don't want to jinx it, or because nothing is for sure. But I don't tell them anything.

I do contact Stephanie Rayner and set up a phone interview, during which I find myself almost underselling my qualifications. It's not my intention when I dial the phone, but once we're talking about math, it sounds flat and uninteresting, even to my own ears. It's numbers. Formulas. Dry, perfect calculations.

It's not art. It's not beauty.

Stephanie is kind and flatters me with compliments about my grades and my résumé, but I want to tell her there are more important things than student council and tutoring. There is supporting your family and there is hard work. There is resilience in the face of adversity. There is love. I bite my tongue and try to accept her compliments gracefully,

I try to sell myself. I try. But when I hang up the phone I am relieved it's over.

But it's not over. Zenn will do his interview and even though he is charming and funny and his talent is creative and interesting, they may decide that math is practical. They may think somehow my gift is more "important" than his. A young woman interested in STEM may be the trend du jour and they may pick me instead of him.

I'm not sure I can let that happen.

I spend a lot of time thinking about Zenn. Not just horny thoughts about his mouth and his skin and his eyelashes, but about *him* — how hard he works, how talented he is, how much he's had to struggle. I keep thinking about how much he really, really needs the scholarship. Without it, he won't go to college, period. He will be stuck painting motorcycle fuel tanks or working at the Piggly Wiggly or raking the lawns of other people's mansions. He deserves better than that. He deserves everything.

I think about how it would feel if I got the scholarship instead of him. I imagine getting the call or the email, and my heart clenches. Instead of feeling happy or excited I just feel sad. Guilty and undeserving.

It's funny how I could want something so badly just a couple months ago, and now feel physically sick when I think about getting it. All I can think about is Zenn and how to give him a chance at his best future. If I wait to see who wins, it will be too late. If I win I won't be able to just give it to him; there are rules against that kind of thing, though I doubt anyone has been stupid enough to win the scholarship and then give it away before. Even if I could, there's no way in hell he would accept it. I know if things were reversed, I wouldn't.

There is no good solution other than him winning the scholarship flat out, and there's no way for me to make sure that happens. But there is a way for me to increase the odds.

Two days after my interview with Stephanie Rayner, I send her an email to withdraw my application. I'm not sure how I've become this kind of girl — the kind of girl who ignores her friends or lies to her family or gives up her dream for a boy. A part of me hates that girl.

But a part of me is proud of her because I'm not sure I've ever done a truly selfless thing in my whole life. I help my parents because I'm a decent kid and I love my brothers and sisters. I do philanthropic work through church and school because it's all arranged for me, and it looks good on college applications. But truly selfless, generous acts? I can't think of any. Until now.

It almost feels like I need to do this as much for me as for him, like maybe this is what love feels like. Like maybe this is what growing up feels like.

CHAPTER 34

ALTHOUGH ZENN HAS BEEN COMING to school, it's been snowing a lot and during his non-school hours he's been shoveling sidewalks for the landscaping company. We haven't seen much of each other and every single part of me misses him. He does drive me home from school today and pulls over before he gets to my house so we can make out for a couple of minutes before he has to rush off. It almost makes it worse, though, to have a taste of him and then have it taken away. His truck windows are a little steamy and the snow is coming down hard when he drops me off. He doesn't come in — he doesn't really have time, and the minivan is in the driveway. We're actively trying to keep him away from my mom.

When I walk in the house, my lips still swollen from his kisses, my mom is waiting for me at the kitchen table. The house is silent, which is creepy and unusual.

"Where are the kids?" I ask, plopping my backpack onto an empty chair.

"They're at Bethany's."

I nod and try not to look panicked. Bethany is a neighbor my mom only uses in desperate circumstances. Something is going down here.

She doesn't beat around the bush. "Do you have something you want to tell me?"

A knot of anxiety twists in my stomach. She's not smiling. She's not happy. She knows I sabotaged myself, somehow. She's going to give me a big-ass speech about giving up a hundred thousand dollars for a boy.

"How could you ..." she starts, but doesn't finish her sentence. She's barely holding it together, her jaw clenched, her hands folded tightly in some sort of prayer under the table.

I don't confess to anything yet. Teenager 101: never offer up more than you need to.

She rubs her forehead with her fingertips. "You know, don't you?"

Wait. What? Know what?

"Who Zenn's father is?"

It's not about me giving up the scholarship. I try to keep my face neutral, which is nearly impossible.

She studies me for a moment. I look away.

This is it. The end of the line. I think about playing dumb, but I am a smart girl. Nearly a genius on some levels. I don't think I can get away with that.

I nod, just barely.

My mom's head drops, her shoulders sag.

"Eva." Her voice is pained.

"I know, Mom. It's messed up. But ... we didn't know at first."

"But you do now. You've known for a while now, haven't you?"

I want to ask her how she found out, but there are too many ways. Fuzzy memories that became clearer, Google searches, a connection between a last name and an old newspaper article, Zenn's vaguely exotic looks reminding her of an old mug shot. Who knows? There are a million ways she could have found out. Most likely she just looked, like I did. She may not be my mother by birth, but she's still my aunt and we share some of the same curiosity genes.

"It doesn't matter to you? That his father killed your parents?" I can tell it is taking everything to keep her voice calm.

"Zenn had nothing to do with it, Mom. He wasn't even *born* yet."

"His father killed my sister!"

"It was an accident," I offer weakly.

"He drove drunk! He *chose* to drive drunk! That's not an accident. It's murder with a car!"

I take a deep breath, trying to stay calm and rational, trying to see this from her point of view. But I can't. I think of Zenn growing up without a dad. I think of Michael's sad eyes. His jacket. The fractal.

"He spent eighteen years in jail, Mom. Zenn's life has been totally screwed up because of that accident."

My mom looks at me incredulously and I realize I've said exactly the wrong thing.

"*His* life has been screwed up? *His* life?" She stands up and starts pacing around the kitchen. "I lost my sister. My *best* friend. I quit college. I moved home and became a mom at nineteen. Don't tell me *his* life was screwed up."

These are the feelings I've always gotten from touching her: sadness, resentment, guilty regret. I know she loves me. I know she wouldn't trade me or the E's for what might have been, but it must be hard to let go of the plans you had for yourself.

"You cannot see him, Eva. I cannot have you involved with that *family*." She spits out the last word, like it tastes bad on her tongue.

"Mom. I've waited my whole life for someone I could have a real relationship with. I'm not going to give him up because you have an issue with his dad."

"*You* should have an issue with his dad! *You* should have an issue with his whole family!"

"Well, I don't. I don't feel the same way that you do."

"You can't even touch him, Eva!" I can tell she didn't think that through by the way she averts her eyes as soon as it's out of her mouth.

I stare at her for a second, almost not believing I heard those words. It's a low blow, like my touch is the only thing that would keep a guy interested. I toss the dish towel onto the counter and walk away. We're not going to make any progress with this discussion.

She follows me.

"I'm serious, Eva. Dating *any* boy could end in heartbreak for you. But *that* boy?!"

"Dating any boy could end in heartbreak for *anyone* — not just me."

"You are not to see him anymore." Ha! Like she can stop me.

I try to stay calm. "I don't think that's fair."

"Yeah, well ... I don't think it's fair that I lost my sister. Life isn't fair."

"His dad took your sister, so you take my boyfriend?"

My mom sighs in frustration. "It's not like you're going to marry this kid, Eva. He's your first real boyfriend. Why not just save us all some aggravation?"

"Okay, first? I never said I was going to marry him. We just started dating! But I like him. He's amazing and I don't see why your feelings about his dad should matter. What is this, *Romeo and Juliet*?"

"*His father killed your parents!*"

"You're my parents! You and dad! I never knew my other parents! I know you miss them, I know you're angry. But I am just trying to live the life that I have!"

I wish so much that my dad were here. He'd get what I'm saying. He'd understand because he didn't know my parents either, and he might be able to talk my mom down from her anger. But he's not here.

I grab my coat and head for the front door.

"We are not done with this discussion!" she threatens.

I walk out of the house and slam the door and she can't really follow me because it's close to dinnertime and she has four little mouths to feed, just down the street at Bethany's. She's stuck, but I'm not. I head straight to Zenn's. Of course, he's not home. I knew he wouldn't be, but I don't have anywhere else to go. I try to text him. He doesn't answer.

I wander around in the snow for a while before I get too cold and head to Java Dock, hoping Zenn will get back before it closes.

It's nearly eight when he finally responds.

> Zenn: Sorry. Fucking blizzard. What's up?
> Me: My mom knows.

There is a text lag.

> Me: I'll say it for you — fuckity fuck
> Zenn: Where are u?
> Me: Java Dock
> Zenn: Be there in a few

When he comes in he goes straight to the counter for a coffee. He's been outside for hours and I'm sure he's frozen through. His coat is covered in a fine layer of ice, and although his skin looks paler than usual, his cheeks and nose are red.

Once he gets his coffee and takes a warming sip, he sits down next to me on the couch and reaches for my hand. I'm not sure whose hand is colder, his or mine.

My mom is crazy if she thinks I'm letting him go.

"So what happened?" he asks.

I tell him what I know, that my mom somehow found out about his dad.

"She doesn't want me to see you anymore." I swear my voice sounds calm and collected, but something must give away my real feelings because Zenn gathers me into his arms and pulls me against his chest. I press my face into his coat, into his clean, hopeful, snowy scent.

"Maybe she's right," he says.

This is not what I want to hear at all.

"You think she's right?"

"I told you, my family is fucked up. You should go off to MIT or wherever and find yourself a nice fellow math genius with a normal family. Your mom would like that."

I pull away. I don't even know where to start with what is wrong with that proposal. "First of all, I would never do that to my future children. Two math-geek parents? Please."

This makes him smile.

"Plus, I'm not going to MIT. Or ... wherever."

This surprises him.

"Yes, you are."

He sounds so sure, but he doesn't know about the email I sent to Stephanie Rayner.

"I'm eighteen. My mom can't tell me who to date."

"But you do live in her house."

"She needs me as much as I need her. The E's need me. And deep down, she still loves me." My voice cracks a little, my throat tightens. She still loves me.

"Well, what do you want to do? Lie to her? Sneak around? That doesn't seem like you."

I sit on my hands, out of habit. He's right. I'm not the kind of daughter who would normally lie and sneak. But ... I look up at him, at his irresistible mouth, his eyelashes that practically fan me every time he blinks. The strongest and most resilient, determined boy I've ever met. The only person I can touch. The only person I *want* to touch. Desperate times may call for some sneaking.

He stares at the floor. I slide my hand across his shoulders and down his back. The more I touch him, the more I believe in the power of touch.

"Hey," I say. "She'll get over it," I reassure him, even though I'm not sure she will. But if she doesn't ... we're adults now. Or almost adults. We get to make our own decisions. It's a scary thought, but also liberating. I get to choose for myself. He gives me an uncertain look, so I kiss him. For the first time since we've been together, it feels like he resists, so I kiss him with more — with my mouth and my body and my soul, ignoring the fact that we're in a coffee shop. Who cares? He's the only thing that matters.

And then he kisses me back like I'm the only thing that matters.

Without saying much else we leave and go back to his place. His mom is not home and the emptiness of the apartment and its boundless possibilities hang heavy in the air.

"This is where you sleep?" I ask, gesturing to the couch. I've never asked him before, but the tiny apartment only has one bedroom and I assume it's his mom's, even if she's rarely there to use it.

He nods and must sense some pity in my voice because he adds, "It ... folds out. To a bed." I could swear he blushes a little, but in the dim light I can't be sure.

"It does?" My voice is amazingly calm. "Show me."

He looks at me for a moment, direct and questioning. I don't look away.

He reaches down to take the cushions off.

And that is how we find ourselves on his couch-bed, half-naked, praying his mom doesn't choose tonight to be responsible and come home early. We reach a point — somewhere after my shirt comes off and his jeans become unbuttoned — where we don't know whether to go forward or back. Thinking that I could lose him makes me feel desperate and he kisses me back like he's feeling a little desperate himself, which makes me feel confident and, dare I say, sexy. Everything about being with him is new and yet somehow vaguely familiar. I want every inch of him pressed against every inch of me. I want his rough, tormented hands to never leave my skin. I want, I want, I want ...

When it seems like maybe we've gone too long without moving one direction or another and it feels like maybe Zenn is going to pull away, I whisper, my heart in my throat, "I would fucking *love* a cup of tea."

And he looks at me, searching and sincere.

"If you're ... making tea, I mean," I add.

His head falls back and he laughs quietly and I feel this embarrassed, awkward weight lift from my shoulders.

He goes up on one elbow, his other hand resting lightly just below my belly button. "I would fucking love to make you a cup of tea," he says quietly and I'm not sure I've ever heard anything so oddly sexy. But then there's this awful moment of hesitation where I think he's going to get up and make me a cup of *actual* tea, but he doesn't.

Thank God, he doesn't.

He's kissing me again and then the last few pieces of our clothes come off and we're fumbling with a condom and then he's moving slow and gentle over me and it hurts a little, but then it hurts less as he's a little less slow and slightly less gentle and everything becomes somehow *more*. He quietly asks me if I'm okay once or twice and I nod fiercely because I'm not sure what will come out if I open my mouth.

I'm not stupid enough to think sex is supposed to be

perfect the first time, but oh, my God, it's still pretty damn amazing. Maybe it's not the actual sex that's amazing ... yet, anyway ... but the closeness? The touching? The intimacy?

Amazing.

⊙⊙

"What would my fractal look like?" His voice is quiet and rough and rouses me from a near sleep.

"Hmmm?"

He wraps his arms more tightly around me and I press my face against the warmth of his chest.

"If I did give you a fractal ... what do you think it would be like?"

I open my eyes and inhale his clean, simple smell. I consider everything I know about him: his dad, his mom, his childhood, his struggles. Even his loneliness. And I think about all the things I *don't* yet know about him: his past relationships, his insecurities, his doubts.

"I don't know ..." I press my hand against his skin, still amazed that I can. "It would probably be purple. And, like, busy." I'm not describing this well at all.

"Purple?" he asks, somewhat surprised, like purple is not his color or something.

I nod and try to think of how to explain. "I sense certain colors more with certain ... emotions, I guess. Green for jealousy, insecurity. Blue is generally kind of sad, which I guess is obvious. Red is angry. Yellow is ... like, bitter? But purple is more ... hurt."

After a moment he asks: "And busy?"

"When people deal with one issue over and over again, the patterns are simpler. Like, concentric squares or maybe spirals. Something structured like that. But when there are a lot of different issues, it's busy. Like organized scribbling."

"You think I have a lot of issues?"

"Naaahhh," I answer sarcastically, and I trace my fingers across the solid flat plane of his stomach.

"Would it have scared you away from me?"

"Your fractal?" I think about this for a minute. "I don't think anything could have."

He kisses my forehead and I'm tempted to stay at his apartment all night, just to freak my mom out a little bit. I mean, that's not the only reason I want to stay with him. I want to stay with him because his warm body wrapped around mine, his breath on my skin, his roughly calloused hand stroking my hair are probably the most amazing things I've ever felt. Why would I ever want to leave? But scaring my mom a little bit at this point would be an added bonus. She's had it pretty easy during my teenage years. I've never had boyfriends, I've helped her with the quads, I get straight As and have been nothing but obedient. Maybe me spending the night with a boy would be enough to shake her out of her power play.

But when it comes down to it, I'm a good girl to the core. Well, aside from the unexpected premarital sex. And after the tragedies my mom has had to deal with, I don't like scaring her unnecessarily.

Zenn's mom doesn't seem to practice the same courtesy because she's still not back, even after we allow ourselves to lie tangled together on his couch-bed for an hour. Even after we get dressed and Zenn devours a sandwich and finally drives me home. In my driveway he kisses me long and slow and sweet and I groan when I pull away and force myself to get out of the truck. I brace for the third degree when I open the front door, but the house is quiet. I sneak past my mom, who is dead asleep on the couch.

Well. So much for scaring her unnecessarily.

◯◯

I get out of the house early in the morning, before my parents or the quads are even up. I'm usually up before them on school days, but sometimes I'll stick around as long as possible to try to help my mom with the kids. Today I'm up and out the door before anyone else's feet hit the ground. I'm not sure what I'm trying to do exactly. This teenage rebellion thing is new to me. But maybe I want my mom to think about what she's asking me to give up. Maybe I want her to realize how easy I've tried to make things on her. Being responsible, getting good grades, staying out of trouble. Maybe I just want her to remember what it's like to be young.

She must have gotten up during the night and checked my room to see if I was home. But who knows. Maybe she doesn't know I was ever here.

I anticipate fifth period with an unfamiliar glowing feeling low in my stomach. I wonder how I'll look Zenn in the eye, how I'll manage to *not* undress him in the art room. But fifth hour comes and Zenn is not there. I eat my lunch alone and try not to let self-doubt get the best of me when he doesn't text me back.

CHAPTER 35

WHEN I GET HOME FROM SCHOOL, both my mom and dad are there. When my mom feels out-argued, she likes to bring him in for backup. I'm guessing they've laid out a game plan on how to deal with me when it comes to Zenn. My mom treats me civilly and doesn't say anything about Zenn during dinner, but I know the storm is brewing. My dad has been brought in as chief negotiator, and I suspect we'll be having some kind of sit-down before bed.

Sure enough, once the quads are asleep they call me into the living room.

"We need to talk," my mom says.

"I thought we did this already." My, am I sassy for a change. It feels kind of good.

"We'd *both* like to talk with you," my dad says.

I poke a thumb in my mom's direction. "Will she listen?"

"We'll both listen. But I think we should pray first."

I try not to roll my eyes. Not that prayer won't help, because it might at this point. But I'm sure my dad is partially doing it because he hopes the awkwardness will diffuse some of my anger. He makes us hold hands, even though that means I have to endure their fractals while we pray. My mom's is ugly mustard yellow, tightly twisted like a helix. My dad's is pale blue, swirly and endless.

"Lord, please be with us as we work through some difficult feelings. Help us remember to be patient and loving, and not stubborn or bitter. Let Jesus guide our words and actions, so that we can love like he loved and forgive like he forgave. Amen."

My mom and I mumble "Amen," and drop each other's hand. I don't think either of us is feeling very Jesus-y at the moment.

My dad starts the conversation. "Mom told me that Zenn's dad is Michael Franklin."

I nod. It's weird to be a teenager and not be denying things, but the truth is the truth.

"Obviously, that's hard for Mom, considering that he is responsible for Lynn's ... and Tom's ... deaths."

"Right. But Zenn *isn't.*"

My dad holds up his hand to cut me off. "We know it's not his fault. But can you understand how your being involved with him would stir up Mom's feelings?"

I cross my arms. I don't want to give up any ground.

"How do you feel about it?" he asks.

"It's weird, I guess, but I really like him. And he likes me. And I don't know why something that happened eighteen years ago should matter."

My mom makes a derisive noise. "Something that happened? His father *killed* your parents in a horrific car accident that could have been avoided. That's not a little thing, Eva. And you are *more* than friends."

I ignore the last part of her statement. "I told you before, Mom. *You* guys are my parents. Lynn and Thomas Scheurich are just ... ghosts to me. I don't remember them. I don't miss them. You and Dad have done too good a job raising me, I guess, because I'm not heartbroken every minute about being orphaned. It worked out okay for me overall. I mean ... I wish I had known them, but I didn't. And it's hard to miss what you never knew."

This seems to shut my mom up for a second.

"And I get that you had to sacrifice a lot for me, Mom. I do. I can't imagine having to take in a child that isn't mine, like, *next* year. I can't. You gave up your own plans and raised me instead, and I can't repay you for that. But ... I'm not going to stop seeing Zenn because you hold a grudge."

My dad clears his throat and I think he's going to agree with me. He's big on forgiveness, obviously, and he's been working on my mom to forgive Michael Franklin for years. But instead of backing me up he says, "Your mom and I also recently learned that you gave up that scholarship opportunity."

Oh, no. How did they find out? I've done all the communicating through email. No phone calls or messages, no letters. No evidence.

Except ...

Wait.

My mom made me sign a contract when I got my first cell

phone at fourteen: no sexting, no cyberbullying, she could check it at any time ... that kind of stuff. I'd signed it without hesitation. At fourteen, I had nothing to hide from her. Hell, at eighteen I had nothing to hide from her. I figured she had stopped checking years ago. But now I wonder if she still slips into my room at night and checks my phone, especially now that I've been seeing Zenn. I've never even changed my screen lock: 3141. (Pi. Yeah, I'm that big of a nerd.)

She could have seen my email to Stephanie, or her reply back, asking me why I was withdrawing, or my second reply, which was vague ... something about circumstances changing, me wanting to give the opportunity to someone who might need it more. I was slippery with my pronouns, I didn't mention names. But still ...

Now the shame settles in. They can kiss my ass if they want me to stop seeing Zenn because of who his dad is, but my giving up a hundred thousand dollars for him admittedly gives them more valid ammunition. Not that I regret giving up the scholarship, because I don't, but I really didn't think about how it would affect my parents when I did it. I didn't think about them at all.

"It's a hundred thousand dollars, Eva!" My mom's voice is bordering on crazy now. "That's more than your father *makes*!"

I don't have any defense. I want to argue that Zenn needs it more than I do, that he's had a difficult life, but I predict that would fall on deaf ears at the moment.

"I can't believe you gave up this opportunity for a *boy*!"

My dad holds up his hand, trying to calm her down. She ignores him.

"A boy whose father *killed* your parents!"

"I get it, Mom! I know who his dad is!" I'm not sure I've ever actually yelled at my mom before, but I'm matching her tone decibel for decibel.

My dad interrupts. "We just don't want to see you get hurt."

"Are you concerned about me getting hurt? Or the money?"

"*Both!*" my mom insists. "Boys your age can be ... selfish."

"Yeah? Tell me something I don't know."

"With your ..." — my dad searches for the word — "condition ... I wonder how long he will be understanding."

"What, because I can't touch him?" I force a straight face. I don't know how they can't sense what happened last night, that my eyes don't give away my lost virginity like flashing neon.

My mom is unfazed, but my dad looks mortified, even though he's the one who brought it up.

"That's what you're saying, right? Because I can't touch him, he'll dump me? And then I'll have given up the scholarship for nothing?"

"I'm just saying —"

"I know what you're saying."

There's a dark part of me that wants to mention that Zenn can still touch *me*. Remind them that my mouth still works, and my other parts, but that would be way over the top. They both might have a stroke.

"What if I *could* touch him?" I ask. "Would that be better, or worse?"

My mom looks at me blankly.

"I mean, would you be happy for me, that I could? Or would you just be *more* upset because he wouldn't have an excuse to break up with me? You just want a reason that doesn't make you look like the bad guys."

My dad speaks up. "Eva, we worry about you. All the time. That's what being a parent is. We don't see how this can end any way but badly."

"Why do we have to figure out how it will end right now? We just started dating. Do I have to plan for the worst already?"

"Eva —"

"Seriously. I mean, I don't have plans to marry the guy, but isn't the point of being young trying to figure out who you want to be with? And how am I supposed to do that if I don't get to be with anyone? I mean, it's not like there's a *line* of guys wanting to go out with me."

This shuts them up. I don't do it on purpose, but reminding them how lonely my life can be always stuns them into silence.

"Maybe what we really should be talking about is how you can forgive Michael Franklin and move on, rather than punishing the son for the sins of the father?" I turn to my dad. "That's in the ol' Good Book, isn't it, Dad?"

And with that I get up and go to my room and shut the door. I'm done discussing this for the night. Maybe for the year. Maybe forever.

Later, my dad knocks on my door. I can tell it's him by his gentle, thoughtful tapping. I suspect my mom would pound tonight. He peeks his head in and holds up his hands in a sign of surrender.

"Hi."

"It's just me. Mom is cooling off."

"Good."

He comes into my room and sits in the chair next to my desk. "Have *you* cooled off?"

"I don't think I need to cool off. I'm the perfect temperature."

"She's just having a hard time, Ev. She still has a lot of complicated feelings about … everything."

"No kidding."

"She lost a lot that night. And I know we have a good life now, but it's maybe not the life she planned. And Michael Franklin brings up those feelings all over again."

"I get it, Dad. I do. But that's between her and Michael Franklin, or God, or whoever. She can't dictate my life just because hers didn't turn out as expected."

He nods. "She'll realize that. Eventually. You just have to give it some time." He moves on to a heavier topic. "But the scholarship, Eva … That's a pretty big deal."

"I wouldn't have won it anyway, Dad. It wasn't a sure thing."

"That's not the point." He takes out the tiny wooden cross he carries in his pocket and rubs it between his fingers. "I wish I could send you wherever you want to go to college. But I can't, Eva. Being a pastor and having five kids has made that kind of impossible."

I feel a surge of embarrassment, for him and his honesty, and for my actions.

"You are a strong and smart young woman. That was a great opportunity. I'm upset that you gave up your chance." He puts the cross back in his pocket. "I'm just ... disappointed."

My teenage rebellion melts away. I hate letting him down. How do I explain it was a selfless act, rooted in everything he cares about most? Before I can start, he pats my leg and leaves.

CHAPTER 36

STILL NO ZENN. BUT WHY NO TEXT? How long does it take to shoot out a quick text?

Charlotte tries to reassure me. Maybe he's just freaked out by his feelings for me, she suggests. I give her a look.

"What?" she says.

"He's a *guy*, Charlotte. And this isn't a Nicholas Sparks book."

"Guys can get freaked out, too."

I've told Charlotte about the other night — I had to tell someone. She was appropriately stunned and excited, wanting to hear every detail. Considering that up until recently I had never even *kissed* a guy, the speed of my sexual progress is somewhat shocking. But I explained that I'm kind of like a puppy who has been in a crate all day while its owners are at work. When he kissed me, it was like he let me out and I have a *lot* of energy and affection to expend, lots of time to make up for. Charlotte and Josh still haven't had sex, which surprises me a little. I guess I didn't picture Josh as the patient type. But he keeps surprising me. I touched his arm the other day and his fractal felt almost ... content. The fuzzy, drunken feeling was gone and the noise from his dad was drowned out by the pleasant glow that I know comes from Charlotte.

Funny how I was so worried about his negative effect on my friend that I didn't think much about her positive effect on him.

"Maybe he doesn't want to smother you," Charlotte suggests.

"Maybe I was horrible."

"He's a guy," Charlotte says, repeating my words back to me. "Isn't sex like pizza to them? Even when it's bad, it's still pretty good?"

I punch her lightly in the arm. "You're not making me feel any better." But Zenn didn't act like anything about the other night was horrible. His quickened breath on my skin, the intensity of his mouth on mine, the small, quiet, satisfied noise he made ...

So I confess to her about the scholarship.

"Do you think he found out?" I ask her. "That I withdrew? He'd be really pissed ..."

"How would he find out?"

I shrug.

"I'm sure he's just busy, Ev. Didn't you say he works, like, nine jobs?"

I'm sure that's it. He's swamped with work.

My mom and I are rather politely ignoring each other. Since I haven't been leaving the house to see Zenn, maybe she thinks I've ended it. I know that's what she hopes. And I know she's still mad about the scholarship. Whether they think it was a good decision or not, it still feels like the right thing to me. Zenn needs it. I'll survive without it. I treat my mom civilly, but not warmly. Even the kids are picking up on it.

"Is Mommy mad at you?" Essie asks me after my mom and I slip past each other in the kitchen without a word.

"A little," I tell her.

"Did you do somefing naughty?"

I smile at her and run my fingers through her silky hair. "I gave something away that Mommy thinks I should have kept."

Essie looks confused. "But it's nice to give fings away."

"Yeah."

"Like if someone is hungry and we take food to the food panty."

I laugh. "Pantry, Ess. Food pantry."

She nods. "Pantwee," she repeats.

"Close enough."

Zenn finally texts me and apologizes. His phone crapped out and they don't have a landline and it took him two days to get to the Verizon store to get it fixed. He skipped school to work because they're late on their rent, and then spent two days trying to make up the work that he missed at school. He wants to see me but, in a rare incidence of maternal presence, his mom is hanging around the apartment. He can't come to my house and I'm not brave enough to suggest we meet at the church again.

So we just decide to drive around in his truck. I tell my mom I'm meeting Charlotte for coffee and head out on foot before she can ask questions. I'm eighteen years old and maybe she realizes there isn't much she can do to stop me. Zenn meets me three blocks away from my house. I climb into his truck and he circles the downtown twice before pulling into the parking lot by the beach. As soon as he puts the truck in Park we are on each other like lint on black corduroys. We kiss hungrily and awkwardly over the gearshift. It's too cold to go in the bed of the truck. I'm too tall to climb onto his lap. It's a frustrating predicament.

Eventually we resign ourselves to the fact that neither of us is adventurous enough or brave enough (or small enough) to do much in the cab of a pickup truck. We settle for an intense make-out session that leaves me feeling loose and unraveled to my core. Then he drives me home and I slink into my room before my mom can see my sexually frustrated swollen lips and beard-reddened face.

CHAPTER 37

BUT THE NEXT LULL when I don't hear from him is longer — almost three full days — and I know it can't be his phone again. He may be at school, but he doesn't meet me for lunch. I try not to text him too often, but I know I've got to be coming across as a little needy.

> Me: Hey!
> Me: Hey you.
> Me: You work too hard.
> Me: Hey! You know … there's this place called school? You should go sometime.
> Me: I miss you.
> Me: All work and no play …

Nothing.

Finally on day three he texts me back and I feel like an addict who finally got a fix.

Zenn: Hey
Me: Hey! Everything OK?

There is a long pause — maybe three minutes, where he doesn't text back. Finally ...

Zenn: Not really

Oh, crap. Something is up. Something is definitely up.

Me: What's wrong? Want me to come over?
Zenn: My mom is home
Me: Oh ☹
Zenn: Meet at the park?

The park! Where we had our first date! Maybe everything is fine.

Me: OK.

I don't question anything: why we're meeting at the park, why he seems so serious, what has happened in the last three days. I feel confident that everything will be all right once we see each other.

The park is nearly empty. The biting wind and new snow have scared away all the afternoon playgroups, and there isn't even any sun to trick your mind into thinking it's warmer. I see him sitting on a bench rather than the play set. No blanket, no pizza. He looks at his phone and bounces his knee up and down.

I sit down and nudge him with my shoulder.

"Hey, you."

He gives a little half smile. Well ... a quarter smile. Like, the kind of polite smile he might give to a teacher.

His knee starts bouncing again.

"What's going on?"

He stares up at the sky and sighs.

"Eva ..."

Oh, no. His voice is like a funeral. Something bad is coming. I look at those lashes and that smooth skin that is still bronze even as tiny snowflakes swirl around us.

"Is ... your mom okay?" I think about her drinking, about her manic episodes. Could she have gone off the deep end?

"Yeah, she's fine. I guess. As good as she gets."

"Then what's wrong?"

"We can't —" His voice cracks a little and he clears his throat. "I don't think we should see each other anymore." He is calm and quiet, but he doesn't sound like himself.

I couldn't have possibly heard him right and I don't want to panic. I don't want to freak out. But ... what the actual fuck?! I had *tea* with him less than a week ago, for the very first time, and now he's saying we should break up?

Was he using me? Tricking me out of my virginity somehow? Does that even happen in real life?

"Why do you say that?" I wonder if his parents found out. But if I didn't let my parents dictate our relationship, I'm not sure why he thinks his parents should have a say.

"I know about the scholarship," he says. "How could you *do* that, Eva?" He sounds angry with me, which I guess I knew he would be. But I did it for him! Surely he must see that.

I try to make light of it. "You deserve it, Zenn. I was afraid they'd hold your dad's past against you, and I'd get the orphan pity."

His voice is tight. "That's for them to decide. Not you."

Suddenly I remember the conversation we had at his kitchen table, about his mom letting that woman pay for his school supplies. He works three jobs so he doesn't have to accept help from anyone. And here I try to "help."

Oh, man. What have I done?

"You shouldn't have to pay for what he did," I tell him. "You've already paid enough."

"So have you."

"Zenn. Come on. Your situation is much worse than mine."

"Eva. You can't *touch anything!*"

I put my hand on his. "I can touch you."

He pulls away. "That's not enough. Not forever."

"It's enough for me."

"No, it's not. You are *not* the kind of girl who gives up everything for a guy. That is not the kind of girl I would fall in love with."

Wait. Did he just admit he has fallen in love with me? Or did he say that he wouldn't because I'm that kind of girl?

"I'm not letting you give up anything for me."

"I'm *not* giving up. I'll still go to college. I'll figure something out. We don't need to break up ..."

"Have you finished even one application since we met?"

My silence becomes my answer. He's right. I've been a little distracted.

"I am *not* enough," he says forcefully. "*This* is not enough for the rest of your *life.*"

I feel like he has slapped me. He doesn't know how

"enough" this is, how long I've waited.

"How do you know what's enough for me?"

"Because I know, Eva. You are bigger than this ..." — he searches for words — "this *barricaded* life you've been living. You deserve everything."

"But not you."

"You deserve *more* than me."

"I think I should decide —"

"But you won't. Because this feels good now. But someday you'll resent me. This is your chance. I'm not going to let you throw it away for me."

We sit in silence for a minute and my mind is spinning with a million different arguments. His eyes are glistening from the wind, or maybe from something else.

"So. You're breaking up with me?"

He swallows. "I have to."

I take off my glasses and press my mittened fingers to my eyes. I'm not crying — not yet, anyway — but it's only a matter of time. I feel it threatening, like nausea.

"For my own good, huh?"

"Eva —"

I swallow, nod and put my glasses back on. A part of me wants to reason with him, to beg, to make him change his mind. But what's the point?

"Okay. Fair enough." One tear escapes my treacherous eyes and I swipe at it with my mitten. I get up to walk away.

"Eva," he says. But when I pause, he doesn't say anything else. So I keep walking.

CHAPTER 38

I DON'T CRY ON THE WAY HOME because I don't actually believe this has happened. He really likes me. I know it. We are amazing together. You just don't break up with someone when things are that good.

But he doesn't follow me. He doesn't chase me down, offer me a ride, tell me he was just kidding. He lets me walk away. So when I get back to my house and he still hasn't texted me to say *I changed my mind*, I lose it. I close the door to my room and collapse on my bed and sob like my life depends on it.

My mom knocks first and walks in. "Honey?" Her voice is soft, concerned. "What happened?"

I don't answer, but I bet she already knows. She rubs my back and I let her.

"Well," I say, my voice pitifully clogged with snot, "you got what you wanted."

"Eva. This is not remotely what I wanted."

I don't want to believe her — I want to wallow in my teenage self-pity — but she doesn't look smug. She doesn't look happy.

"He dumped me. And not because I couldn't touch him, like you thought. No. Because I *sacrificed* something for him. What the *fuck*?!"

"Eva." Her voice is stern. I don't usually swear in front of adults.

"No, Mom. Seriously. All my life I've been preached to about sacrificing. Jesus made the ultimate sacrifice, right? But I sacrifice and what do I get for it? Kicked to the curb."

"I don't think giving up your future for a cute boy is exactly what Jesus would do."

I try not to lose my temper. "Wow. You guys all must really think I'm an idiot."

"We don't —"

I cut her off. "I didn't give up the scholarship because Zenn is *cute*. Give me a *little* credit. I did it because he *needs* it more than me. He *deserves* it more than me. My life has been a cakewalk compared to his. He basically lost his dad, too. And his mom, really, and he didn't have you and dad to rescue him. And now he has a chance to start over, to have a future. And I could maybe help give that to him. Why is that such a horrible thing?"

My mom doesn't answer.

"Seriously. I may not have learned a lot from church — hell, I don't even *believe* most of it — but I learned that love is putting someone else's needs ahead of your own. It's what Jesus did. It's what you did for me. Is it all just a load of crap?"

My mom sighs and strokes my hair. "No. You're right."

I look up at her through tears. "I'm right?"

"You're right. That's what love is. It's what we've taught you. It's what we've tried to live."

"Yeah," I say sarcastically. "You also taught me about forgiveness. And how's that working out for you?"

"One lesson at a time, Eva."

I smile a little.

She sections my hair and starts to braid it, like she used to. I close my eyes and wish I were little again, back before love and heartache and complications.

"I could touch him, you know." I surprise myself by saying it out loud. I hadn't planned on telling her, but something about her braiding my hair makes me feel young and safe, like back when I would tell her everything. And what does it matter now, anyway? My days of touching him are over.

"Hmmm?"

"I could touch him and he didn't give me fractals."

Her hands still mid-braid. "What? Are you serious?"

I nod and watch a hundred different emotions cross her face: confusion, joy, fear, panic.

"Nothing?"

I shake my head. "Nothing."

I wait for her to process what I've said because I know there will be a lot more questions: what we've done, how far we've gone. But she surprises me. She doesn't dive in to the parental inquisition, just thinks for at least a full minute and then asks rhetorically, almost as if she's asking herself, "Why him?"

There is a trace of jealousy in her voice. All these years she has wanted me to be able to reach out and hold her hand.

All this time she has tried so hard to help me with my fractals, and here this boy — whose dad killed my parents — is the one I can touch.

"I don't know. The only thing I can think is that he was there the night of the accident. His mom was pregnant." Am I about to cry again? "She held me, did you know that?"

A tear rolls down my mom's cheek and she swipes at it with one hand.

"She held me until the police came, and Zenn was ..." Now a tear slides down my cheek as well. "He was there. Inside her, I mean. And I know it sounds weird and impossible and just ... crazy, but maybe he comforted me? Like, maybe she held me against her belly and somehow ..." I can't finish the thought because I'm full-on crying now, and so is my mom.

"I didn't know she held you," my mom says through her tears. "I didn't know that."

I nod, and my mom wraps her arms around me and I press my face into her softness.

"They are so sorry, Mom. All of them."

"I know," she says. "I know they are." And I can tell she believes it, finally.

She holds me until eventually our tears subside.

"Do you think he can ... cure you?" she asks.

It's not something I've even thought about.

"I mean, do you think him not giving you fractals is a start? Like maybe, eventually ..."

I shrug. I'm still getting fractals, but they don't bother me as much now. They are the stories of people's lives and maybe it's better to know people's truths than the false faces they sometimes put on. Maybe I should just embrace the fractals a little. Let them help me understand people better. A few years ago I saw a meme that said, *Be kind, for everyone you meet is fighting a battle you know nothing about*. At the time I bitterly thought, *Yeah, no kidding*. But maybe it's okay to know what battles people are fighting. Maybe that's how it should be — all of us with our struggles on display.

My mom is waiting for my answer. I touch her arm and her fractal is still there. But it feels different somehow. Some of the yellow — the bitterness — has mellowed to a softer gold. Some of the red anger is just pink now. Her fractal is changing, not my ability to feel it.

"They're still there," I tell her, and her hopeful look disappears. "But it's better, Mom. I'm not really afraid of them anymore."

I lace my fingers through hers, something I haven't done in years.

She clears her throat. "I wasn't going to tell you this."

I let go of her hand to wipe my nose with a tissue. "Tell me what?"

"Someone from the *Telegraph* called. They want to run some kind of story about us, about how your parents died and I adopted you. How you and Zenn became friends without knowing how everything was connected. I assume someone from the scholarship committee put two and two together and they thought it would be a good 'human interest' story."

My mom does sarcastic air quotes, and I can tell she doesn't like the idea of our story being used as some kind of bait for people to buy the newspaper.

"Anyway, I was angry. I was trying to figure out why you would give up the chance at a huge scholarship to stay here for the son of the guy who killed your parents, and I told the reporter, 'Well, you know how teenagers are when they think they're in love.' And I'm not proud of it, I'm not, but I was angry and frustrated and I suggested that maybe Zenn convinced you to —"

"Mom! He had nothing to do with it! He didn't even know!"

"I know. Honey, to be honest, at that point I didn't even know he was one of the other finalists. I just thought you gave it up so you could stay here and be near him."

"What? That would be so ... stupid."

"I know! And I was so disappointed you would do that. But when that reporter called, I realized that you gave it up for *him* to have the chance."

Am I supposed to feel more or less foolish now?

"How did you figure that out? Did they tell you?" I try to remember my reply to Stephanie Rayner. I'm almost positive I never said anything about Zenn.

My mom shakes her head. "The reporter said that he withdrew his name, too."

This surprises me at first. But Zenn is proud and I'm sure when he found out that I had pulled out, he did the same. I explain to my mom.

"No, honey. He did it before."

"Before when?"

"Before you did."

"What?"

"She said he actually withdrew first."

I just stare at her.

"He gave it up for me?"

⊙⊙

I drive by his place, but his truck isn't there. Of course it isn't. Even if he is as heartbroken as I am, he still has to go to work and pay the bills. Self-pity is a luxury he doesn't have. But I know his schedule by now and I know that if he did go to work, he's at the grocery store today.

I pull into the parking lot and wait next to the cart-return rack, watching the store's automatic door from the minivan. My heart races every time it opens. Finally Zenn comes out, orange safety vest over his winter coat, knit hat pulled down, no gloves. No gloves in this weather? No wonder his hands are such a beautiful disaster.

The wind has picked up and he hunches against the cold as he makes his way toward the rack. I don't get out right away and he doesn't notice me sitting in my mom's van.

I am a wreck, a jumble of devastation and hope and anger. I have no idea what to say.

He starts to collect the carts from the rack. I take a deep breath and open the door.

When he sees it's me, he pauses, letting his hands drop from the cart he was pulling from its metal cage.

"You left out some important information this afternoon." My voice is so smooth I almost can't believe it.

I think he knows what I'm talking about. I can see it in his eyes.

"I can't believe you gave me that high-and-mighty speech when you did the exact same thing." I can hear the anger creeping into my voice. I am a mess of conflicting emotions: angry at him, but also grateful and touched. Disappointed that we've both screwed up our chance, and petrified of losing him.

He looks up at the sky, which is dark already, before five o'clock. He doesn't ask how I found out. I don't suppose it matters.

"It's different, Eva."

"No. It's not different at all."

"It is. You ..." His hands go up to his head in frustration, grabbing his hat and pulling it farther back on his head. "My family ruined your life —"

"No one ruined my life. My life is just fine." And I realize that it is. Fractals or no.

"They wouldn't have given me the scholarship anyway."

"That's for them to decide." I kind of like throwing his own words back at him. "You are not the kind of guy who gives up everything for a girl," I say, trying to remember his exact phrasing. "I wouldn't fall in love with a guy like that."

I see the hint of a smile.

He looks down at his feet and shoves his hands into his pockets. He sighs. "Well, shit. We really fucked this up good, didn't we?"

I step a little closer to him. "Yep."

"Maybe we should talk before we do anything idiotic next time."

I'm happy he's referring to the future. "Probably a good idea."

He smirks a little and my heart skips. "Who do you think would have gotten it?"

"Definitely me," I say. "I mean, who could resist my mad math skills? It's *super* fun to watch me use the Chebyshev method."

"I'll bet." He takes his hands out of his pockets, like he wants to reach for me. But he doesn't.

"I'm sorry," he says. "I really didn't want to break up with you."

"Of course you didn't." I reach out and tug at his sexy orange vest.

His arms slip around me, encircling me.

I think about when we met and I asked him his name and he made that Venn diagram with his hands. I probably fell in love with him right on the spot. I think about how our circles once seemed to barely overlap. Two separate lives with a tiny sliver of math tutoring in common. But now it's like my whole circle and his whole circle are the same: our past, our present and maybe even our future.

EPILOGUE

STUDENTS WHO SACRIFICED SCHOLARSHIP
MAY GET COLLEGE MONEY AFTER ALL

A tragic car accident leaves a young couple dead, their infant daughter orphaned. A war veteran is sent to jail for manslaughter, leaving his unborn son to grow up without a father. They are heartbreaking stories pulled straight from the headlines, and they definitely caught the attention of the committee who reviews applications for the prestigious Ingenuity Scholarship, which awards a gifted Wisconsin teen $100,000 for their college education. Two applicants with these exact stories — Eva Walker and Zenn Bennett — were chosen as finalists for the scholarship from a pool of thousands.

When it was discovered that Bennett's father was actually responsible for the death of Walker's parents, and then both teens withdrew their names from scholarship consideration within days of being named as finalists, truth quickly became stranger than fiction.

After Walker and Bennett withdrew, the scholarship was awarded to the third finalist: Jason Barber of Maple Grove. But Scholarship Chairperson Stephanie Rayner wondered if the first two finalists had each withdrawn to give the other a better chance of winning.

"That possibility seemed very 'Gift of the Magi,'" Rayner points out, referring to the story by O. Henry in which a poor husband and wife each sell their most prized possession to buy a gift for the other.

The *Milwaukee Sentinel* ran an article announcing the winner, with a small sidebar about the unusual connection between Bennett and Walker.

Their story gained immediate and national attention. Since that time, social media has worked its magic and to date, their story has been shared on Facebook alone over 500,000 times. A Go-FundMe account was anonymously established for both of them, and money started pouring in.

Both Walker and Bennett declined to be interviewed for this article, stating that they've gotten far too much undeserved attention already, but they thanked the public for their generous support.

If the GoFundMe account keeps growing, Walker, with the help of some academic-merit aid, hopes to attend Northwestern University in the fall and major in engineering science and applied mathematics with plans to eventually get her PhD in neuroscience. Bennett, a gifted artist, hopes to attend the Art Institute of Chicago in the future.

The two remain very close.

ACKNOWLEDGMENTS

So many, many thanks to so many wonderful people:

My original agent, Bethany Buck of Sanford J. Green-burger Associates, who first believed in this book and sold it faster than I could have hoped. Thank you for loving my story and taking a chance on me. You're wonderful.

My current agent, Wendi Gu, for all of your thoughtful feedback on my upcoming projects. Go Cats!

All the people at Kids Can Press and KCP Loft: Lisa Lyons Johnston, Michaela Cornell, Naseem Hrab, Kate Patrick and anyone else who helped behind the scenes. I'm not sure I've ever met a more kind, funny and intelligent group. Thank you for lovingly and beautifully bringing *Zenn Diagram* into the world.

My amazing editor: the talented, smart and awesome-in-every-way Kate Egan. Working with her has been a dream come true and she made this book so much better. Trust me.

My lifelong friend, Cindy Malin, who has always shared my nerdy love for words and has helped me get this book out into the world.

The talented Cindy Kennedy for taking my headshot (which was probably the most daunting part of this process — no lie).

My friends and "life coaches," Sara Reddington and Amy Miller, for years of encouragement, support and gentle pushes toward my dream.

The family and friends who have read my work over the years, for being kind, generous and gentle with your feedback: Jon Aguilar, Suzanne Burns, Susan Cain, Kym Garcia, Amy Gold, Pam Griffin, Heather Horita, Rachel and Mollie Hughes, Betty Jones, Dierdre Kelleher, Jackie Kieltyka, Sam Lanham, Chloe Leith, Rebecca Levenberg, Nancy May, Mary Jo Pape, Deb Price, Chris Rayner, Zoe and Wendy Rudd, Mackenzie and Deb Russ, Jennifer Russell, Doug Sabo, Gina Seaton and Eric Zorn.

My loving and generous parents, Barbara and Dennis Walters, who have always encouraged creativity, hard work and balance.

My brothers, Rich and Glenn Walters. We have different talents, but you both understand the desire to make things from the stuff that runs around in our brains.

All of my extended family for their loving support: Jackie, Kit, Evan, Kaylee, Landon and Teagan Walters; Jerry, Ceil, Kevin, Danny, Kathy, Michaela, Joey and Alaina Brant; and Theresa, Pat, Jack, Andrew, Mary and Danielle McCluskey.

My beloved grandparents, who I miss dearly: Fred and Nessie Bartels, Elmer Walters and especially Esther Walters, who loved to read and would be so proud.

Lastly, to my patient husband, Jim, who often gets ignored in favor of a computer screen and loves me anyway, and my amazing children, Emma and Nathan. You guys inspire me to dream big and set an example of what it means to be brave and live fully. Love you forever.

ABOUT THE AUTHOR

At age ten, Wendy Brant wrote her first book, *My Mysterious Double*, the story of a girl and an imposter pretending to be her. Wendy put not one but *two* copies of her glorious fourth-grade school picture on the cover. Toni Tennille bowl haircut, yellow turtleneck, denim vest with wide lapels. Brave might be one word to describe her ...

Years later, after graduating with a degree in journalism from Northwestern University and completing the Publishing Institute at the University of Denver, Wendy wrote adult fiction (albeit unpublished) while working as an HR manager and being a mom. But when she started reading the same YA books as her kids, her attention and passion shifted. Now she likes to write about isolated teenagers who somehow find a way to connect with others, and she's also a sucker for a little romance.

Though Wendy miraculously manages to keep her kids and pets alive and well, she has a brown thumb and kills plants indiscriminately. She likes to bake but not to cook. She loves the smell of coffee but not the taste. One of her favorite things is videos of unlikely animal friends. Wendy has always been somewhat of an introverted nerd, but she was also a cheerleader in high school ... so figure that one out.

Wendy lives in the Chicago area in the best neighborhood in America (as crowned by *Good Morning America* in 2010) with her husband, teenage daughter and son, and guinea pigs Mac and Tosh.

You can find out more about Wendy on her website and blog (wendybrant.net) or on her Facebook page (ZennDiagram), or follow her on Twitter @wendyjobrant.

Praise for *Just a Normal Tuesday*

"There is grief and there is grace, and this book is full of both. A look at love, loss, and learning to live with questions that have no answers. Kim Turrisi is an exquisite new voice."

— Martha Brockenbrough,
author of THE GAME OF LOVE AND DEATH

kcploft.com

FAME. LOVE. FRIENDS. PICK ANY TWO.

MARIE POWELL
& JEFF NORTON

"You're the drummer," she said to herself. "It's your job to keep them on beat. To hold it all together."

But how the bloody hell was she supposed to do that?

KCP Loft

kcploft.com

DON'T MISS THE DEBUT NOVEL FROM WATTPAD SENSATION
DoNotMicrowave

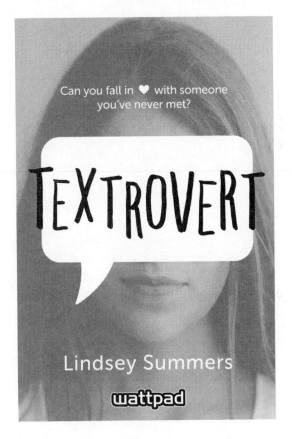

Can you fall in 🖤 with someone you've never met?

TEXTROVERT

Lindsey Summers

wattpad

KCP Loft

kcploft.com